The Accident

Rich Myers

For my wife and daughter whose love and support sustain me in all endeavors.
Special thanks to my life-long friend Dick Cussen whose willingness to read drafts and suggest improvements helped me to navigate this story.

ONE

The absence of sound. It would have been less frightening had there been noise on the level of a steel foundry. There were no brakes screeching against the road surface or horns blaring in the frigid air in an attempt to avoid catastrophe. Instinctively, he felt there should be. But locked tires' passing over ice at increasing speed was more of a whisper. There was simply no warning of the impending crash to come. In the space of only a few seconds, Michael Fitzpatrick knew that impact was inevitable. His heart rate accelerated and his breathing became shallow as he used his hands on the steering wheel of his sports car as a brace, pushing his upper body into the driver's seat, anticipating the opposite forces to come. He was able to see the driver of the Mercedes he was about to strike for only a moment and, if asked, would only be able to say that the driver was a woman with blond hair. The event, in his opinion, was moving at warp speed as first the bumper, then the hood of his car ,made impact with a force that broke the morning stillness with metal bending metal, rendering the type of noise where one knows for a certainty something bad has just happened without having to have witnessed it. Michael watched the hood of his car ripple with waves and rush towards his head at the same instant. A millisecond later his windshield exploded as the seat belt dug deep into his left shoulder and diagonally across his chest, violently preventing him from continuing his forward motion.

Then there was silence again. It retuned as suddenly as the impact, and was every bit as unnerving.

Michael sat stunned staring at the hood of his car, preventing him from seeing the other vehicle, and noticed his knees were higher than they should be. The impact had shortened the length of his Alfa Romero Spider by nearly one third, pushing his knees up and to either side of the steering wheel which nearly had him pinned against the seat. Reaching to unclip his seat belt, he felt the first pangs of discomfit from the bruise it had left on his body. Internalizing a fear he never knew could exist, he pushed, then punched at the damaged door with his fist and aching shoulder until it opened enough for him to squeeze through. The first thing he noticed was the blood on the driver's side window of the car he had hit. But the blond woman who had been driving was not behind the wheel. Moving closer, he saw that she was lying sideways towards the passenger seat with her seat belt keeping her from completing her fall. And then he saw more blood. A lot of it. He stood frozen in place as a dozen people seemed to suddenly materialize. People came from their apartments to offer what help they could while some had cell phones to their ears calling 911.

A man dressed in jeans and a ski jacket rushed from his car, parked crookedly at the curb, and opened the passenger door of the Mercedes while stating, "I'm a medic!"

"They're on their way," one of the cell phone users yelled.

Michael pulled his cell phone out of his parker and hit the speed dial for his father. Thankfully, he answered on the first ring.

The medic unclipped the seat belt and guided the unconscious driver gently to his lap and examined the laceration on her scalp. Appearing satisfied, he placed a finger to the side of her neck searching for a pulse.

"She's just unconscious," he yelled to the people gathered about the wreckage. "She's bleeding but not from the accident, I don't think."

"Huh?" Mike asked, closing his cell phone after having just spoken with father. "What did you say?" He raised his voice, realizing he wouldn't be heard otherwise. "She'll be all right won't she?"

"I'm an EMT and she sustained some bruising when her head hit the driver's side window, but her bag deployed and…wait! She's coming 'round." He knelt closer to her and gently brushed her forehead. "Lady? Lady, are you all right? Can you hear me?"

Her eyes flickered as they opened all the way. Her first reaction was to gasp as the big white bag took up most of her vision. Turning her head to the right, she could see a face before her and several people behind him. In the background a siren wailed as it made its way up the hill to the scene of the accident.

"What happened?" she asked.

"You've been in an accident and an ambulance is nearly here. Just relax. They'll have you out of your car in a few minutes. In the meantime, try not to move."

He turned his head to check the progress of the ambulance, which he felt should have been there by now. It was still coming up the hill, but more slowly than he would have anticipated. His ambulance crew often went too fast, at least in his opinion, when responding to an accident scene. This one appeared to be taking its time.

At last, it came to a stop two feet from the damaged Mercedes.

Jumping out from the passenger seat he told the arriving EMT's what he knew of her condition adding, "She may be bleeding from her uterus. We'll know for sure when you get her out of there."

Fear was coming at Michael in waves as he turned from the wrecked Mercedes to the street surrounding him in hopes his father had arrived.

Francis Fitzpatrick, Congressman from the 9th Congressional District of Massachusetts, was only a few blocks away at the State House when his son started his trek down Anderson Street on Beacon Hill. He was meeting with one of the local representatives from his district, Bradford Sullivan, who unbeknownst to him, was to become his main challenger in the next election. He called Sullivan last night and asked to drop by his home, but the Rep said he was on his way out the door but could make time to meet him at his office in the State House tomorrow morning where he spent most weekends. Fitzpatrick agreed, knowing it was more likely a case of not wanting to be seen having a conservative Republican in his home.

It was a shame, he thought, that Massachusetts was a liberal state from head to toe while he was one of the rare congressional Republicans to serve the state. The list of Republican Congressman from Massachusetts was few. But apparently, even a Republican Congressman was worth a photo-op. He stood holding the representative's right hand in both of his as the cameraman measured the room lighting.

"Make it snappy Sean," Sullivan said, "I'm sure the Congressman is a busy man with a full agenda. Even on a blustery Saturday, hey Congressman?"

"Oh, not so busy as to miss a photo op with an up and coming representative of my own district." He may be a one term congressman, but Fitzpatrick knew politics and the weakness of flattery. He also knew this particular representative as a member of his church and was hoping to get him to say something positive about the bill he had before the US House of Representatives. Nothing in the way of all out support of course, but maybe an utterance that he could use in the newsletter he sent to his constituents each year.

His "Faith for Life" bill was languishing in the House of Representatives and he knew he needed something to bring it to the forefront of the House members for a vote. Only one thing could make that happen; when the people the House members represented were expecting, and on rare occasions, demanded action. It was as controversial a bill as came before the House in many years and perhaps since the 3/5ths voting bill prior to the Civil War.

His bill addressed the unborn fetus right to life from conception to delivery. It stated the right of the unborn to the full protection of the Constitution to include every federal law related to every US citizen to the extent that no state law could override it. He realized his time as a Massachusetts Congressman was limited. He was elected due to circumstance, not platform or party affiliation. His opponent was a well known, well respected liberal from Brookline and a shoe-in for re-election until his 14 year old babysitter became pregnant. Something the incumbent vigorously denied being responsible for. He almost pulled it off, but once the parents demanded a DNA test, the game was over. And so was his political future.

Fitzpatrick senior may be a Catholic in a predominantly Catholic state, but he was a politician, a Republican at that, who actively supported church doctrine. For reasons that he and the Church would never understand, the two no longer went together. To be a religious person was a good thing, a sign of character. But to bring the teachings of that faith to a public office? You may have gotten a fair amount of votes based solely on your religious affiliation, but don't even think that we would want you basing decisions on what you believe, he mused. In Catholicism, as with most Christian faiths, the protection and nurturing of life was paramount. There's nothing more to discuss, the Congressman thought with anger. Thank you for your vote. Well, your last one anyway. They wouldn't make that mistake again, he was certain. He instinctively knew that 90% of them would deny to their neighbors they voted for him in the first place. Fine! It turned his stomach to think what this wonderful country had become. And the questions he was asked to submit answers to from various special interest groups! He thought again of the questions and how he would like to be able to answer them

Would you vote in favor of a federal bill to support same-sex marriage?

"Massachusetts already recognizes same sex marriage and I am confident it won't be long before every state makes the same mistake."

In your opinion, should people facing foreclosures be made to evacuate their home prior to having a six month grace period to catch up on their missed payments? Twelve months?

"Why not suspend payments indefinitely? I'm sure their properties will be paid off once they have the money. In the meantime, we'll let the banks go into foreclosure and see how they like it."

Do you support universal healthcare?

"I would, but then where would the Canadians go when they needed immediate treatment? I feel it's important that we don't start thinking of only ourselves."

Should undocumented aliens be giving preference on civil service exams?

"You did say undocumented, as in illegal, didn't you? Sure, sure. I never understood the reason for firemen and policemen needing to speak English anyway."

Do you support a larger or smaller military presence in the world?

"Did you know that the California National Guard has more soldiers than the entire Mexican army? You don't see Mexico worrying about invasion do you?"

As a Catholic, are you in favor of women being ordained?

"I'll answer that when I'm Pope Fitzpatrick."

Are you willing to ban Christmas displays in schools to protect the sensitivity of non-Christians?

Yeah, he thought. That last one had a chance where he was

concerned. It seemed to him that people these days made their decisions on who would best serve their country based solely on their specific needs, not the country's needs. A politician may be willing to open the borders to all foreigners, even those with a known criminal past, no questions asked. You might think a platform like that would make a candidate's chances of being elected slim to none. But if that same candidate supports gay marriage, he'll win the majority of that voting-block and to hell with the country's security.

Well he may be a one term Congressman, but he wasn't going to waste his opportunity while he had the chance to support what he felt with his whole heart to be right. Life began in the womb at conception. To think otherwise was the result of another "special interest group", namely pregnant women, who didn't want to be held responsible for their actions.

Truth be told, he had his doubts where rape was concerned. Serious doubts. But when you started making exceptions, there was no stopping them. He felt he did his best to ease his conscience regarding rape by supporting a bill that made rape a mandatory sentence of life in prison. And his Faith for Life bill went a step further by punishing the doctors who performed an abortion by up to six months of imprisonment and forfeiture of their medical license. Let's see how far they'll be willing to stand on their liberal positions with that hanging over their head, he mused. And if the procedure was done in a back-alley by someone working with only a fundamental knowledge of medical procedures? Life imprisonment. So sad, too bad.

The flash from the camera brought the Congressman back to the present.

"One more for safeties sake," the cameraman said and the next flash had him backing out of the room.

"Thank you Sean," said the Rep and turning to Fitzpatrick, "And thank you, Congressman. Please take a seat. Would you care for coffee?"

"No thank you, Brad," Fitzpatrick replied as he took a seat near the window, farthest from the Representative's desk. He didn't want the man to feel pressured.

"I wouldn't have thought the State House would have a media representative available on a Saturday," he said as a way of breaking the ice.

"Who? Sean?" Sullivan grinned. "He's my wife's brother. He was unemployed and running bingo games at the church before I got elected."

"I thought he looked familiar!" Fitzpatrick believed he never set eyes on him before today, but where they went to the same church, what's the chance of being called on it?

Sullivan fidgeted with a pencil on his desk and glanced at the wall clock. He agreed to this meeting only to get a better measure of the man.

It was apparent to everyone in the Congressman's district and in Washington, too, for that matter, that Fitzpatrick was a lame duck congressman from the day of his swearing in. His seat was available to anyone, especially a democrat that cared to go after it. Sullivan was certain there would be several contenders and he was planning to be one of them. After only a few minutes he knew he was dealing with a light weight here.

"I'm honored you dropped by Congressman, but as I mentioned last night, I have a lot of work ahead of me and—"

"Brad, I'll come right to the point. Last week in Mass you heard Bishop Connor talk about the need to protect life, all life, from conception and—"

"You mean he preached," Representative Sullivan interrupted.

"Well yes. I believe that's his job, to preach." The Congressman paused, wondering where to pick up. "You may not know this Brad, but I have a bill before the House that supports that very principle. Fully backed by our Bishop Connor, I needn't remind you. In fact, I'm scheduled to meet with the Bishop this afternoon," he added in the hopes it would give weight to his visit here this morning. "Anyway, it calls for stiff penalties for those who prefer to measure right from wrong based on their own selfish needs. What's more—"

"I am familiar, at least somewhat familiar, with your bill, Congressman," Sullivan interrupted. "And you ought to know how necessary it is for me distance myself from it. My god man! If I uttered a word in support of that bill I'd be tarred and feathered. And if you remember your history, they know something about that in this town." Sullivan offered a smile as a way to soften his rejection. He just wanted the Congressman out of his office.

"You go to the same church as me Brad," the Congressman tried again. "You listen to the same sermons, and they are unequivocal about the right to life." He stopped realizing he might be pushing too hard too early. "Look," he tried another tack. "I know you believe as I do about abortion and-"

"Whoa there Congressman! Just because we go to the same church, I doubt very much we are in agreement on abortion, anymore than on how to go about the war on terror, or how taxes must be raised and, with all due respect Congressman, how the wealthy are getting a free ride on that score. I respect your office Congressman, but I will not be used to advance your beliefs."

Fitzpatrick sat there staring at him. He didn't really come here believing he'd get whole hearted support, but a complete rebuff of everything he said?

"Another thing you are obviously not aware of Congressman," Sullivan could sense blood as he did with all of his political opponents, and as he felt certain Sullivan would soon be one of them, he went for the throat. "My wife Maggie was recently elected as the President of the Massachusetts NOW Chapter." He watched the congressman's face for a twitch, any sign that would tell him the man knew what a blunder he had made coming here. Fitzpatrick's expression remained open. "Does the idiot even knows what NOW stands for", Sullivan wondered. Not willing to take the chance he explained. "The National Organization for Women totally supports the right of women-"

"I know what that organization stands for," Fitzpatrick said brusquely.

The two locked eyes waiting for the other to speak. Sullivan began again.

"Let me tell you what my wife thinks of your bill, she thinks you're in league with the devil. Now if the local president of an organization as large and powerful as NOW is so vehemently opposed to your bill, how many in the total organization feel that way? In short, Congressman, your bill will never reach the floor for a vote, let alone be passed."

The congressman took a deep breath.

"One question Brad. Just the one," Fitzpatrick looked down at is hands. "What do you think about when you're listening to the Bishop or to any sermon on a Sunday?"

"The thoughts of one with a clear conscience, Congressman", he smiled. "Oh! And if the Patriots will win their division," you pompous ass, thought Sullivan.

The Congressman rose to leave and in act of good heartedness, Sullivan offered his hand in parting. Fitzpatrick ignored the offer of a handshake and walked out of the office closing the door behind him.

I'm not a vindictive man, thought Fitzpatrick, but if the opportunity should come up where I have the chance to knock that man down a peg, I don't believe I could stop myself.

Representative Sullivan picked up his telephone as soon as the door to his office closed. "Sean? It's me Brad. Get a reporter up to my office as soon as you can think of something that will get one of those bastards in here. I need to make a statement about Congressman Fitzpatrick being out of step with the times and the good people of his district. There's no way he'll keep his seat and it occurs to me that I know someone from his very district ready to lead. Me, you ass! Call me back when you've arranged something. I don't know! Try something like a statement concerning the war on terror and its effect on Massachusetts' taxpayers. They jump at that shit. And Sean, remind me again. What am I paying you for?"

Sullivan sat back in his chair and closed his eyes to envision how he would handle the remainder of his day. First of all, he would have to cancel his rendezvous which was due within the hour. That may be just as well, he realized, when he thought how moody she'd been lately. But damn, he thought, she was a beauty and wealthy, too. He involuntarily pictured her lying nude on the hotel bed this last Tuesday afternoon. She said she wanted to talk, but he successfully ignored that request when he lay down beside her. Just as suddenly his thoughts turned to his wife Maggie, nude on their bed. She was certainly still pretty, with a great figure, but the bottom line for him was that nothing could match the excitement of making love to a new women. Preferably a beautiful woman, thank you.

He thought of reconsidering and keeping his appointment for one last time. No! It was time to end it. Besides, his run for Congress was going to take his full attention for the foreseeable future. In fact, now just might be the perfect time to break off the affair. He'd tell her they could meet again when he was in Washington as a congressman. There'll be plenty of time to talk then, he smiled. He would require two residencies, one in Boston and one in the DC area. Maggie would be spending most of her time here while he was free to enact laws, fight the opposition, and find release at a more leisurely pace.

His run for congress created the biggest reason of all for separating himself from her, he rationalized. Not the time pressures, the planning meetings, nor the fundraisers, but the press. Along with his run for Congress and his wife now being the president of the state chapter of National Organization for Women, the press would be all over them. There was just too much riding on the future to chance it on his hormones. Of course, there was one other reason that superseded all of the others; her husband was his biggest supporter and benefactor. So wealthy and well connected was he that should he decide to support another candidate, Sullivan knew he'd be finished.

How'd I let this happen? He wondered, knowing it was a matter of circumstance and, at least at one time, shared desire.

"I'll call her and end it as soon as I hear back from Sean," he spoke aloud.

Thinking of Sean brought another problem to the front. The people of his district loved Sean Foley and he was a great at arranging meet-the-candidate meetings held at private homes during his run for state representative. But this was going to be different. Sean couldn't get close and personal with even a small percentage of voters the 9th district held.

There was going to be a lot of planning sessions and high-level meetings in the coming months, he knew, and he would need to find someone to replace Sean. Maybe he could do it while convincing Sean he was being promoted. That was going to be a dicey game. Maggie would go ballistic if he tossed Sean out. But getting into Congress was big time politics and it required a lot of money, the right party connections, a ruthless determination to win, and, oh yeah, a lot of money. He'd have to announce his candidacy and start fund raising right away. I have eighteen months to vanquish the dinosaur that just left my office, he mused.

"Not bad", he thought. "Maybe I can work that 'dinosaur' thing into my campaign".

Congressman Fitzpatrick stopped on his way to the exit of the State House and looked at the walls of the grand rotunda called the Hall of Flags. Hanging upon them were 18th-century banners. The hall's murals included depictions of the Pilgrims landing in Plymouth and redcoats getting their comeuppance in 1775. If you close your eyes you can easily imagine the minutemen drilling with their muskets on the Commons, he thought. So much history in a country still so young.

The vibration of his cell phone brought him out of his reverie. Looking at the cell phone window he read, "Michael". He hoped this wasn't another call from his son cancelling a planned visit home.

"Hello?" the Congressman sighed into the hand piece already accepting the inevitable.

"Dad?" Mike's voice was strained and it sounded as if he was trying to catch his breath.

"What is it, Michael? What's wrong?"

"There's been an accident, dad. I've been in an accident!" he emphasized. "She isn't moving. And there's a lot of blood."

TWO

"License and registration," a voice suddenly invaded Mike's consciousness. He was so intent on watching the EMT deflate the driver's bag he didn't see the police arrive.

"Ah, yes sir." Mike leaned into his car and removed his registration from the glove compartment and fumbled with his wallet to extract his license. He handed them to the officer who undoubtedly went through each day with the same bored expression. But today, with the cold biting at everyone, he looked peeved.

"Fitzpatrick, huh?" the officer asked lifting his gaze from the documents to Mike's unshaven face and noticing his bloodshot eyes. Leaning back a fraction he took in the wrinkled pants. He leaned in closer to sniff the haze of air near Michael that was visible with each exhaled breath.

"Have you been drinking, Mr. Fitzpatrick?"

"Only a shot. Honest! I..."

"Only a shot? And here it is nearly eight-thirty in the morning," the officer said in a mocking, nonchalant tone.

"Well, it was Tim's idea. I didn't want to have one but..."

"It says here you live in Cambridge. You a student over there?"

"Yes sir. Harvard."

"Did you call 911?" he asked noticing Mike still held his cell phone in one hand.

"No. I called my father. He said he would be here any minute. He's at the statehouse." Mike was still confused by what had happened and looked around to see where his father was.

"The statehouse? Are you related to Congressman Fitzpatrick?"

"Yes sir. I'm his son."

Glancing at the ambulance, Mike saw that they had the lady lying on a stretcher and answering the questions of another police officer on the scene. That's got to be a good sign, Mike thought. She's awake and able to talk so maybe she just fainted. But the blood, he remembered seeing. So much of it.

"Okay. Let's go over to my car and keep warm while I take your statement." He rested his hand on Mike's elbow and led him to his police car.

Settling in beside the officer, he scanned the faces of the many people who had gathered while he was looking for his father. The two-way radio squawked with information on who was where, who could respond, what was your status. Mike watched as the officer picked up his mike and reported his current status by describing the accident scene and, as an afterthought, who he was sitting with. This would undoubtedly create some gossip at the station house.

The officer and Mike stared out the front window of the car as the ambulance maneuvered around the Mercedes to take a right on to Phillips Street. It was going to be a short ride to Mass General hospital.

Turning to face Mike the officer spoke, "Before you tell me what happened, I'm going to administer a breathalyzer test."

"Why? What for?" Mike stammered.

"You already admitted to have been drinking and we need to determine if it impaired your ability to operate a vehicle."

Mike was shaken his head from side to side as he tried to recall all of the advice he had heard through the years regarding his rights to refuse a breathalyzer test and what that would mean legally.

"Look Mr. Fitzpatrick," the officer could see where this was headed. "We're not talking about a standard 'pull-over you appear to be weaving' incident here. If you refuse to take the breathalyzer, you will automatically lose your license for one year and attend mandatory AA meetings. If you agree to the test and it shows that your alcohol level is below the legal limit to operate a vehicle, nothing more happens in that regard."

Mike thought of the shot he shared with Tim just a short time ago but he couldn't stop himself from thinking of all he had to drink the night before. Was it still in his system, he wondered? Of course it would be!

"No," he said more loudly than he intended. "No sir," he brought his voice down and tried to sound reasonable and polite. "I don't believe a breathalyzer would be in my best interests. Not at this time anyway." Damn! That came out wrong! "I mean I don't think it's fair the way that breathalyzer works. I mean, how far back does it measure what you had to drink?"

The officer sighed and passed Mike a form to sign indicating he knowingly refused to have the test administered.

Placing the signed paperwork under his clipboard he looked again at Mike and said, "Tell me what happened."

Suddenly there was a rap on the driver's side window that had both occupants jump.

"I'm Congressman Fitzpatrick. I'd like to join my son if I may."

The officer pointed to the backdoor and the Congressman jumped in.

"My name is John Doyle, Congressman," the policeman introduced himself. "Pleasure to meet you, sir." Doyle was a member of the force long enough to see careers rise and fall on who they knew. "It makes me wonder with names like ours if weren't related somewhere along the past."

The Congressman nodded at Doyle and turned his attention to his son.

"What happened, Mike" the Congressman asked while scanning his son's face for any signs of injury.

"I was about to take his statement, sir," the officer said. "As to what happened," he added.

The officer and Congressman both waited for Mike to speak.

"I couldn't stop," Mike said.

"Your brakes failed." the officer stated.

"No. It was the ice. I couldn't stop."

The officer turned his body to look back up the hill were Mike says he made his turn onto Anderson. It was quite a distance.

"You're saying from the time you turned onto Anderson Street you were unable to stop?" He looked straight at Mike and added, "And you couldn't slow down?"

"Yes. Yes, that's right. I tried to slow down, but when I touched the brakes the car started to slide. I was able to keep it pointed straight down the hill if I didn't use the brakes, you see," he added as a way of explaining.

The officer turned his head slightly to exchange a glance with the Congressman.

"You should know Congressman that your son has refused to be administered a breathalyzer test and he has admitted to drinking this morning."

"One drink!" Mike said.

"What?" the Congressman stated. "You were drinking alcohol this morning?"

"One drink, dad. With Tim. I wasn't binging or anything. It was just..." He realized there was nothing he could say to justify it. "It was just the one shot."

"A shot?" the congressman stated more than asked, while shaking his head.

"What about the other driver," Congressman Fitzpatrick asked the officer.

"If you'll wait here, Congressman, I'll find out."

Leaving his vehicle, the officer walked briskly to where the other policeman was finishing up a witness statement. The high and mighty, Doyle thought, you'd think he's respond to my good nature, but no, he's a bastard just like they write about him.

Mike and the Congressman watched the two uniformed men converse. After taking down a few notes on what he was being told he headed back to his car and jumped in.

Rubbing his hands for warmth he said, "As far as we know, she was bleeding heavily due to what appeared, according to the lead EMT, to be a miscarriage."

"Oh my God," the Congressman muttered.

"Will she be Okay?" Mike asked.

"No idea," the officer answered. "They took her to Mass General."

"Do you have her name?" the Congressman asked.

Checking his notes he answered, "Jessica Brackton."

The Congressman's eyes widened upon hearing the name. He was sure it was Jessica Billington-Brackton.

"Do you have her address?" he asked.

"Not with me at the moment, but I wouldn't be able to give it to you anyway."

"Yes, of course," answered the Congressman. "Well, what happens now?"

"I will need to bring your son to the station and book him for reckless driving while under-the-influence." Doyle felt some kind of internal satisfaction at being able to do that.

"But I'm not impaired in any way!" Mike protested.

"You've been drinking, and judging from your appearance, I can tell you that it looks like more than one to me, you refused a breathalyzer, and you've been in a major accident. Do I need to add "uncooperative" to the list?"

"No officer," the Congressman answered for Mike. "I'll walk back to my car and meet you at the station, Mike."

"Is losing my license for a year pretty much the extent of all of this, officer?"

"It could be," the officer conceded. "But I'd be willing to bet money Ms. Brackton won't agree to that being the end of this."

THREE

Bishop Seamus Connor sat in his study. He was having a hard time tearing his thoughts from his latest meeting with Congressman Fitzpatrick and all of the good this one bill could do. He had grown tired of the non-aggressive response the Church had taken on abortion leading to what had become a routine Christian belief that ending the life of a fetus was nothing more than an individual's choice. Perhaps, the Faith for Life Bill would wake people up. And, even if it didn't, he mused, it would be a good start. The Church would have something that they could openly, vigorously, and loudly support. He was scheduled to meet with the Congressman later that afternoon but it was to be, like all of their meetings, a clandestine affair. Even his superiors were leaning on him to distance himself from the Congressman for fear that the Bill would appear to have originated from the Church and not a statesman. What if it did originate from the Church? But, they argued, the separation of Church and State needed to be observed, lest the people reject it out of hand.

He shook his head to clear his thoughts to focus on the gathering before him; five young men that stood before his desk, fresh from seminary and recently ordained. Boys really, he thought. Like he himself must have looked lo those many years ago. He was pleased to see them as young as they were as the Church desperately needed young blood. But the trend these past couple of decades pointed toward later commitment to the priesthood. Candidates spent their first several years out of college pursuing another profession before entering seminary. It was not the path he had followed, but he had to agree it undoubtedly brought greater experience to the job. If only we had more of each, he thought.

It was his job to assign these men to parishes and it was one duty he was happy to fulfill. With the recent spate of lawsuits and accusations of sexual misconduct against the Church, it was important to know who may pose a threat among these men and who would not. But it simply wasn't easy to say who might have pedophile leanings. They didn't have horns, for goodness sake. But oh how I wish they did, he thought.

Looking from one face to the other, he saw clean-cut, handsome young men. Gay? Some perhaps, like the one standing to his left, but that was for their own conscience to deal with. Being gay didn't provide greater access to opportunity just because you were a priest. But a pedophile? That was very different. There was a Catholic Youth Organization at every parish. Parochial schools, family gatherings and family illnesses where attendance was necessary, were gratefully accepted. The facts were that too much opportunity presented itself. But would a twisted soul enter the priesthood with that in mind, or was it their way of serving penance for wrongs already committed, only to find that when presented with the next opportunity, the body was indeed weaker than the spirit? No matter. He would have two weeks to determine who would be working with people and who would be assigned clerical duties that kept them away from the faithful.

The two-week "get acquainted" policy was something he instituted himself. They came assigned to him from the seminaries based on the needs of the diocese, which of course could never be met. He would like to have more time with them, but the parishes were crying for new blood to the point that Cardinal Monroe told him, in no uncertain terms, he was displeased with his program. During the past three decades the number of priests in United States and Canada had dropped from over 60,000 to under 50,000. And as was evidenced when he last attended the National Federation of Priests' Council in Toronto, the median age of his fellow clergy was 60 years old—up from the age of 47 as recently as 1970. During the same time, the Catholic population in the United States had risen above 61 million. Doing more with less had become a way of life for the clergy.

The Cardinal's displeasure with him for the delay in assigning priests was understandable in many respects, Connor knew, but it was not the only point of contention. Both the Cardinal and the Archbishop were displeased with his continued association with Congressman Fitzpatrick. "Distance yourself form him and his bill, Seamus," Archbishop Pollock instructed. "The closer you get to it, the more we have to lose if the bill fails, as it most certainly will. We can't start relying on politicians to do our job."

The Bishop's purple Zucchetto, or skull cap, sat on one corner of his desk. His neatly trimmed white hair contrasted with his deep blue eyes that held depth and knowledge. So intriguing were their color that some people found it hard to stop looking at the Bishop's eyes, even when he was not looking at them. Arthritis had recently introduced itself to his right knee, but not to the extent that the condition had affected his own father. Perhaps due to inheriting his mother's genes, he was able to stay relatively thin. His dad, on the other hand, carried extra weight like he was born with a spare tire around his waist.

He remembered his father, a car salesman with a seventh grade education, waking each day with moans and hobbling from one room to the next as he prepared himself for work. His mother would not his tie and help him into his shoes as early morning tasks were the hardest to perform. His father's only concern, beyond his family's health and safety, as far as Seamus could recall, was earning enough money to keep his family comfortable. Being a car salesman required a lot of standing and walking from the showroom to the car lot, but his father was very good at his job, earning top salesman nine out of twelve months each year. His arthritis was a hindrance, not an excuse. His sales performance provided his family with good income, better than average shelter, nice clothes, a new car every other year, and the ability to send Seamus to Notre Dame, where Seamus' first year there was marked by the bombing at Pearl Harbor. Many of the first and second year students quit the university the day following the attack and enrolled in one branch of service or another. Seamus would've followed them but for a letter he received the week prior from his father, stating what he felt was the country's obvious upcoming involvement and that Seamus should stick to his studies. "No one will pay you for simply being patriotic and even less opportunity lay in being dead," he warned.

It was during his second year at Notre Dame, while the war in Europe raged on, that he changed from a business major to philosophy.

On his visit home during a Thanksgiving break from classes that year, Seamus was sitting on his bed reading The Guardian. His father appeared at his door and hobbled over to the desk where Seamus spent most nights during his high school years doing homework. While half leaning and half sitting on the edge of the desk, his father reached down and rubbed his aching knees.

"I've been wondering what you plan to do for a living when you leave college, Seamus," his father stated. "Are you planning on being a philosopher? If so, I can't imagine there being much money in it."

"Your right, dad," Seamus nodded and smiled at his father. "There's not much money in it as far as I can see either. But it's what priests study, good ones anyway, and I believe that's what I am supposed to be."

"What about your plans for having your own business? Truth be told, I was hoping you and I could open our own car lot. There's a good spot available and...."

"I can't do that dad," Seamus interrupted. "Whenever I'm at church, or even read the papers, especially about the war, I feel a presence, something telling me that I'm needed. I tried to ignore it, but that doesn't work. I spoke to Father McAdams about it, a lot," he said, referring to his counselor at the school.

"And he said you were to become a priest?" His father asked.

"No," Seamus shook his head, "not at all. He said I should keep listening."

His father nodded while he contemplated this. "Well," he sighed, "they'll feed and clothe ya, and give you a roof over your head. That's all a man can hope for."

He straightened himself in preparation to leave.

"I'm sorry, dad," Seamus offered. "I may change my mind yet, ya know?"

"I don't think so, Seamus. All I ask is that you be a good one, good at being a priest I mean." Father and son looked at each other for a moment and then laughed at the same time.

"It'll make your mother happy knowing your plans," he said as he hobbled toward the exit. "And just so you know," he turned at the door to face his son, "it ain't making your old man too sad either."

Whenever he thought of his father, his mind always returned to that conversation. What kind of life would he be living now had he embraced his father's idea to open their own business selling cars as a team? And that thought always led to Katie, his high school sweetheart, and the family he might have had with her as his wife. But now was not the time for memories.

Bishop Connor nodded to his assistant as he spoke to the men before him. "You know me as Bishop Connor and this is Father Anthony Canalli. When Father Canalli tells you to do something, it is coming from me. Never question that. He will show you to your rooms and explain what is expected of you during your brief visit with us.

"First, I want to congratulate you on your recent ordination and wish each of you the very best of luck in the many years ahead. Who knows," he smiled warmly, "a future pope may be amongst you." The priests tittered at that, but they had already heard such things from family and friends.

Bishop Connor took a deep, relaxing breath and let it out slowly as he pondered what he was about to say. He was widely noted for using stories to make a point and they were eagerly anticipated when he spoke to an audience. He had been using the same story he was about to narrate for three years and only for the new priests he was about to assign. It was still the best one he knew and it always hit the mark he aimed for.

"Before you leave me to settle in I have a story for you. It concerns a family. It comes to me from a priest from one of my parishes who recently visited me for guidance. Don't worry; it's not from a confessional." The Bishop paused to be sure he had their attention.

"He tells me that a young girl of fourteen of his church became pregnant. Let's call her Sarah and yes, she was only fourteen," he slowly shook his head in concentration. It was imperative that he convey how important a story this was.

"The girl came to him after Mass one Sunday afternoon. You can imagine how distraught she was; fourteen and pregnant! She asked if she could speak to him alone and, when the door to his office was closed, she burst into tears. He said it took him fifteen minutes to calm her down enough to tell him what was wrong. Once she did, he needed to know a lot more before he could decide what to do.

"Did her parents know of this? No.

"Who was responsible for this? Her seventeen year old boyfriend.

"Did he know? Yes, but he was no longer talking to her.

"How far along was she? About six months, she guessed. She was quite overweight, apparently, which aided her in covering up her condition.

"Why did she wait so long to make her pregnancy known? She didn't really want a baby now, but someday she did. And she couldn't tell her parents. She didn't know what to do.

"First, of course, both sets of parents must be told. Unfortunately, the boy was of a different faith, making it a bit more problematic." He glanced up from his table and recognized their full attention on him. Good, he thought, and continued.

"He wasted no time in calling her parents and arranging for them to come straight to the church. He was less successful with the boy and his parents. When he called their home, the boy answered. Once told the reason for the call, he said the girl was lying; she was available to anyone who wanted her. And no, his parents weren't home. You can expect the same response from many of your future parishioners. Denial comes with the human race, not just a faith.

"Anyway, once the girl's parents were seated with their daughter, who was cowering in a corner chair, he dropped the bomb, so to speak. Now keep in mind that this is a devout family. This is especially true of the mother. Never misses a Sunday Mass, always participates in church functions, volunteers wherever she's needed, tithes her husband's salary, and has taught catechism to elementary school children for many years. Sounds like a dream parishioner, doesn't she? Would anyone like to guess what the mother's first words were when her parish priest finished explaining the situation?" The Bishop paused, but the men stood transfixed, staring at him.

"Well, I'll tell you. She said, 'Sarah will have an abortion.'" One of the newly ordained actually gasped. The Bishop took note of him, a good sign.

"Now Sarah's priest was as shocked, as I'm sure you are, when he heard this and he began to lecture Sarah's parents, especially the mother, who obviously called the shots in that family, that abortion was not an option. At which point the mother stood and motioned to her husband and daughter to follow her. The meeting was over.

"Naturally, the priest tried to reach the family many times over the next couple of weeks to provide counseling and guidance. But they weren't having it. The family stopped attending church completely and the mother dropped her catechism duties the next day. They simply went missing. At least, as far as Father Sh...as far as their parish priest was concerned," the Bishop caught himself in time.

"Then, quite unexpectedly, the mother appeared at his door. Several weeks had passed since he had last seen her. That was the night he told her of her daughter's condition. He said she looked ragged, like she had not slept in days and indeed that was the case. You see, she found someone to abort her daughter's pregnancy. I don't know who she could have gotten to agree to do it. Sarah was so late in her pregnancy, so I can only suspect money played a significant role.

"Now she stood before the priest contrite, ashamed, and broken in as many ways as a human spirit can be." Bishop Connor paused to sip from his water glass. He knew he had them totally bound to his every word.

"There was a complication during the procedure she said. Her daughter's doctor came to her in the waiting room and, medical reasons aside, he could possibly save the daughter or her baby, but not both. The mother chose her daughter. The next thing she remembered was the doctor before her again, explaining how sorry he was but due to her advance pregnancy, her being overweight, blah, blah, blah, the daughter had died. And...her baby died as well."

His audience's eyes were like saucers and their breaths shallow.

"She was, as I said, before him now asking for forgiveness and to pray with her for her daughter's soul. He asked of her husband and learned that he was leaving her. She said the one time she really needed him, he chose to leave. No, she wouldn't miss him. But her daughter? Oh, how she missed her.

"The burial was scheduled for the very next day and if she hadn't been so busy with arrangements, she would have come sooner. But, of course, she needed the church and his service for the funeral Mass. And while she already had her daughter's name on the prayer line, could she impose upon him to lead the congregation in a prayer for her daughter during Mass next Sunday?

"I'm telling you this story as a way to prepare you for what you can expect. It's not all weddings, christenings, and funeral masses for the aged. Father Canalli and I have only two weeks to prepare you for "the real world". To that end, we offer a prayer each night before dinner that typically asks for mercy for one of our own recently departed. However, in light of what you now know concerning Sarah and her family, I am going to suggest we say a prayer each night for the coming week devoted entirely to Sarah's mother. For her soul."

As he expected, his students' faces took on one of consternation.

"Any questions?" he asked. "Go ahead. There's nothing to be afraid of."

"Excuse me Bishop Connor," the one who gasped earlier asked, "but isn't it Sarah and her poor baby whose souls we should be praying for?" The others in line nodded slightly to show their agreement.

"Sarah and her baby?" the Bishop repeated. "Didn't I explain that her parish priest was providing the funeral Mass for their souls? Besides, they're innocent," he waved his hand in a dismissive manner. "Family and friends are praying for them as we speak. It's their *murderer* who needs our prayers boys." He paused to let his statement sink in.

"As it stands now, the soul of Sarah's mother is in great peril."

FOUR

Jeff Sailor, editorial reporter for the state's largest newspaper, The Hub, sat at his desk fiddling with the digital batteries to his new miniature tape recorder. At 52 years of age, a hairline just beginning to recede, a stomach only two inches beyond where it should be, and a job that most journalist aspired to have, he felt only a mild contentment. His "Man at Large" articles were a big hit and he only had to submit two a week. He enjoyed how easy his job had become over the years, but was becoming less enthused about it. He had interviewed prostitutes, AIDS sufferers, gang members, honest politicians believing they could make a difference, as well as corrupt ones looking for money and power. And he had the power to make a career, or seriously hamper one. But it was no longer rewarding.

His style was to report in third person, making his columns more readable and less personal. There was a time that he could expect a couple of job offers a year from competing news agencies with some coming from as far away as California. But, he was a Boston boy born and bred and after the New York Times, The Hub was the paper to work for on the east coast.

Sailor still remembered how to use the old manual typewriters and could use a pad and pencil when occasion demanded. But, Jeff also loved technology and the new gadgets that made his job easier. This recorder was of miniature size and had so many "extras" it required two batteries the size of eraser heads to be inserted in the back. The fact that the batteries were expensive, and Jeff didn't want to pay for them out-of-pocket, had him dropping by the office this Saturday morning. He knew his associate, Bill Gaynor, had recently purchased the same device so he had hopes of lifting a couple batteries from Bill's desk. He was in luck.

He had just passed Gaynor standing by Angela's desk. Probably hoping to snag a date with her, he reasoned. Angela, like all recent journalism graduates, was assigned to answer the phone, track staff whereabouts, and generally do secretarial work during their internship. If she lasted through that, she may just be lucky enough to do background research on stories for an established reporter, like himself.

Sailor closed the battery cover, pressed power-on, and nothing happened. He must have them in backwards. It was easy to be distracted with that damn police scanner squawking away, he grimaced. He liked gadgets as much as Gaynor, but who wanted to listen to babble all morning? Closing the battery cover to his recorder once again, he powered it up and heard a click. He pressed the record button, noticed a small green light come on near the power switch, and slid it into his sports jacket pocket. He'd test it on Gaynor and Angela on his way towards the elevators. But first he checked Gaynor's desk for any telltale signs of his theft.

As he stood, he moved a few items around, trying to remember if he had even touched them, when he heard the name 'Fitzpatrick'. He looked around for the source and realized it came from the police scanner speakers. Leaning closer, he hoped to hear more, but the dispatcher had already moved on. That was when Jeff's own inner power light came on. Reaching into his pocket, he removed the recorder and hit the rewind button. Playing back what the recorder held in its memory provided him with what he missed being said on the scanner. So Michael Fitzpatrick had been in accident, he mused. He knew who Michael was related to without the arresting officer having to state it to the dispatcher.

This could be just the boost his career needed. He did an occasional guest appearance on local cable news and found that he liked the spotlight it provided. A job offer from them, he knew, would have him thinking seriously about his continuing career in print.

He replaced the recorder in his jacket pocket and headed for the door. "Angela?" he called out over the office dividers. "If anyone is looking for me I'll be at Mass General."

"You sick?" a male voice, Bill Gaynor's, came to him as he pressed the elevator button.

"Nope, chasing a story. Be back later to write about it. Ought to make tomorrow's edition if I'm lucky."

"You got to be kidding me!" Gaynor exclaimed. "You're not even on duty."

"Your Sunday's piece is already to bed," Angela reminded him, using an industry term.

"Then we may be seeing two pieces from me," he whispered to himself as he stepped into the elevator.

FIVE

Congressman Fitzpatrick was driving his son towards his apartment, although he would rather pull on his thinning hair and scream. Jessica Billington-Brackton for goodness sake! Of all the people. He took a deep breath and reminded himself it was his son who was important, not some society dame. He smiled to himself realizing the police officer didn't even recognize her name. That's the way it was with blue bloods. Unless you were *tres* important, they didn't *want* you to know who they were. Still, Billington kept her maiden name so those who should know wouldn't miss it.

A couple of hours later, after Mike's photo had been taken, his fingerprints recorded, and his bail set — it took a few strings being pulled to get that to happen pronto — he was dropping Mike off at his apartment.

"Go and get yourself cleaned-up," he told Mike.

"You're leaving me?" Mike asked incredulously. "Take me home, dad. I want to stay with you and mom tonight."

"I can't take you home looking like that," his father snapped. "Get a shower, shave, and change into something other than jeans and a sweater. I'll be back after I pay a visit to the hospital."

"You know her?" Mike asked. "The lady I hit, you know her?"

"I know of her and with any luck, she'll know of me," he sighed. "Go on now, get cleaned up. I'll be back to pick you up."

Arriving at the hospital parking lot he contemplated calling one of his congressional aides. Have them hunt down some colleagues who could help Mike out of this jam. But then he realized he was jumping the gun. Nothing happened that couldn't be handled by the two of them. At least, not yet.

He approached the reception desk and, as quietly as possible, mentioned he was there to see Mrs. Billington-Brackton.

The receptionist scanned the computer console before her and shook her head.

"Not registered, sir. Sorry."

"She was in a car accident and brought here maybe three hours ago?"

"Oh. Wait a sec." She clicked a few keys and looked up at him. "Are you family?"

"No, but I was involved in the accident that brought her here," he lied. "Did you find her?"

"She's in recovery now. That's why I couldn't locate her; she hasn't been assigned a room yet. But visiting hours aren't until six p.m. and even then, I'm afraid only family until the doctor says otherwise."

"I understand," the Congressman said, realizing it was time to pull rank. "However, I'd like to make a special request. You see, I'm Congressman Fitzpatrick and I have a confession to make. I wasn't really part of Mrs. Brackton's accident, but she is a dear friend of mine and if I am unable to see her while she's recovering, I'd like a word with her doctor. Can you arrange that, or perhaps point me to someone who can?"

"One moment please," the receptionist left her station and could be seen speaking to what appeared to be a senior nurse behind a glass partition. Both of them returned to the front desk.

"Hello, I'm Nurse Frankton, nurse in-charge. How can I help you?"

Fitzpatrick introduced himself to Nurse Frankton and handed her one his cards with the dome of the capital embossed on it. He repeated his request to speak to Brackton's doctor if he was unable to meet with Brackton herself.

Nurse Frankton brought him to a private sitting area and asked him to wait while she notified Doctor Hayes that he had a visitor.

Taking stock of his surroundings, soft colored walls, low lighting, and no TV or magazines, he realized this was probably a room where they brought loved ones when bad news was to be told. He offered a quick prayer that wouldn't be the case today.

After several minutes, the door opened and the doctor entered. Doctor Hayes looked tired and at the same time, suspicious of the Congressman's visit. Wearing the typical white jacket over jeans and a stethoscope draped around his neck, he looked to be up most of the night.

"How can I help you?" the doctor asked scratching the four o'clock shadow on his chin.

"My son was involved in a car accident this morning that necessitated Mrs. Bellingham-Brackton's visit here. I'd like to know everything you can tell me about her condition."

"Are you family?" Doctor Hayes asked.

Fitzpatrick could feel his blood rising. "Look doctor," he said. "If necessary, I will make some calls that will have your boss calling you."

"It's just that we are still trying to reach her husband," the doctor explained.

"Perhaps I can help with that," Fitzpatrick said. "I'll make some calls."

The doctor's stance altered slightly as he knew this was not a fight worth taking on.

"She came to us with minor face lacerations and some bruising to her left check. That was easily bandaged. However, she also experienced a miscarriage; most likely the result of the accident. At this time, all I can tell you is that she lost a lot blood and will be staying with us for another day, and possibly two. Are you all right?"

Fitzpatrick's own face drained of blood as he contemplated what he had just heard. The sponsor of the bill "Faith for Life" felt nauseous at what he knew would follow when this leaked out.

The split between the two political parties had been growing wider with each presidential election. Conservative radio talk show hosts used any information that could undermine a Democrat, while mainstream television and print did their best to disparage Republicans, with each side accusing the other of being biased. It had reached a point, he feared, that the media would decide who was best qualified to serve the country and any other opinions to the contrary were not welcomed, nor would they be shared with their audience. Even Hollywood, with their liberal leanings, in the congressman's opinion, wrote screenplays that undermined and distorted a conservative candidate's position and worse, undermined the values of his country as a whole. You only had to watch Letterman or Leno each night to see who the left considered fodder for a good laugh. Goodness knows, he had been their main focal point since he introduced his bill.

"I'll be fine," he answered the doctor. "When will she be able to receive visitors?"

"Tomorrow will be the soonest," he said. "Congressman or not, I can't allow you near her until her condition improves."

"Yes," he nodded. "I understand. Thank you, doctor."

As Fitzpatrick was leaving the hospital parking lot to pick up his son, Jeff Sailor of The Hub was watching him from where he sat in his car. Once he found a nurse willing to take one hundred dollars to confirm that Billington-Brackton was a patient, he was elated. That feeling was soon pushed aside when the nurse mentioned the miscarriage. Elation became nirvana. This story just went from a scoop to a significant pay raise. Until he could get his thoughts under control, he knew it would be best to think things out, have a plan. He went back to his car and waited. That was just about an hour ago. He recognized the Congressman's car as soon it pulled into the lot and he congratulated himself on being patient. He was hoping he would see the Congressman's son Michael paying a visit, but this might play better. "Congressman Rushes to Hospital to Visit Son's Victim" he envisioned the headline.

Normally, he would have waited by the door of the hospital and attempt to get a statement. But this had all the makings of a big story, of Kennedy-Chappaquiddick proportions. And, as far as he could tell, he was still the only reporter onto it. He knew that wouldn't last so he had to play his cards carefully if he was to be nothing more than the man who alerted the public to what had happened. He wanted to be the media's go-to man as this story made national headlines, as he was sure it would.

But timing was everything, and it was growing short. Forget about making Sunday's paper, he thought. This warranted careful handling.

After spending four years as a congressman, he knew that Fitzpatrick was as close to professionally handling reporters as you can get. The man he would ambush was the son, Michael. Sailor loved to see that deer-in-the-headlights look when he posed an unexpected question. And if he was right, the question he would be asking Michael Fitzpatrick just might result in a coronary.

Dialing the office, he started speaking as soon as he heard Angela's voice. "Who's available to do research today?"

"It's Saturday afternoon, Jeff. Skeleton crew, remember?"

"Wrong! You're available. Go the archives and pull out whatever we have on Congressman Fitzpatrick: school, family history, wife, and, this next part is important, his son Michael. You getting all of this?"

"Jeff, I'd love to do this for you, but I don't have access to the archives and I was just about to head home. I can maybe call—"

"I'll smooth it for you, Angela. Listen kid, the chances of you doing anything but answering phones there are slim. I'm offering you something most kids in your position would give their eye teeth for; a chance to be a reporter!"

"Gee. Okay, Jeff."

He was pleased to hear excitement creeping into her voice.

"But about the access to the archives?" she asked.

"Give me five minutes and I'll call you back with the code to the door. And Angela?"

"Yes?"

"Not a word to Gaynor, or anyone else. You understand? If anyone asks anything just tell them you got permission to access the archives to help with your graduate paper."

Hanging up on Angela, he speed dialed his boss and explained he was on a big story. A very big story, but he needed a little more time and a little more background before it was ready for the presses. He traded the pass code to the archives with Angela for Michael Fitzpatrick's apartment address and nearly got into an accident himself as he sped from the parking lot.

Thank goodness this is Saturday, he thought, as he made his way down Mass Avenue passing Harvard University. The streets and one way's were so complex at this point he contemplated parking his car and going on foot. Although walking from Harvard Square to Hilliard Street, where Michael had an apartment, was tempting, he knew he needed his car to remain nearby.

Turning onto Hilliard Street from Mt Auburn Street, he slowed his car, keeping an eye on the house numbers. Coming to the one he wanted, he pulled over at the first spot that provided enough space.

"You can't park there!" a guy suddenly appearing in a doorway yelled.

"Sorry, I'll only be a minute," Sailor yelled back as he ran back up the street where he drove past the address he wanted. As an afterthought he added, "Police business!"

Maybe that would put him a little time before the tow truck appeared.

Standing on the front porch of an old Victorian, used now to house multiple tenants, he scanned the names next to the buttons that would ring his presence. He found Fitzpatrick's name near the bottom. Did that mean Michael lived on the top floor or the bottom, Sailor wondered? Ringing the bell, he took a deep breath to compose himself. He'd use that 'police business' line again. Had a nice official ring to it that would open most doors, he smiled.

No answer. He pushed again, holding his finger on the button for a full 10 count.

Suddenly the front door opened and a couple in their twenties was passing him.

"Excuse me," he touched the sleeve of the parka the young man was wearing. The bearded face and dark eyes with darker bags beneath them spoke of music, free-love, and drugs. "Would you know if Mike Fitzpatrick is in? He asked me to pick him up. I hope I've got the right address."

"No idea, dude," the man answered as he walked towards the stairs. Sailor could see by the man's expression he was leery of a stranger being there asking for Fitzpatrick. Probably thinks I'm a cop, he thought.

"Wait," the girl said, making her companion glare at her. "I heard him leave his apartment about five or ten minutes ago."

"He must have hopped a ride with someone else, I guess," Sailor offered knowing Michael's car was no longer available. He headed down the steps and turned towards his own car.

"Who should we say came by?" the man asked.

"His uncle Festus," Sailor replied as he suddenly broke into a run upon seeing a tow truck coming down the street.

Jumping behind the wheel and pulling away as soon as possible, he cursed himself, realizing that he should have trailed the Congressman as soon as he left the hospital. Now there was only one place to go. He was off to Medfield, the home of the Congressman and his next victim.

SIX

While he headed down route 109 to Medfield, Sailor tried calling Angela at The Hub without success. He was about to try again when he remembered she was probably in archives.

Noticing a gas station at the corner of what had to be Medfield's town center, he checked his near empty gas gage and pulled in.

"This Medfield is some beautiful town", Sailor said to the gas station attended. "I understand Congressman Fitzpatrick lives here. He ever drop by for gas?"

"Sure does. His wife, Emily, too," It was obvious to Sailor that the attendant felt proud about knowing the Congressman. This could work to his advantage.

"Ya know I knew the Congressman at one time. But heck, that was when he'd visit my dad at our home in Somerville. They served together."

"No kidding?" the attendant said while nodding. "Your dad was in Nam?"

"Yes sir," Sailor said. "Died from his wounds, too, but it took a few years for the shrapnel to finish him off. He and Fitzpatrick would be up till all hours of the morning drinking, laughing, and telling stories. Drove mom nuts. That was long before he was a congressman of course!"

"Sure, of course," the attendant went along. "You ain't seen him since then?"

"No, but I got to tell ya, me being in his home town and all, he sure would get a kick if I dropped in on him out of the blue. My being so close an all." Sailor added a chuckle while he slowly shook his head to show he was imagining just how surprised the congressman would be.

"You ought to do it," the attendant said.

"Do what?"

"Drop in on him. His house is just up the street."

"No kidding? It is, huh?" Sailor adopted a look of concentration then shook his head saying, "He probably isn't even home."

"Yeah, he is. I saw him go by with his son not long ago. He's there."

"How far up the street did you say?" Sailor asked the payoff question.

"Just a coupla miles. You leave here and stay on North Street. Take a right on East Circle and there it is. Only house in the cul-de-sac."

"Well I just might do that. Thanks."

A little more than three miles down North Street he found East Circle. He stayed just south of the entrance where he could see the house between the trees. Two cars were in the driveway, a Lexus and a Ford Suburban. He checked his rearview and saw two cars coming along the road. He wouldn't be able to stay here long without drawing attention to himself.

He jumped when his cell phone rang.

"Jeff? It's Angela. I think I have everything you could use."

"Good work. Tell me what you learned about the Congressman."

"What do you want to know?" she asked.

Rolling his eyes, he kept his voice measured and asked, "Where'd he go to school? How'd he make his money?"

"He graduated from Medfield High where he was the lead rusher on the football team. Got his undergrad and graduate degrees from Boston College where he majored in business. Spent three years in the Army with one tour in Viet Nam where he earned the bronze star. He took over his father's cable manufacturing business in '78 and sold it for undisclosed sum in 1998. According to Hoover's, the company grosses more than 150 million a year these days."

Sailor let out a whistle. "Good work kid. Seal what you have in an envelope, a dozen if you need them, and leave them in the bottom right drawer of my desk. It should be empty enough to hold them. If not, throw out whatever is in there. I'll be by later."

"You're coming back to work tonight?" She asked incredulously.

He closed the phone lid and slid it back into its belt holder as he wondered just what was required to win the Pulitzer Prize for reporting.

Turning the ignition, he watched in shock as the Congressman drove out of his driveway, stared directly at him as he took a left, and headed towards the town center.

"Who was that dad?" Mike asked.

"Beats me. Maybe just a gawker. Some people are under the impression politicians are like movie stars or something."

They reached the center of town and parked behind a row of stores that were facing the street. On the second floor was their family attorney's office. Climbing the steps, Fitzpatrick Sr. said, "You can trust Stan, Mike. We grew up together."

"Stanley Ross, at your service," the attorney said as they opened the office door. His hair was curly and needed a cut; gray was beginning to show on the sides. He was thin and had a small mole on his most prominent feature, his nose, which seemed too large for his face. Wearing a corduroy sports coat with patches on the elbows, he came from behind his desk and embraced the congressman.

"It's been a while, huh, Frank? Or is it Congressman Frank?" he smiled at Mike and winked.

"Too long, Stan."

"And will you look at the tree that came in with you! How are you Mikey?"

"I'm good Mr. Ross. Thank you." Mike caught himself staring at Ross, who reminded him of Kozmo Kramer from the Seinfeld show, and quickly shifted his gaze.

"It's Stan. You hear me Mike? You're of age now and from what the grapevine tells me, such as it is in this town, you'll be my competitor soon. Law school, huh? You have one picked out?"

"Ah, Stan," the Congressman said. "I don't mean to be rude ol' buddy, but this is more of an official visit than a social one."

"Sure, sure. Take some seats. We can chat later, huh?"

Mike and the Congressman sat facing Stan who returned to the seat behind his desk.

"Perhaps we should discuss my fees first?" Stan said. When they only stared at him for a response, he burst out laughing. "Geez you guys! A joke! I was joking! What can I do you for, congressman? You buying some property? Need to revise your will? Just tell me."

"I think we may need a defense attorney, Stan."

Stan looked from face to face waiting for a laugh. When it didn't come he said, "Go on, Frank."

"Mike was in a car accident today. The lady in the other car had a miscarriage as a result. I'm afraid charges may be brought against Mike and if that should happen, I want to be prepared. Mike was driving down—"

"Whoa! Stop there. I want to hear it from Mikey."

"You're right," his congressman conceded. "Go ahead, Mike."

After more than an hour of relating the story of his morning and answering questions, they were coming to the end. That's when the Congressman added, "I went to the hospital to visit with her, but they wouldn't let me see her."

"You went to the hospital to see her? Alone?"

"Yeah, I wanted to express my concern and sympathy. See if there was anything I could do for her," he answered.

"Like to pay her off you mean?" Ross suggested.

"What?" Fitzpatrick yelled.

"You're an idiot, Frank," Ross replied. "What I meant by that question is the very question every person who hates you and your political party will be asking. You should have come to me first."

"Oh damn," Fitzpatrick shook his head.

"Who have either of you spoke to about this?"

"No one," Father and son spoke in unison.

"See that it stays that way. The only person you'll answer to is your attorney. I can't stress that enough."

Stan Ross waited until they both acknowledged they understood with a nod of their heads.

"Any who, I'm obviously not qualified to represent you. But I can make a recommendation or two. Without hearing your story, I wouldn't be able to do that and don't worry, client attorney privilege still exists. I can't tell a soul about this without your permission."

"Okay, Stan. Who do you recommend?" the congressman asked.

"Normally, I would say Tom Cranks. I've known him since law school and he specializes in criminal law. But I got to tell you. I was at a law seminar in Sturbridge last fall and heard the most amazing young woman speak. She really knew her stuff when it came to criminal law. One of the reasons I didn't take that route was the minutia you need to know, not only about the law, but it helps a great deal to know more than a little about anatomy, psychology, forensics, the list just keeps getting longer. Any who, this lady reviewed a case she handled where her client was going down big time and would have, too, but for her knowledge in ballistics. She was able to show...."

"Ballistics, Stan?" The congressman asked. "We're talking about a car accident here."

"No, you're not," Stan emphasized 'not'. "You're talking about your son's life and the opportunities he'll have or not have as a result of this *accident*. Not to mention a first term congressman's reputation. Trust me on this. They're gonna go for your jugular Frank. And Mike's, too."

"Maybe I should call Carl Brunner. He's a big name attorney and has enough experience, for goodness sake," the congressman said. "Look how he handled that movie star shooting. The lady was guilty as hell and he had her walking free."

"You can go the Brunner route, Frank, but think about this; you put a big name like Brunner up against these guys, and by guys I mean the district attorney, and everyone starts thinking maybe you're looking to buy your son a way out. Hell, a lot of people will convince themselves you were the one driving! Don't ever forget that it's Mike whose feet are in the proverbial fire. Your role is one of a concerned dad."

Fitzpatrick turned to look at his son who remained silent throughout the exchange. "What do you think Mike?"

Mike shook his head. "I don't know, dad. She's not dead or anything, just a little bruised. She lost her baby and I feel as bad as a person can about that. But it's not my fault. The ice..."

"Yes it is your fault, Mike," Stan interrupted. "Don't say that again. At least not in public. You go around saying that and people will start thinking you believe you shouldn't be held responsible for your actions."

"But," Mike started to protest.

"Hold on," Stan raised his palm facing Mike. "Let me give you an example. Say you have a pit bull you're crazy about, but he's one mean son of a gun. Knowing this, you put up a chained linked fence that circles your property. Every few feet you put up alternate warning signs, glow in the dark type, stating "Beware of Dog!" and "Keep Out! Private Property". Unfortunately, Bob, your idiot neighbor, comes through the gate to lodge a personal complaint with you about your dog barking during supper hour. He gets mauled and, of course, sues. Who do you think the court is going to side with? The owner did everything he could to keep his dog enclosed and away from the public.

"Now think about this, what if it had been a child who entered that gate to retrieve her ball? You may see that as a big difference, but the law doesn't. It may not be the dog owner's fault his neighbor's a moron, but he's held responsible anyway."

"But anybody could have been driving my car," Mike argued. "There was no stopping it."

"From what you've told me, Mike, you slid quite a ways before making contact with her car. Is that right?" Ross asked.

"Yeah, it seemed like I was sliding forever."

"That street has a sidewalk on both sides? Buildings on either side? Cars parked lining the street?"

"Yeah, of course. It was all I could do to keep the car straight to avoid hitting them," Mike answered.

"So you admit to making every effort to avoid hitting an empty parked car while confessing to ramming your car into one occupied with a pregnant lady? That about sum it up?"

"No, no," Mike protested. "You're twisting things!"

"And I'm not even good at this stuff," Ross smiled.

Making their way back down the stairs towards the congressman's car, they both felt drained. They left it with Ross to contact the lady in Sturbridge to see what she thought of defending them against the charges that Ross assured them would come, and if she was available.

Mike reached out and stopped his father before he could open the door to the parking area.

"Stan's a real good guy dad. Thanks for arranging for me to meet with him."

"Let me tell you something, Mike. I've known Stanley Ross since grade school. He was the most obnoxious little kid you could hope to avoid meeting. Hell, he was the only first grader I've ever known to get beat up on his way home from school. And it shames me to say it now, but at the time, I believed he earned it!

"Well Stan finally made it to high school in one piece but, he hadn't changed his personality one lick. He was the smartest kid in school and his arrogance wouldn't let anyone forget it. Then one day at football practice, I look over and there's Stan, standing on the sidelines in full uniform. I almost laughed aloud and would have if coach Edelstein wasn't watching us".

"Boys," the coach announces, "this is Stanley Ross, our new linesman.

"We learned later that Stan was Edelstein's nephew. Not that it helped him. He took a beating at every practice, but always pushed himself back up. He never missed a practice and never saw action during an actual game, except for one. During the last game of the season, the coach gives Stanley a play number and tells him to get in the game. He runs out onto the field where a collective moan came from those of us in the huddle. It was a close game at this point and a win would put us over the 500 mark for the season.

"It was third and eight with the ball on their 25 yard line. Too far for our punter to try and we already lost the ball twice earlier to interceptions. Stanley throws his arms around me and another guy and hunches down with the rest of us. "Twenty-five Red Frame," he announces and we just stare at him. Twenty-five Red Frame was not a play we had heard of.

"Come again, Ross? Gary, our quarterback barked at him.

"25 Red Frame. What?" he looked at us. It was the only time I ever saw Stanley nervous.

Gary turns his head to glance at each of us and says, "95 Red Flame on 2!"

"I couldn't believe my ears. He was calling a play that had never worked for us, a reverse lateral. The quarterback laterals the ball to a runner headed in one direction who laterals it to another runner, me in this case, headed in the other direction. The idea is get the defenders headed in the wrong direction of the man with the ball."

"Ah, I know what a reverse lateral is, dad," Michael grinned.

"Well the first part of the play went as scripted; the ball was slammed into my gut as I ran past Tom Bower. But we seldom ran the play, even in practice, and the result was ugly. Instead of running in the direction of the first ball carrier to give the impression that was where the ball runner was headed, half our defenders stayed on the line waiting for me to get behind them. The play didn't fool anyone but Stanley. He ran to the left, got knocked on his butt, when he saw me take the ball. He got up and ran to the right to defend again, but got knocked flat on his back. As I made my turn to head up field, Stanley had somehow made his way closer to my side where I saw him take a monster hit from a guy I spent the game hoping to avoid. He was one of those linebackers who, by the very look on their face, you knew had an IQ no higher than a snail's, but encased in a head the size of a ripe melon. He was huge, all muscle, and fast. If it hadn't been for Stanley taking that hit I, would have taken it."

"Did you score?" Mike asked.

"I fumbled," the father snickered. "Lost that game and the school ended the season below 500 for the first time in years. And Stanley suffered two broken ribs, ending his football career in high school.

"Fortunately, a new defensive coach made some drastic cuts and recruited some pretty tough kids to play defense. He helped them to stay in school, too. As a result, I was able to make longer runs and a number of touchdowns.

"Where I'm going with this Mike is after that day on the field, watching Stanley take a beating and standing again for more, I knew he had a quality to him that deserved greater respect. I let it be known that if anyone had a problem with Stanley, they had a problem with me. Since then, Stanley thinks of me as his best friend in life. Hell, maybe I am, but the fact of the matter, is he remains the smartest son-of-a-bitch I ever met."

Opening the door, they were met with a bright flash to their eyes and Jeff Sailor's voice.

"Hello Congressman, I'm Jeff Sailor with The Hub. I wondered if you'd care to make a statement regarding your son Michael's car accident today."

"Wha... How did you know about the accident?" the congressman asked.

"Dad, no! Let's just go." Michael prompted.

"Michael! Perhaps you'd like to give your side of events as you see them?" Sailor asked. "You know she suffered a miscarriage don't you?"

The congressman was fumbling with car keys trying to get to the auto-unlock button.

"Without a statement from one of you, I'm going to have to write what I learn from others. Is that what you want?"

They got into the car and the congressman made a swift exit back onto North Street with another camera flash lighting up the car from behind.

"Nice picture, Congressman," Sailor chuckled. "Oh yeah, this just keeps getting better."

SEVEN

"I'll go myself. Thank you for calling, father." Bishop Connor placed the phone in the cradle and stared at the headlines of The Hub newspaper sitting before him. His assistant, Father Canalli, came into the room with a pot of coffee.

"Freshly brewed," he smiled and raised an eyebrow to the Bishop waiting for an invitation to pour.

"No thank you, Father. That was Father Coughlin from our Medfield parish on the line. He got a call from Congressman Fitzpatrick asking if he could drop by his home after Mass this morning."

"I read the news this morning, Bishop. A terrible thing for any family to have to endure," Father Canalli said.

"Indeed. I have a visit to make and no time to waste."

"On Sunday morning?" Father Canalli asked. He had received two calls in the past week alone from Archbishop Pollock instructing him to keep a tight leash on Connor and to convince him to drop his ties to the Congressman. As if I'm *his* superior, thought Canalli angrily. It was Bishop Connor who, ten years earlier, invited him to be his assistant. The invitation came at a time when Canalli was beginning to question his ability to instruct his congregation. Week after frustrating week, he would recite the homily and watch as eyes glazed over in anticipation of Mass ending. Being so closely associated with a Bishop, he thought, might help him to recharge, but that proved not to be the case. If anything, his time with Bishop Connor had led him to believe his talents would better serve the Church doing anything but being a parish priest and leave the weekly homily's to those better suited for it. He was indebted to Bishop Connor, but he had little choice but to follow the orders of Connor's superiors.

"Is it wise, Bishop, to be seen with them just now? According to the article, the Fitzpatrick boy may have been drunk and the Brackton lady plans to see that charges are brought against the boy for murdering her child. There'll be press all over their property and you'll be walking into a firestorm. Besides," he added, "you normally provide Mass the first Sunday for new arrivals," referring to the newly ordained priests.

"I'll be leaving that in your capable hands, father. The congressman is a friend and one of our most ardent supporters and I won't have him swinging in the breeze," Bishop Conner said as he rose and stretched, silently thanking the Congressman for not calling him directly.

"Ah me," the Bishop sighed. "What is it with this great country of ours? So much potential and yet, we elect a president who starts a war with foreigners and the next one who wants to kill our own unborn. It's gotten to the point where every four years my sermon makes reference to voting for the less of two evils."

"War will always be with us, Bishop," Father Canalli offered.

"True enough, father. History certainly bears that out."

"Oh," he continued, "You might want to use the homily about Jesus healing the son of the Roman Soldier. I always liked your interpretation of it. And after lunch, instruct the boys to work as a group to present to me one agreed upon reason why there can be no God. That'll stretch their minds and faith. We'll review it as a group tonight."

With that, he walked from the room allowing Father Canalli to place a call to Archbishop Pollock. Once he completed what he felt was the role of a Judas, he sat and contemplated what the Bishop had meant by "your interpretation."

Arriving in Medfield, Bishop Connor realized how correct Father Canalli had been. There were so many reporters and curiosity seekers by the Congressman's house he needed to park nearly a quarter of a mile away from the driveway. Walking towards the Fitzpatrick's front door, he went pretty much unnoticed until a reporter, just finishing a live report for TV, noticed his collar.

"Keep that camera rolling!" He yelled at his cameraman and literally jumped in front of the Bishop's path.

"Excuse me Bishop Connor," the reporter spoke into his microphone. "Are you here at the request of the Fitzpatrick family?"

Several other reporters noticed the new-comer being interviewed and ran to get near him. A dozen microphones were shoved near his face with cameras being lifted over the heads of those in front.

"Are you here to take confession, Bishop?"

"Will you perform a private mass for them, Bishop?"

Bishop Connor pushed his way through them and climbed the steps. Reaching for the doorbell, he heard one of throng behind him say, "Have we tried to get a statement from the Cardinal? Well let's do it!"

Turning to face the reporters the Bishop took a breath and said, "I am here to visit a friend. It may surprise some of you to know that, yes, even Bishops have friends."

A moment later, the door swung open and Congressman Fitzpatrick pulled the Bishop inside and swung the door closed as voices began to ring out with more questions.

"If I hadn't been walking by the door when the bell rang I would have ignored it," Fitzpatrick said. "I couldn't believe my eyes when I looked through the peephole! I still can't. Thank you for coming Bishop Connor."

The Bishop was a bit disorientated. It was much darker in here than outside where snow from the last storm brightened everything. Looking up the stairway to the second floor, he noticed the lights from lamps glowing on the walls. The Congressman noticed his look and explained.

"The first thing that greeted us this morning was having our pictures taken while we descended the stairs. Photographers were leaning against our windows! Since then, we've gone into blackout mode."

"Good thinking," the Bishop nodded. After what he just experienced outside he could almost imagine the windows being shattered by overzealous news people.

"I'm honored by your visit Bishop Connor, but" the Congressman hesitated, not sure how to mention their pack to appear have nothing more than passing familiarity with each other while he fought to have his Bill advance in the House of Representatives. Finally, he said. "I was expecting our Parish Priest, Father Coughlin," he explained.

"Yes, I know," the Bishop said. "He called me and explained your request and I decided to drop by myself."

"Emily? Mike?" the Congressman called up the stairs. "Come down here and see who came to visit us." He ushered the Bishop into the living room turning lights on as he passed them. He indicated a winged chair near the fireplace where a stack of wood was ready for match. As Fitzpatrick knelt to light the kindling, his wife and son came into the room.

"Bishop Connor?" Emily Fitzpatrick asked having recognized him from his visit to their church last Sunday. She may have been the only person in New England who wasn't aware of the close ties he shared with her husband these past several months. The Bishop stood from his chair and took her hand. "What a pleasant surprise!" She half turned and pointed to Michael. "And my son, Michael."

"A pleasure to meet you Bishop Connor," Michael said as he awkwardly offered his hand.

"So you're the Fitzpatrick they're so eager to speak with," the Bishop said nodding towards the windows.

"I'm afraid so, Bishop Connor," Michael answered while looking at his shoes.

"Although I suspect that bunch outside would be disappointed to learn of it," the Bishop said as resumed his seat, "I'm not here to offer you absolution, Michael. But perhaps I can provide you and your parents with some comfort. Please, everyone take a seat." He paused while the parents shared a spot together on the sofa and Michael, sitting on an ottoman, stared at the fire. Once they were settled he spoke again.

"Now, I've found over the years that the best place to start offering comfort is first knowing what's causing the pain," the Bishop smiled. "And there's nothing like a warm fire and comfortable chair to set the mood. What say you tell me a story, Michael?"

For nearly an hour, Michael retold of his car's slide down the hill, the crash, the police questioning and the likelihood of his being arrested for murder. The Bishop listened without interruption and when it was apparent Michael had come to the end, he asked his first question.

"They say, The Hub that is," he clarified, "that you refused to take a breathalyzer. Is that true?"

"Yes, Bishop," Mike answered. "I took part in a toast to the future with two friends that morning. I was afraid I might fail the test even though I didn't feel the least bit impaired. I can tell you this much, though, I will never drink again. Not ever!" He took a breath and sighed, "I just want to be able to forget about all of this."

"And you think by never tasting alcohol again you'll be making up in some small way for the problems your last drink caused you? That with time, this will all just go away?"

"Well, yeah," Michael answered tentatively. "My dad says time can heal most every wrong."

"I suppose it's my turn to tell you a story, Michael," the Bishop eased back in his chair.

"An old man had a very young boy for a neighbor. The boy was spirited and seemed to find disappointment only when he wasn't planning mischief or found himself neck deep in it. He appeared to hate everything and everybody. The old man noticed one day that the boy had picked up the habit of cursing and practiced at it every spare moment. His favorite curse was using our savior's name and often added a middle initial to it for effect.

"This bothered the old man considerably and, truth be told, he was somewhat afraid of the boy and what might happen if he fell on the wrong side of his spitefulness. But, he determined, something had to be done. Just overhearing the boy made him feel his own soul was being jeopardized. So he went to the boy and made him an offer.

"How would you like to earn five dollars?" he offered the boy.

"Well that was quite bit of money for a boy his age and he was eager to have it."

"What do I have to do? He asked, and I've omitted a word of two from the boy's actual answer," the Bishop smiled.

The old man answered, "I have a board that I will give you and for each day for the next week that you use the Lord's name in vain, I want you to drive one nail halfway into this board."

"Well, sure!" the kid said and immediately took the board, cursed mightily, and ran for a hammer and nail.

A week passed and the old man went out to the yard when he saw the boy and asked, "How'd you make out with my request?"

"The boy ran into his house and a moment later returned with a board that had seven nails sticking into it.

"Well done," said the man and handed the boy five dollars.

"Want to try it again for this week?" the boy eagerly asked.

"No, you did what I asked. It's just that I feel bad in having had you do it."

"Why? I didn't mind," the boy said.

"You see," the old man said, "every time you use the Lord's name in vain, you take a step closer to Hell where you'll burn for eternity. And those nails are there to remind us both that you spent the past several days making sure that will happen to you."

The boy thought about what the man said and came up with a plan.

"What if I take one of these nails out for each day I don't use the Lord's name in vain?" he asked. "Will you give me another five dollars?"

The old man thought a moment, secretly happy the boy had taken the bait, and answered, "I doubt you'll be able to do it. But it's a deal."

A week later, the old man once again had the boy fetch the board and was surprised to see the nails were all gone.

"You see," said the boy triumphantly, "the nails are gone and I am no longer in danger of going to Hell."

"Yes," the old man agreed, "the nails are gone but, the holes are still there."

The Bishop looked at Michael who stared back with an empty expression. The telephone rang. Mrs. Fitzpatrick reached for the phone on an end table, but once she lifted the receiver, she froze to hear what the Bishop would say next,

"You see, Michael, the point is that while we need to ask for forgiveness for damage done and guidance in how to atone for that damage, we must never forget the holes we've left behind."

"Hello?" She asked absently while digesting what the Bishop said. Oh! Yes, yes he is. One moment please."

She passed the receiver to the Bishop explaining, "It's Cardinal Pollock."

EIGHT

Unlike the general public, Jeff Sailor felt he had no restrictions upon him to visit Jessica Billington-Brackton at the hospital. It was simply a matter of getting to her room. He arrived at the hospital entrance, coming directly from his office where he spent the night preparing his story in time for Monday morning's paper. He grabbed a few hours sleep on the reception room sofa before heading for the hospital. His hope was to get to Brackton before she had a chance to see the morning news. And just as importantly, speak to her before every news media had a journalist shouting questions at her.

Instead of stopping at the receptionist, where he knew he wouldn't gain access to the patients' floors, he walked into the near-by waiting room. It was early, but there was already quite a few people lounging about. Some would be there many hours more, he knew, to await the results of emergency operations being performed on their loved ones. Looking back at the receptionist, his worst fear was realized as two cameramen and four reporters were standing at the reception desk asking about access to Brackton.

"Well, let us speak to her doctor," one of them demanded.

"He's not on duty," was the reply.

One the reporters held up a hundred dollar bill and winked at the receptionist.

"That does it," she snapped. "I'm going to get my supervisor and recommend she call the police to escort you out!"

As she was headed for the glass partitioned office behind her, one of them said, "Lady, you ain't seen nothing yet," provoking a harsh laugh from his comrades.

Sailor saw his chance and walked behind them heading for the elevator bank straight ahead. Luck was on his side when the doors opened to one of the lifts just as he arrived. Scanning the floor buttons, he found two with "Recovery" beside them and pushed the higher one. He'd work his way down if necessary.

The doors opened to an empty nurse's station where he spotted a stethoscope sitting on the desk. Her walked to the desk and casually placed the stethoscope around his neck. Walking leisurely and confidently, he started to stroll by each room. As he passed each room he'd glance in and noticed two patients for each room with their names on a whiteboard pinned beside the door. All he needed to do to find her was look for the "Billingsly-Brackton" name. Four doors down, he found it. Hers was the only name on the whiteboard.

With the curtain by her bed pulled halfway, he could only see her feet under the sheet covers. Moving quietly, he entered the room and found her lying in the bed, staring at the ceiling. Glistening tear tracks lined either side of her cheeks. He thought she looked like Grace Kelly, with only a string of pearls missing from her neck to complete the picture. The left side of her face was bruised and her overall complexion suggested she never saw the sun.

Noticing his arrival, she swiped at her face to dry it and said, "Good morning, Doctor."

Sailor smiled at her and was about to correct her when he realized what a gift she just handed him. Improvising was his strong suit.

"Good morning. I'm Doctor Bragg. How are you feeling this morning?"

"A lot better than yesterday I can assure you," she answered.

"I'm happy to hear that. It makes my job much easier when my patients are on the mend physically."

"What do mean?" she asked.

"Oh! Sorry. I'm one the psychologist on staff. My job is to come by and speak to those people who have experienced serious accidents to help them mend psychologically. It's been found to speed up body healing as well. And I can assure you," he smiled using her words, "it's a much better task than speaking to the loved ones of the recently deceased."

Realizing his error, he blurted, "Oh I'm sorry! I should have started by letting you know how sorry I am for your losing your baby. That was so insensitive of me. I truly am—"

"It's Okay doctor," she interrupted. "It's not like I lost a real baby."

In an effort to assure him that she was not upset with his statement, she gave a smile. He seemed so much nicer and less brusque than the doctors who kept coming by to check on her vital signs and asking where it hurt. He hadn't even used his stethoscope to monitor her heart. She found that she wanted his company a while longer.

Sailor realized he was near babbling, but stopped to take her statement into account. If she didn't feel badly about hemorrhaging out her baby, this story may die a quick death.

While Sailor's face still felt hot, he slid a chair that was against the wall and scooted it near her bed. Sitting down, he reached into the inside pocket of his sports jacket and activated the tape recorder. He crossed his legs and locked his hands over one knee. A perfectly innocent and relaxing pose for his patient. After that last gaff, he would need to stay sharp, he realized.

"Do you remember the accident?" he asked.

"Of course I do." she answered.

He hoped he hadn't overplayed his hand with that question. Maybe he should have kept up the small talk a while longer. But he knew he was running the risk of being tossed out on his ear at any minute. He decided a gamble was worth it.

"And?" He asked.

"I was driving down Phillips Street and when I passed through the intersection where Anderson Street intersects, a red car slammed into the driver's side of my car. He must have gone right through his stop sign," she slowly shook her head trying to comprehend why someone would do that. "I think I may have blacked out for a minute or two, but not for long. She paused and looked directly at him. "Is that what you wanted to know?" she asked.

"It's a good start," he smiled again. "It shows you haven't lost any memory."

He was thinking furiously, trying to determine not only what to ask next but how to ask it. 'It's not like a real baby' kept running through his head.

"According to the police 'accident report,' the man who hit you is the son of a prominent politician. Do you know Michael Fitzpatrick?" he asked.

"Is that usual," she asked in reply.

"That you might know him?" he was genuinely confused.

"That a psychologist would read a police report," she answered.

"Why certainly, "he bluffed. "Answers can often be found in the details, as they say."

She turned her head and looked back at the ceiling. "No, I don't know who he is. Is he related to congressman Fitzpatrick, the zealot?"

Oh! That was a good one, thought Sailor.

"His son, in fact" he answered. "Do you know the family?"

"I know of them, doctor. I have no desire to actually meet them."

"If that's the case," Sailor measured his words carefully, "it doesn't sound like you'll be seeking damages against them."

"Jessica? Should I come back?" A man who appeared at the end of the bed asked. He was tall, at least six foot two, Sailor guessed, and dressed in a Brooks Brothers suit. His dark hair was brushed back in the style of the movie star, Andy Garcia.

"John, meet Doctor Craig, hospital psychologist" she said, nodding towards Sailor. "And this is my husband John Brackton."

"It's Bragg, actually," Sailor corrected her. "How do you do, Mr. Brackton?"

"Fine thank you," Brackton said as he shook Sailor's hand. "I can pop down to the cafeteria and grab a coffee and leave you two alone."

"The doctor was just asking if we planned to press charges. You don't think that's necessary, do you? Did you know it was congressman Fitzpatrick's son that hit me, John?"

"I learned it this morning. Damn Hub has his picture next to yours on the front page."

Sailor blanched and turned in his chair to make a hurried exit through the door, if necessary.

"Oh dear," she said, turning her head away. "I'm sorry, John. You don't like publicity of any kind, I know."

"Don't be silly," Brackton said as he squeezed her toe through the sheet. "This is different. And yes, I plan to see Fitzpatrick pay handsomely to keep his precious son out of jail while ours lies buried. But he won't succeed, you know. I've personally contacted the DA, Jack O'Brien as soon as I read the article. I supported him big time when he ran for that office and he owes me."

"I could use a coffee, John, if you don't mind?" Jessica Brackton asked her husband. She was beginning to look even paler, in Sailor's opinion.

"Not a problem, darling," Brackton answered. "And you doctor? Care for a coffee?"

"No thank you. We were just finishing up."

"Nice meeting you," Brackton said as he strolled out the door before Sailor could return the compliment.

"He's the youngest billionaire on Wall Street you know," Jessica Brackton said while looking at the empty doorway.

"What?" Sailor wasn't sure he heard her correctly.

"He'll fly back tonight and make more millions during the week and return to our home here on Saturday where he will lock himself in his study," she said. "I hate New York City. Is there something wrong with me for hating New York City, doctor?"

"If there were, I'd have many more patients," Sailor smiled. He studied her face, noting her far-away look. He was getting nervous for her.

"It's John you should be speaking with, you know. Not me," she said.

"Oh? Why's that?" Sailor asked, knowing he was getting in way over his head.

"He didn't know I was pregnant until the accident. He learned of it yesterday after I was brought here," a tear began to form in her eye. "I wonder what he's thinking," she said, more to herself than Sailor. "Wouldn't you want to know, doctor? What he must be thinking?"

"I think we've covered enough for today," he answered while placing his chair back against the wall. Her pallor was becoming alarmingly pasty as her face seemed to appear made of alabaster. "I'll check back with you later."

Turning, he headed out the door and towards the elevators. Realizing the nurse's station was no longer vacant; he decided to use the stairs instead. Taking the stethoscope from around his neck, he tossed it at the nurse who sat staring at him as he walked down the hall. "The Brackton women may need attention. Check on her, will you?"

The nurse studied him a moment and said, "I don't recognize you, doctor. Are you the family's private physician? If so, you know you need to check in here first and..." Suddenly a series of bleeps and buzzers had her turn her attention to the control panel behind her. Reaching for the microphone, she repeated in strong but controlled tones, "Code Blue, Room 525. Code Blue, Room 525."

Sailor used the opportunity to slip through the exit to the stairs as he heard steps running down the corridor responding to what he felt sure was a response to Code blue; a cardiac arrest.

NINE

As the Bishop drove towards Fitzpatrick's home in Medfield, Sailor attempted to reach Jack O'Brien at his home from his office at The Hub. On the third ring a voice responded, "This is O'Brien."

"Good morning Mr. O'Brien, this is Jack Sailor calling. I—"

"Sailor?" the attorney interrupted. "From The Hub?"

"Yes, sir. I was—"

"I wondered how long it would take you people," O'Brien said. "I'll have a complete statement for you tomorrow morning. Come by my offices on State Street at noon."

"Of course, Mr. O'Brien but in the meantime..." The phone line went dead.

Sailor snapped his cell phone shut and returned his attention to his PC and the piece he had already started.

"Jack O'Brien, district attorney for the state, will make a statement to the press at 10 o'clock this morning from his law offices." He saw no reason to hide that fact knowing O'Brien would have word out to every news media outlet by the end of today.

"District Attorney Jack O'Brien has been at the helm of the biggest cases the Commonwealth has seen these past three years. Unlike his predecessors, who typically would farm out cases for his staff to prosecute, he took a personal interest in high-profile cases where he is the lead prosecutor.

"He's won several convictions in court, but last spring he went up against Carl Brunner who successfully defended a local woman from a murder indictment involving a love triangle, money, and the death of film star, Stephanie Fench."

Leaning back in his chair he stretched his arms above his head, gyrated his shoulders, and thought of his next call.

The phone was answered on the first ring, "Fitzpatrick residence," a female voice said.

"Good morning, may I speak to Mike please?" Sailor asked in what he hoped was an innocent voice.

"Who's calling please?" then added, "He's not really taking calls today."

Sailor turned to the one skill besides reporting that he excelled at; he improvised, "It's about his car."

"Oh. One moment please," was the answer, and Sailor could hear Michael being summoned to the phone call concerning his car.

A moment later he was on the line, "This is Michael Fitzpatrick."

Sailor swallowed, then plunged right in. "Michael, this is Jeff Sailor from The Hub. Before you hang up on me you ought to know that I can help you. What I choose to write and don't write will have an impact on your case. I was hoping you could shed some light on what happened. You can ignore my request, but that will leave me to write a piece based on assumptions. I don't like having to do that and I'm sure you don't want that either, do you?"

His question was met with silence and Sailor began to wonder if Michael had disconnected after all. Finally, he heard a sigh, followed by a sharp intake of breath.

"The road was all ice! I tried to stop the car but couldn't. No one could have! And I didn't take the breathalyzer because I had just left my friend's apartment and…it didn't seem right to have to take it. It was Jenkins's idea and it was only one shot… Oh damn!" And with that last uncompleted statement the line went dead.

Sailor jotted down the response verbatim, and sat staring at the words.

"The road was covered in ice?" he wondered. He tried to remember the road conditions on Saturday morning. Cold, he recalled, but no snow. He was drinking? And then, "who the hell is Jenkins?"

Reaching for the phone book kept at the bottom of his desk drawer, he flipped through the pages until he found a suitable suspect.

"Timothy Jenkins", he read aloud, "15 Revere Street, Boston." He highlighted the listing and ripped the page from the phone book. While about to pass Angela's reception desk, he stopped and smiled at her.

"Wonderful piece of work you did," he told her. "I plan to mention it to your boss. I've no doubt we'll be sharing an office ourselves soon."

"Really?" she blushed.

"For certain! If anyone asks, I'm out on the Fitzpatrick story." He turned and several moments later he was stepping into the open elevator door.

Sailor found a parking spot just doors down from Jenkins' address on Beacon Hill, dismissing his luck on this being a weekday morning. He rang the bell and waited.

"Who is it?" a tinny female voice asked.

"Good morning," Sailor answered. "Is Timothy Jenkins home?"

"No, he's at class. Can I help?"

"Well perhaps," he said while thanking his luck. "May I have a moment or two of your time?"

A buzzing sound indicated the door was being unlocked and that he could enter. Running up the stairs, he stopped before a door with a young blonde peering out over the door chain. He stood there a moment catching his breath. He needed to calm down, he thought. Be more professional!

"Thank you, Ms…"

"I'm Carla," she said. "A friend of Tim's. I'm not supposed to let anyone in when Tim's not here."

"No problem," he assured her.

"What do you want with Tim?" she asked.

"Oh, it's nothing important really. Mike mentioned Tim to me last night and I wanted to come by and introduce myself."

"Mike Fitzpatrick?" she asked.

"That's right. I'm his uncle. My sister, Mike's mother," he said while rolling his palm face up for her clarification, "asked me to do a little investigative work on my own. Before things have a chance to get muddied."

"Yeah, well," she said hesitantly," Mike stayed here Friday night is all I know. He slept on the couch."

"That's what he said," Sailor nodded. "Big party wasn't it?"

That question made her blink.

"If Mike calls a party of three big," she frowned. "I wanted to go out but Tim said we had to stay and support Mike. 'Cause of his girl breaking up with him?" she said it as a statement.

"Right," Sailor said and tilted his head to the side to indicate he was thinking. "His girlfriend…"

"Ann," Carla said.

"Right! Ann. You know, the way Mike described the drinking, I just assumed it was a big party." Sailor knew he went out on a limb with that statement but he was following his intuition, which often proved correct.

"He certainly drank plenty," she nodded while obviously remembering. "Tim kind of encouraged him. At least in my opinion, Mr…?"

"Carlisle," Sailor answered. "Tom Carlisle."

"Anyway," she continued, "I didn't know Ann broke up with him until the next morning. I'm sorry for him and all, but I think it's for the best."

Sailor lifted his eyebrows.

"She's nice and everything but…"

"It's okay. Just between us," Sailor encouraged.

"She's so stuck up. You could tell she didn't want to be around Tim and me. Like the Cranston name was special or something. Oh! I'm sorry! You probably liked her."

"Actually, I've never met her. But no worries, I won't mention this to Mike," he assured her.

"So, Mike left here Saturday morning. What time was that?"

"Didn't he tell you?" she asked.

"Of course, just corroborating stories is all. Makes me feel so Robert Parker," he laughed having referenced the local detective author.

"About 8:15 or 8:30 I guess. Jim came by to borrow Tim's ski poles," she said while studying the door chain. She was trying to recollect that morning. "Oh! Then they all had a shot and Mike left," she looked back at Sailor smiling.

"Just the one shot, huh?" he nodded. "What was that about anyway? I didn't think to ask Mike."

"About?" she asked.

"Well, 8 o'clock in the morning's a little early to start drinking shots, even for the young and fit," he smiled.

"I don't know," she shook her head. "I was in the bedroom and heard them talking. That's how I learned about Ann breaking up with Mike. And it was bourbon!" she suddenly volunteered. "I remember Tim saying Bourbon never hurt anyone."

"Gee, you have a real good memory," Sailor complimented her. He would have kissed her, too, for all that she told him.

"Thanks for meeting with me," he added and turned to head down the stairs.

"I'll mention you to Tim," she said. "Will you be dropping back to see him?"

"No, I don't think so," he turned to answer her. "You've pretty much told me everything I needed," he smiled at her and skipped down the stairs towards the street.

He hit the rewind button of his recorder as he rushed back to his office.

TEN

Representative Brad Sullivan came out of his home office, went to the den, and sat in his easy chair facing the television. It was quarter to twelve so he had fifteen minutes before he would turn on the television for the noon news. He was up half the night documenting his plan to win the congressional seat of Fitzpatrick in the next election, eighteen months away. He had a lot more work to do, he knew, but he needed to give his head a rest. He hadn't used his mind so hard on anything since his law exams and that was nearly ten years ago.

He was making good progress on a list of potential supporters he would contact when Jessica, "that's Mrs. Billington-Brackton to everyone else, thank you," crossed his mind. They were to meet for some "fun" the very day of her accident. Oddly, he thought, twice in the same week wasn't something she wanted since their early meetings, when they first started seeing each other. But events had changed things quickly and he never had a chance to call her to tell her it was over, that he didn't want to meet with her again. At least until he was a congressman. Calling her now, he knew, would be dangerous and fraught with risks. Depending on her condition, her husband might even be answering her cell phone. Unlikely, he knew, but possible. And her condition! According to the local newspaper, she was pregnant for goodness sake! What kind of a sick-o gets knocked up and continues with an affair? The poor bastard, Sullivan thought, acknowledging her husband for the first time that morning. It would have been their first child, too.

Sullivan thought of how things had started so innocently between them. No, not innocently, he corrected himself. From the moment they met, he wanted to share a bed with her. At the time, their first meeting at a modest fund raising event for his run at becoming a representative, he would have given the chances of a carnal experiencing with Jessica a thousand to one shot. She, a Boston Brahmin and he, the son of immigrants. But something clicked between them from the moment they met.

His brother-in-law, Sean Foley, arranged for him to hold the fundraiser in the back room of Gardelli's Restaurant, in the north end of Boston. Sean enhanced his meager income by booking numbers for one of the main clientele of the restaurant.

As a result, a word to the restaurant owner resulted in the fee for the room being waived. What's more, the owner had the tables set with white linen table clothes, potted flowers, and he served appetizers prior to Sullivan giving his campaign speech.

Not long after speaking to the crowd of about fifty people, he felt a touch on his shoulder, turned and saw her. He took her hand in greeting and felt the squeeze, the minuscule difference in pressure that signaled there may be something more to her; to them, if he pursued it. Which, of course, he did.

"My husband tells me good things about you, Mr. Sullivan," she said while still holding his hand. It was her husband, John Brackton, who had arranged for many of the wealthier guests to be seated there tonight.

"Please, call me Brad. I can't tell you how much I appreciate your support. I never realized the costs involved in running a campaign! It's a shame your husband couldn't make it here tonight."

"He's in New York, and as long as you deliver on what my husband expects of you, you needn't worry about cost. Did he tell you what that was?" She asked looking him in the eyes.

"I'm sorry, Mrs. Brackton, I lost you. What was?"

"It's Jessica," she replied. "And I'm asking if my husband told you what he wanted in return for supporting you?"

"Ah, no. I think it's more a matter of seeing eye-to-eye as to what our district needs and—"

"I'm sure he'll get around to it then," she interrupted while suddenly seeming to be bored with him. She dropped her hand from his and scanned the room while Sullivan tried to think of something to keep her near him.

"I wish my wife didn't have to leave so early," he said. "She's on the planning committee of NOW and their budgets are due next week."

"Have you met Carl Hanlon yet?" she asked him, overlooking the comment about his wife.

"Carl Hanlon?" he repeated trying to remember. "No, not yet. Doesn't he own that chain of dry cleaners you see everywhere?"

"Yes, that's one of his businesses. I'm sure he's here at my husband's request. Let me introduce you to him. And let me warn you," she lowered her already soft voice, "he hates to see new faces moving to the neighborhood, if you know what I mean."

"This is Boston," Sullivan answered, "there's new faces in the city every day."

"But not living here," she replied. "Working here is one thing, but living next door?"

"Oh! I see what you mean," Sullivan said. "You're referring to immigrants."

"Not me!" she answered in mock surprise. "Mr. Hanlon. Come on, let's go speak with him. I'm sure you'll find him colorful." With that she took his arm and they walked to where Carl Hanlon stood leaning against the wall sipping from the beer bottle in his hand.

The only remarkable thing that Sullivan could recall about his meeting Hanlon was his preference to use the F word. He found it to be distasteful and was shocked to see Jessica Brackton remain standing by while Hanson spoke about "the invasion of immigrants" and how Cambridge should be bombed.

Later, after most of the guest had left he was surprised to see that Jessica Brackton was still there. She was seated alone at a table watching him as he shook hands and said goodbye to the last of the guests. Sean was busy bussing the tables and placing the potted flowers, those not taken by the guests, in boxes.

Walking over to her table, he took a seat next to her.

"When is your husband due back?" he asked. "I must thank him personally for his support tonight."

"I can relay that message, Brad. But it's still early, don't you think? Would you have any interests in buying me a drink?"

"Of course! Let's go to the front, the restaurant bar is—"

"Not here. It's a nice place but, I was thinking of someplace more cosmopolitan. Like the Black Orchid or Fiddlers."

He recognized the first as a bar packed with Irish immigrants and the other a college hangout for near dropouts. But both served well if they were looking for anonymity.

"I'm game," he smiled and offered to drive.

She chose the Black Orchid as it was relatively close by and, being a Thursday night, crowded with the newly arrived Irishmen drinking alongside their recently established cousins who had jobs, but felt ill-used.

"I love to listen to Irishmen speak," she spoke close to his ear to be heard. "It's like a song, a lilt or something."

"I know what you mean," Sullivan nodded. "I grew up with it. My grandparents were both from Ireland."

Leaning against the bar, sipping a black and tan, was an older man with grizzled whiskers and an eye that claimed it didn't miss much. He was looking at Sullivan and Brackton and instinctively knew where their night was headed.

"Hey Flaherty!" the bartender yelled over the noise of the crowd at him. "I'd better be seeing some coin from you soon or this'll be the last night you'll be cuffing."

"I told you the hotel pays by the fortnight!" The old man yelled back. "Can you count to fourteen?"

When the band came on to play the noise level went up another several decibels, requiring Sullivan and Brackton to lean into each other to be heard.

Several gimlets later, they were trashing the back of his SUV where he deliberately parked it, the rear of a parking garage where the light overhead had burnt out.

The next morning, Brad awoke to a headache and lightness to his step he hadn't experienced in years. He found a note on the kitchen counter from his wife stating he had better have a good reason for being out so late and that she would be home about six o'clock that evening and to "be sure to watch the news at noon!" His next thought was the SUV.

Going directly to the van, he opened the doors and inspected the back seat for any signs it had been used for anything but sitting. He was grateful it appeared normal. But, as he was about to close the door, he noticed something shiny, a metal object nearly out of sight under the passenger seat. It was a cell phone. Opening it and scrolling through the numbers he realized that it must belong to Jessica Brackton.

He returned to the kitchen, thumbed through the phone book, and found her home number. She answered on the third ring.

He explained what he had found, while deliberately not mentioning any details from the previous night, and wanted to know how she would like to have him return it to her.

"My practice isn't that far from you, so if the timing is good," he offered, "I could swing by this afternoon."

"I have a meeting I'm expected to attend at my church this afternoon. Besides, that would be awfully inconvenient for you. I'm so sorry. But I do plan to be near Quincy Market tomorrow night. Perhaps we could meet there?"

Sullivan hesitated, not being sure another meeting would be in his interests. Her husband represented an unfathomable depth of wealth to his campaign. But that was the same reason he was unable to deny any request she may have of him. He knew that he had made a mistake of gigantic proportions last night that jeopardize his marriage and political ambitions, but as long as they both remained discreet, everything should be fine.

"Of course, just name the place and time," he said.

"Why don't you give me your cell phone number and I'll call you when I'm on my way there?"

"Good idea," he responded and as it turned out, it was a good idea. Right up until her accident.

Glancing at his watch, he picked up the remote and turned on the wall mounted wide-screen to the local 12 o'clock news. He didn't want to disappoint Maggie by ignoring the request she made on the note she left for him. No matter. He was looking forward to O'Brien's statement regarding the case the state would bring against the son of his soon-to-be Republican challenger for Congress. He was sure that any other surprises Maggie thought awaited him would pale in comparison.

The talking head behind the anchor's desk was doing his best to look serious when a picture of Jack O'Brien, beside one of Michael Fitzpatrick, showed on the screen behind him. Sullivan turned up the volume.

"Two days ago we reported on the terrible accident involving Congressman Fitzpatrick's son, Michael, and socialite Jessica Billington-Brackton. We go live now to State Street where our own Carrie Banks is awaiting an announcement from the district attorney's office."

Sullivan watched as the anchorman's image changed to what appeared to be a conference room full of reporters. The camera panned the room and came to rest on the face of Carrie Banks.

"Thank you, Walt. I, along with several colleagues," she smiled at the camera, "am standing here in district attorney Jack O'Brien's conference room awaiting word on a promised announcement concerning the status of charges that, may or may not, be brought against Michael Fitzpatrick, the son of congressman...hold on! Here he comes."

The camera turns to face the front of the room where Jack O'Brien stands at the head of the table and is smiling for the cameras. The cameramen edge nearer for a close up of the attorney's face.

"I wish to thank you all for coming on such short notice," he stated, causing several reporters to be heard chuckling off screen.

"I will try to make this brief," several more chuckles could be heard as O'Brien was known to be a camera hound. It was thought amongst many local journalists that he would host a news conference on his latest shoe shine if it meant getting on camera. It was also widely believed he had his sights set on a higher political office, most likely the governor's, once he garnered enough notoriety as DA.

"No doubt you are all aware of the recent, horrific loss suffered by the Brackton's at the hands of an errant, possibly drunk driver. I want to assure the Brackton family, as well as the good citizens of Massachusetts, that this office does not play politics or favorites when justice is demanded. To that end, I have instructed this office to pursue legal action against Michael Fitzpatrick, who will be charged with willful negligence resulting in the death of Taylor Brackton.

"Thank you."

As the camera was turning to capture the face of Carrie Banks again, it caught the image of several reporters fleeing the room with cell phones pressed to their ears.

"Well Walt," Carrie spoke loudly while smiling, "you heard it live, Michael Fitzpatrick will be facing a murder conviction in the loss of the Brackton's infant son, Taylor."

"Any idea what happens now, Carrie?" the anchorman asked.

"The only thing I know for certain, Walt, is that this reporter is going to join the crowd you may have seen rushing out of here and will try to get a statement from the Fitzpatrick's, specifically the Congressman!"

"Thanks, Carrie and keep us informed.

"In a related story, NOW is staging a demonstration in Medfield Center, home of Congressman Fitzpatrick, where we'll join Tom Sander with a 'live' broadcast of that event after the following messages."

"Oh, oh," Sullivan straightened in his chair. "Please tell me" he whispered into his hands, "my wife is not staging a protest against the man I will be running against. What have you done, Maggie?"

ELEVEN

Maggie looked into her compact mirror and smiled at the male reporter facing her, who was waiting for the cue that they were 'live'. Around them marched nearly fifty NOW members holding hand painted signs reading, "Fight for Right!" and "Equality for Fitzy, too!" Not a bad number of people, Maggie thought, on such short notice.

She glanced to the cameraman standing beside the reporter while adjusting knobs as he panned from the reporter to her. Was it just my face he'd capture, she wondered. Forcing herself to focus, she thought of how this would not only help her cause, but her husband Brad's as well. Although she would never say it, she wanted him to be a congressman more than he did. Being near all that power gave her stomach butterflies. He simply had to take Fitzpatrick's seat from him and she was going to do everything within her power to help. He was just too good a man, who involved himself in issues that mattered to the country.

The first action Brad Sullivan took upon passing his bar exam was to become a member of the American Civil Liberties Union, better known as the ACLU. While his ACLU membership was a topic of conversation when Maggie and he first met, it was not how Maggie chose to remember it. She enjoyed telling potential NOW candidates that she met her future husband during a NOW Membership drive where he stood on the outskirts of the crowd listening to NOW's sales pitch. She knew right away that he was the man for her. Accurate or not, it made for a good story and often helped young single women in their decision to enroll.

But Maggie had noticed for some time now that those women showing the most reluctance to enroll had issues with one article of the six that made up their Constitutionality Equality Amendment or CEA, as they called it. And Article Three was pretty much the corner stone of their organization. She knew it by heart:

This article prohibits pregnancy discrimination and guarantees the absolute right of a woman to make her own reproductive decisions including the termination of pregnancy.

The rest of the articles were simply common sense, she felt, but this one, this one was the primary reason a lot of potential members backed away. Most of her colleagues would shake their heads at what they felt was a display of simple stupidity for not joining. "It's our body," they'd reason, "why let a judge decide what we can and cannot do with it? Most men won't take responsibility for a pregnancy, let alone help raise the child. You want them to continue to tell us we must bear and raise their mistakes?"

We have such a long way to go in educating the public, she knew. A case in point was that the declining enrollment in recent years could be clearly traced to the organizations support of Bill Clinton during the Monica Lewinski scandal. What scandal, damn it!

But Maggie knew that many women and men were still under the spell of the Church which, she came to learn after Google-ing several sites, stipulated that human life was the most important aspect of Christianity and that it began at conception.

Church, she thought, one of the oldest organizations on earth, ran by men for men.

She had been looking for some way or something that would help soften the organization's hard shell exterior. And, she felt the perfect opportunity presented itself in the Michael Fitzpatrick case.

As the local president for the National Organization for Women, Maggie was responsible for promoting the organization's national agenda at the state and local levels through statewide activities. Being in charge of what those statewide activities would be was a prime reason for her accepting the nomination and ultimate office of state president. She knew in her bones NOW could wield more clout with the right goals, the right marketing, and most importantly, the right leadership.

She spent the previous evening calling the leaders of the local chapters and asking for as many volunteers they could muster to meet at the Medfield town center at 11 o'clock the next day. Her plan was to show how upset NOW membership was with the prospect that if an innocent woman could lose her baby to an irresponsible driver, then that driver should be held to the same standard as the back alley abortionist would receive under the Congressman's Bill.

"Faith for Life," she mused. Have to give credit where it's due, I suppose. Semantics could make or break a cause, she knew. But so could a well organized, well led rebellion.

Her focus shifted to the cameraman who raised the fingers of his left hand and began to drop them one at a time. When the last digit fell, the reporter flashed a bright smile to the lens. Nothing else seemed to be happening, Maggie noticed, but then it occurred to her the reporter was listening to the anchorman.

Maggie suddenly felt a chill of fear as she grasped to remember the reporters name. "John," she remembered. Then just as suddenly, she was sure it was "Tom".

"Thank you, Walt," the reporter suddenly spoke. "I'm here with Margaret Sullivan, recently elected president of the Massachusetts' chapter of National Organization for Women."

With that he moved the microphone closer to Maggie's face obviously expecting a comment.

"Hi," she smiled deciding to give up on using his name. "And its Maggie," she said.

"Okay, Maggie," the reporter smiled wider, "can you tell us what this protest is about?"

"Yes I can. Many viewers may not be aware of this, but Congressman Fitzpatrick has a bill he authored and is trying to bring before Congress to become law. He and his supporters call it the 'Faith for Life!' Bill. But we call it our 'Fight for Right!' Bill."

"Could you explain that a little more?" the reporter asked.

"Certainly. The congressman's bill calls for life imprisonment for any back alley abortionist found to have little or no medical training performing an abortion. Well, I'm fairly certain drinking and driving has little to do with medicine and killing a fetus by car certainly qualifies as a non-medical procedure. Hence, we expect the congressman's son to be held accountable for murder and not some trumped up charge that allows him to walk away with a hand slap, simply because he's a Fitzpatrick."

"So you're saying that because of his "Faith for Life" bill, you want his son to be held to the same standards as a back alley abortionist?"

"That's correct!" Maggie couldn't hold back her excitement having seen that she was making her point. "Maybe this will help the congressman to understand what every women in this great country will face if his bill is enacted into law. We may just as well run in front of a car than to face an untrained abortionist, and yet that is what the congressman will be forcing tens of thousands of women to do each year."

"Thank you," he said. "That was certainly enlightening."

The reporter was being told though his ear piece to stall for time before turning the story back to the anchor desk. Turning to some of the on-lookers he spotted a middle-aged lady looking on quietly but ill-at-ease.

"Excuse me," he said turning his back on Maggie while approaching the on-looker. "I wondered if you cared to share your thoughts on all of this."

"Not sure I even know what they're doing," she answered, "but I can tell you this. I like Congressman Fitzpatrick."

"I'll tell you what I think of it," another lady near-by shouted. She was older than his last subject with grey hair, a moderately wrinkled complexion, wearing jeans and a plaid shirt that she wore untucked.

The reporter moved closer to her. "Yes, ma'am?"

"I'd like to know how many of these women are Democrats and how many are Republicans. I'll bet you a hot lunch that they're democrats trying to bring harm on a Republican politician. It ain't right to hide that under a painted sign, no matter what it says."

"Oh for goodness sakes that's not what this is about!" A lady standing to the right said. The reporter moved to capture her comments.

"These people are with NOW. They support the right for a woman to choose abortion and the congressman is trying to stop them from having that right."

"Thank you, Ms..."

"I'm Joan Riley. Just moved here a short time ago," she said.

"You seem to know the purpose of the protest, so how do you feel about it?"

"I haven't giving it much thought, to tell the truth, but now that I'm standing here watching them and you can bet I'll bone up on it. When I make a decision, I like it to be an informed one and personally, I like to call my own shots. It seems to me that the congressman is trying to take away a right from us women without any idea what he's doing. But like I say, I'll get on-line and read some of their NOW pamphlets and make up my own mind."

"Thank you, Ms Riley," the cameraman said and focused his smile at the camera. "There you have it Walt from Medfield Center."

"Thank you, John," the reporter could hear Walt's voice through his ear piece. "There certainly seems to be varying opinions on that gathering. And there are varying opinions on the Patriots chances to win this weekend. Sports, when we return."

As the cameraman and newscaster prepared to leave, a BMW drove past them headed back towards route 128 which would lead to Boston. Jill Rowe, alias Joan Riley, had to get home in time to drop by the cleaners for a pick-up and to get supper started. The new president, Maggie Sullivan, seemed to be a pretty smart cookie, she had to admit. Thinking to call her to ask to be a plant in the crowd in the event of reporter asking opinions was brilliant. Hopefully, the responses they worked out for her the night before would have many non-members checking their website and possibly enrolling.

TWELVE

Jessica Brackton lay on her couch staring at the china cabinet her mother had given to her as a wedding gift. The cherry wood was polished and reflected back the objects in the room. It was a beautiful piece of wood, she thought. And then, "I wonder if the baby would have been beautiful". She was unable to think of it as 'my baby'. Having had a 'heart scare' as she referred to it, she was ordered to rest. No lifting, no running, nothing to exert herself the doctor ordered, and she nearly laughed in his face.

Turning her gaze from the cabinet, she spied the fresh flowers from her husband that sat in a crystal vase on the coffee table. She reached out and gently rubbed one of the rose petals, enjoying its softness and, as with most things she saw and touched that morning, her mind returned to her pregnancy and the bottomless loneliness she was experiencing.

It wasn't fair that she should be made to bear the brunt of this loss by herself. But that's where it got confusing. Her husband was being stoic and kept telling her that life could play cruel tricks, but the next time it would be different. She knew he was inwardly seething at the Fitzpatrick's and would "make them pay", as he said on his first visit to her hospital room.

She remembered that she had every intention of telling Sullivan she was pregnant when they last met at the Exeter Hotel and even mentioned her need to talk to him. It was time to end their affair. Nothing but a simple dalliance on her part and now, she realized, a mistake.

But he dismissed her request to talk. He was excited about his political future and radiated energy with every step he took and word he uttered. Before she knew what was happening, they were on the bed and what felt like just moments later, alone again. She could kick herself for letting him control the situation, and her. But what was more galling, was the fact that he hadn't even bothered to call her since then. He proved to be about as caring of her as her husband had proved himself to be. "What a fool I am," she thought, and dabbed at her eyes. "Well he's a bigger fool if he thinks I'll be ignored!"

She looked at the telephone resting on the end table and briefly closed her eyes at its garishness. It was an antique model adorned with a silver plated handle and a matching silver rotary dial that her husband paid goodness-knows-what for. It was ostentatious at best, and she had refused to use it. But, remembering her cell phone was in the bedroom; she sat up and begrudgingly reached for the handset. Dialing one number at a time, she waited for an answer at Sullivan's State House

Office.

Representative Brad Sullivan returned to his office at the statehouse in a jubilant mood. He made a mental note to thank his wife for suggesting he make the announcement on the steps of historic Faneuil Hall at Quincy Market. It had always provided a platform for the country's most famous orators, he reflected. It is where colonists first protested the Sugar Act in 1764 and established the doctrine of "no taxation without representation." Firebrand Samuel Adams rallied the citizens of Boston to the cause of independence from Great Britain in the hallowed Hall, and George Washington toasted the nation there on its first birthday. And it can now be said that Bradford Sullivan announced his candidacy for Congress from those very steps.

Even Sean, walking in through the office door at that moment, couldn't dampen his mood. However, it did remind him of the talk he needed to have with him. He felt pretty confident that he could get Frank Ambrasio to work his campaign. But he heard that when Frank ran a campaign, he ran everyone around him as well. That would prove to be a problem with Sean. But that talk could wait until later, maybe tomorrow. Today was the day to kick off his fund raising efforts.

"I thought it went pretty well, Brad," Sean said while fishing through his pockets finally producing a sheet of paper. "No hard questions for you that I could see."

"The great thing about running as a Democrat in a Democratic state, Sean," he said, "is that the reporters never push too hard. Hell, they hate Fitzpatrick as much as I do!"

Sullivan's brow burrowed as he thought for a moment. "No," he said finally, "the only opponent I have to fear will be one from our own party."

"Here's the list you wanted of donors from your last campaign," Sean said handing him the sheet of paper. The type was double spaced with names, phone numbers, and the amount contributed.

"Thanks, Sean. This is a good start. But we're going to need bigger names with bigger wallets if I'm to have a chance. Get me a list of every corporation doing business in Fitzpatrick's district with the names and phone numbers of their management. Also, the names of every college president and political science professor in the state. I think I can make some promises that'll appeal to them if I'm elected. I'll contact ACORN," he added, referring to the Association of Community Organizations for Reform Now.

"What's a political science guy going to want?" Sean asked.

"It's what I want from him, Sean. I'll offer to visit their class and talk to the students of a day-in-the-life of a politician and how much I want to help the little people of this great state." And when I'm done speaking to them, he thought, they'll be begging me let them help me by going to the streets to support my campaign.

Just then, his phone rang.

"I need those names as soon as you can get them to me, Sean," he said, signaling to Sean it was time for him to leave and get started.

Picking up the receiver he said, "Hello, this is Brad Sullivan."

"It's me," came a soft reply, "Jessica."

Damn, thought Sullivan, I'm not ready for this call.

"Hey you," he said, "How are you feeling?" It was the safest comment he could think to make.

"Why haven't I heard from you Brad?" she asked.

"I, I, well I heard about the accident and felt terrible but, you know, we don't want to be together during a time like this. I mean seen together," he corrected himself. There was silence on the line and he cursed himself for not getting a message to her earlier.

"You know I miss you, Jessica," he hastily added. Damn! Where'd that come from?

"No Brad," she said, "I have no idea that you miss me. Perhaps I should drop by your office so you can tell me what you want to say to my face."

What did she mean by that? He wondered. Did she guess that I was going to break off our relationship?

"You aren't afraid that my face was ruined by the accident are you, Brad?"

"Of course not!"

"Then why haven't I heard from you?"

"Your husband," he said. "I assumed he was at the hospital with you and would stay with you when you returned home. What was I supposed to do if he answered? Act like a schoolboy and hang up? How many times would that have worked?" He was becoming more confident as he gave his reason for not calling.

"When can we see each other again?" she asked. "I need to speak to you."

"Well, we're talking now aren't we?" he said. "I think you need to have some time to yourself so soon after what you've been through. Let's give it a few weeks and I'll call you." Sullivan was hoping she'd agree. The more time apart the easier the split.

"I have appointments I can't break for the remainder of this week. Mostly with lawyers," she added. "I will be at the Exeter Hotel at 1:30 this Monday afternoon. Do you recognize that name, the Exeter Hotel, Brad? It's the same place we were to meet the day of my accident." Sullivan could tell by her voice that she was smiling when she said that. Probably some mental mechanism to keep herself together, he figured.

"I expect you to be there," her voice continued through the receiver.

"And let me make it easy for you, I'll be in room 314. You understand me Brad? I've already booked it." With that said, the line went dead.

Sullivan sat there holding the phone receiver still pressed to his ear as his mind went into overdrive considering what he could do and what the ramifications would be as a result of him doing it. Meeting her at the hotel was out of the question. She really was missing a screw, he thought. A week after a miscarriage and she wants to jump in the sack with her lover?

Ex-lover he corrected himself.

He hung up the phone, flipped through his appointment calendar to Monday, and noted he had a lunch with the CEO of Yankee Glass, a potential contributor. It was near the theater district and close to the hotel she mentioned. It would be easy to have a bite to eat, get a pledge for money from the CEO, and then drop in on her. He could have a little fun and get back to his office before anyone missed him. Goodness knows he deserved a break. Especially after the recent fight with his wife over the protest she organized against Fitzpatrick in Medfield. He took a breath trying to relax after that thought. Maggie had been a bear and showed no signs of remorse. He wasn't having any luck getting her to see that by attacking Fitzpatrick, she appeared to be protesting as a way of campaigning for her husband. And just as importantly, it wouldn't help her cause.

Maggie pointed out that not only was she helping her cause, but his as well and if he couldn't see that then he could plan on making future campaign appearances without a wife by his side.

Brad thought back to Jessica. He knew how their hotel meeting would normally work. She'd get there first and take a room under her mother's maiden name, Barbara Sanford, for whom she had an active credit card. She'd then leave a note for her "husband" at the front desk indicating which room she was in. As long as they chose below scale hotels where the staff was made up of half immigrants and half illiterates, there was a better than even chance no one would recognize either one of them. Some of the places they had met at proved to be too ill maintained for a return visit. Once, they found a half used bottle of shampoo next to a tube of Vagisil on the bathroom sink. They left immediately and met two days later at the Exeter Hotel, vowing there'd be no more rendezvous' at hotels that cockroaches called home.

He often wished aloud to her that they could meet in Cambridge where the non-documented alien population was on the rise due to that town's recent campaign to attract illegal immigrants with promises of jobs and free shelter. But Cambridge was too far out of the way.

How many times they had met for sex, he wondered. A couple of dozen at least, he was sure. When it first started, they were meeting twice a week, but over the past couple of months they seemed to mutually agree to scale back. It was now over two weeks since their last meeting. "May as well be married," he muttered aloud.

Meeting with her on Monday would certainly take some of the edge off and allow him to better focus on his campaign. As tempting an idea as that was, he just could not get around the disturbing thought of her wanting sex so soon after a miscarriage. No, he determined, he wouldn't be meeting with her at the hotel on Monday, or any other day. She was smart. Hopefully, she'd get the hint without him having to confront her.

He glanced at the clock and realized he lost nearly an hour since his return from announcing his candidacy. I've got to concentrate, he told himself, if I'm to get this campaign started.

At that moment his office door opened and Sean stuck his head in.

"I need to take the rest of the day off, Brad. Marie's got a hair appointment and I've got to watch the kids," Sean said referring to his wife.

"Watch the kids?" Sullivan asked disbelieving. "Sean, are you aware I just announced my candidacy for Congress? Were you there when I did that?"

"Yeah, Brad. I know, but Marie just let me know this morning. Otherwise, I could have let you know sooner."

"C'mon in a moment, Sean, and take a seat. I've been meaning to talk to you about something and now seems appropriate."

Sean walked all the way into the office closing the door behind him. He crossed the room and took a seat in one of the two chairs situated at the front of Sullivan's desk. He suddenly had the feeling he was stepping into hot water by requesting time away from the office, but wasn't sure why. He often left 'work' early.

"If this is a bad time, Brad, I'll call Marie right now and tell her to reschedule," Sean said. Adding nervously, "No problem. I'll call her from here, okay?"

"That's not necessary, Sean. Let Marie go to her appointment while you watch the kids. Look Sean, my run for congress is going to take some real help. With influential people, I mean." Sean stared at him.

"I'm going to need a professional handler, you understand. Someone who's been successful doing this sort of thing before. Otherwise, we'll, me and you, we'll be just wasting our time."

"Uh huh," Sean agreed.

Sullivan often ran into these situations speaking with Sean. The man had a photographic memory and never forgot a word of conversation whether directed at him or one he overheard, but Sullivan could never tell if he understood what he was being told. "A savant that was unable to connect the dots," he mused.

"I'm thinking of asking Frank Ambrasio to lead us in that effort," he told Sean.

"Geez, Ambrasio, huh? He's a big name, Brad," Sean said. "He ran the Williams campaign."

"Come to think of it, he did," Sullivan said. "And he won that campaign didn't he, Sean? And that's what we need. Someone who knows how to win a big time race."

"Okay, Brad," Sean said as he rose from his chair to leave.

"He's going to need a place to work from, Sean," Sullivan said hastily. "An office, you know?"

Sean thought a moment and shook his head.

"We're only allocated two offices, Brad. Yours and mine. I don't think they change that rule for anyone but the Speaker."

Sullivan was reaching his breaking point. This is what I get, he thought, when you try to help a family member who never finished high school. Dyslexia, his wife told him. But dyslexia doesn't make you dumb, he thought angrily. He didn't know of any other way to make himself known to Sean but to say it.

"He'll need your office Sean. I'll work something out for you," Sullivan said as he wiped at his brow. "You go home now and watch the kids for Marie. I'll work something out for you," he repeated.

"Geez, Brad. You're canning me?" Sean asked.

"Think of it as a reassignment, Sean," Sullivan said as he could feel the tension building throughout his body. "I'll need you even more as we go forward with this Sean. Out there on the streets talking with the common man. Like you did when I ran for Rep." Sullivan tried to put more enthusiasm into his voice. "Only this will be different. This is for a seat in Washington."

"I didn't get paid campaigning for you then, Brad. Is that going to be different?" Sean asked.

"I'll work something out, Sean. Go on home."

Before the door to his office closed, Sullivan was searching through drawers of his desk looking for something to calm his stomach. When Maggie hears that he let her brother go...damn!

THIRTEEN

Congressman Fitzpatrick was in his home study reading a bill that was before the House regarding fishing limits for Cod and Haddock. It was the third time he tried to get through it without his mind wandering to what might happen to his son, Michael. On top of that, his aides were pushing him to make more public appearances, in spite of his son's problem, in preparation for the next campaign. He felt he had little chance of winning another term, but felt his country needed him, despite what his constituents might think. The last presidential election nearly had us being led by a woman who openly admired Margaret Sanger, he grimaced. Someone who not only advocated for abortions, but wanted the country to adopt policies advocating selective breeding, sterilization, and euthanasia! But then, many people had the time to reflect, including himself, if he were to be honest, that maybe she would have been the better choice after all.

He jumped when the phone rang

"Hello," he answered.

"Frank, this is Stan!"

One thing about Stan, he remembered, he was always happy when he was talking.

"Good news, buddy," he continued without waiting for Fitzpatrick to acknowledge him. "I was able to reach Kim Matson. You know? The attorney I spoke to you about the other night?"

"Oh! Sure, I remember," Fitzpatrick spoke for the first time.

"Well, she's interested in your case and wants me to set up a meeting. You, Mike, me, and her. She's on her way to my office now, but won't get here until at least eleven this morning. It's a bit of a ride from Leominster."

Fitzpatrick looked at his watch and saw that it was nine-thirty.

"I gave her the big picture and when she gets here, I'll give her some personal history on Mike and the family. Any who," he said, using a term he adopted from a childhood cartoon character, "what say you bring Mike and yourself to my office at 1:30 today? That work for you?"

"I guess we can do that," the congressman answered.

"Excellent! You know you made it big time when you can do what you're doing, congressman."

"Doing what, Stan?" Fitzpatrick had no idea what Ross meant.

"Here I am bringing you a lawyer, who's already on the clock I should add, and arranging a meeting which is also billable, and you haven't asked me the big question."

Fitzpatrick sighed and played along. "What's the big question, Stan?"

"How much this is going to cost, ya doink!" Ross used an expression that Fitzpatrick hadn't heard since childhood and he had to chuckle.

"Just so you aren't hesitant to make a decision in the future based on what it might cost, let me clear about this Stan; cost does not matter."

"Maybe not for you, Frank, but just so you know, Kim doesn't know any investigators in this neck of the woods so I told her I would play that role. And I'll only be charging you half my normal rate. Plus expenses of course," he hastily added.

"What do mean by you being an investigator?" Fitzpatrick asked. "You're my lawyer."

"You honor me with those words, Frank," Ross replied. "Any who, defense lawyers and prosecutors all use investigators to do the leg work. Interview potential witnesses and cool stuff like that. She's really uncomfortable using a newbie and wanted to use one of her regulars from New York, but I said no need, I would be available."

"You don't have to do this, Stan," Fitzpatrick said. "As I just said, cost is not my primary concern here, protecting Michael is. If she requires someone from *Alaska* to help her then—"

"Stop there, Frank," Ross interrupted. "This may be hard to believe, but the people coming after Michael are a lot tougher and meaner than those asses in high school you protected me from. Now I have a chance to protect you. I can write up a warrant for a search, use big lawyer-like words to intimidate people, and while I may not be a criminal lawyer, I know a hell of a lot more about the law than some gumshoe!"

"Okay, I guess that makes sense." Fitzpatrick said. "Is there anything I should bring with me for the meeting?"

"Are you kidding?" Ross laughed. "You got me for an attorney. You don't need anything else!"

Fitzpatrick could still hear Ross laughing when he broke the connection.

After lunch, the congressman and Mike jumped into the car, used the remote control button to raise the garage door, and eased their way down the driveway to shouts of questions from the reporters gathered about the front of their home.

As they drove down North Street, the Congressman noticed that Michael appeared to be considering something.

"What's up, Mike?" He asked.

Michael thought a moment longer and taking a breath said, "Can't you get rid of them, Dad? You're a congressman. You shouldn't have to put up with this invasion."

"You're right, I shouldn't have to put up with it and yes, I could get them to move far enough away we wouldn't have to see them. But how do you think that would look to the public?"

"Yeah, I guess that wouldn't look too good. Like we were hiding or something."

"Exactly," the congressman answered as he pulled into a parking spot behind the building Stan Ross had his office.

Walking through the open office door they could see Stan speaking to a dark haired women sitting in a chair facing his desk with her back to them.

"Any who," he said to the woman, "we can finish with that later. Right now," he continued while standing, "I wish to introduce you to Congressman Francis Fitzpatrick of the ninth district and his son, Michael."

The woman stood and turned to greet them. The first thing that Fitzpatrick noticed was her oriental features, and then the realization of how young she was. He stood there awkwardly, unable to think of what to say.

"Congressman Fitzpatrick," Ross said, "meet Kim Matson, Michael's lead defense attorney."

"My pleasure, Congressman Fitzpatrick," she shook his hand and turned to Michael. "And you must be Michael Fitzpatrick." She offered her hand and Mike shook it.

"Frank," the congressman said. "Please call me Frank."

"Very well, Frank," she smiled. "Stan was just finishing up with some personal background on Michael and your family. I can probably get everything I need on you by doing a Google search, but nothing beats speaking to a family friend," she said nodding towards Ross.

"If everyone is comfortable and ready," Matson said, "I'd like to start by each of us exchanging cell phone numbers. There may be times when I can't afford to be waiting on a call back and—"

"Don't have one," Ross said

"But you're an attorney," Matson said.

"A business, slash, tax attorney," Ross replied. "If I use a cell phone, half of my clients will be calling to reschedule appointments while I'm walking towards their door. This way, if they want to reschedule and they're not able to reach me here at the office, they get billed for a visit anyway."

"Excuse me," Fitzpatrick interrupted. He looked around the room trying to think of the right words. "I don't mean to be offensive, Kim, but—"

"You want to know something about me?" she asked.

"Yes. That's it," Fitzpatrick said, somewhat relieved with an opening to broach his concern. "Perhaps you could tell us something about your experience, where you went to school, things like that. It's not that you're young or a minority or anything. Oh golly," Fitzpatrick's face visibly reddened realizing he just pointed out the very two things he was most concerned about. "Please forgive me. I'm nervous as hell."

"No need for forgiveness Frank," she said. "I recognized your look of concern the moment you walked in. It's a common reaction, actually. Unless, of course, I'm defending someone with a Chinese heritage." She took a moment to collect her thoughts as Fitzpatrick and Mike took their seats.

"Let's attack my appearance first," she said. "The Chinese are naturally shorter than westerners and have skin smoother, more clear than most westerners. This in turn gives the appearance of youth when sometimes, just the opposite is true. For instance, I had a client, a lady whose family came from China. She was wrongly accused of shop lifting at a major retail store at a local shopping mall. The accusation came from a cosmetician who was trying to sell her, of all things, anti-aging cream. Upon reviewing the tapes this store used to record activities of their staff and patrons, I had to admit the women she described fit my client to a tee. Middle aged looking, about fifty years old, short of stature, with slightly darkened, clear skin. My client, however, was in her eighties."

"Wow," Michael said. "How did you get her off?"

"The tape clearly showed the cosmetician and the lady conversing amiably about the anti-aging cream. Fortunately, the cosmetician couldn't speak Mandarin and my client couldn't speak a word of English. A clear case of mistaken identity. Westerners are not used to seeing Orientals every day so they have a hard time distinguishing one from another.

"As for school, I received my undergrad degree from Suffolk University as well as my law degree."

"I'm sure your parents are very proud of you," Fitzpatrick said. "Michael graduates from Harvard this spring and is also planning on attending their law school in the fall, concentrating on business law."

"That's wonderful, Michael," she said. "And yes, Frank, my parents are very proud. My father is a retired firefighter and my mother a librarian. They adopted me from an orphanage in China when I was still a baby. And while my features are totally Chinese, I can assure you, I am as American as Michael here," she turned to offer Michael a wink.

"Cool," Michael said, totally absorbed in what she said.

"Since graduating from law school I have represented more than seventy-five cases and have a win or no-conviction rate of better than ninety-eight percent."

"Isn't that a bit lopsided?" Fitzpatrick asked. "I mean that's a, a, well, for lack of a better term, that sounds ridiculously high for a win rate."

"Ahem," Ross interrupted. "I have to agree, Kim. Unless you can place a spell on juries I don't see how you could have accomplished that."

"It's really quite simple," she answered smiling. "I only take cases I know I can win."

FOURTEEN

Bishop Connor enjoyed dinner with the newly appointed priests, along with Father Canalli, and suggested they adjourn to the living room to discuss their assignment that day; one sound reason God does not exist. It was his favorite exercise with new charges and he looked forward to it more than dessert. The priests were young, recently ordained, and eager to spread The Word.

Relaxing in his easy chair, he instructed his charges to get as comfortable as possible sitting on the rug. He took the paper from Father Canalli where a statement was hand written explaining why there can be no God. Scanning the document, he was a little disappointed that they couldn't offer anything new. He had seen this same reason, worded differently, before.

"Children, those of us with the least amount of sin that can be credited to us, are allowed to suffer from illness, from abuse at the hands of evil people, and in some cases, die horrible deaths."

"I know this exercise was difficult for you," the Bishop sighed. "But always remember that it is through doubt that faith grows and flourishers. Remember what St. Augustine wrote in his Confessions," the Bishop smiled, "Give me chastity and continence, but not just now."

"But doesn't that attitude allow for doubt to flourish and grow?" he was asked.

The Bishop thought a moment, knowing he had to be careful with his answer.

"I suppose each of you could give me a thousand reasons why God does exist." The Bishop said. "What can we expect to learn from what we already know?

"But here," the Bishop held up the paper he held in his hand, "you've chosen a reason that shakes many a faith and can leave us wondering, what is He thinking?

"Some of you will experience what is stated here first hand while trying to provide comfort to a parent. It won't be pleasant and regardless of how strong you feel your faith is at this moment, it won't be easy. You will be speaking to someone experiencing unfathomable grief, unable to grasp the existence of a god that would allow this."

"What are we to do then, Bishop Connor?"

"Beyond asking that they pray with you, I'm not sure. That will be up to you. Some of you may be gifted and are able to bring comfort just by being present. I've seen that, you know. Some people emit a certain," the Bishop hesitated while he hunted for the right word, "a certain aura, I suppose. While most of us," he smiled again, "have only our faith to see us through."

His audience sat staring at him without offering comment. Perhaps, the Bishop thought, Father Canalli's fears are correct when he mentions I may be pushing too hard in getting them to think about the vocation they've chosen. But better they do it now than later, he determined.

"What I'm trying to tell you is to continue to develop your faith on something other than it being what your mother's instilled in you. Most of you believe you have already done that by completing seminary, but take it from an aging man that it is a lifelong process."

The Bishop noticed one of the men wore a look of consternation. "Yes?" he asked. "What's troubling you?"

"Well Bishop Connor, I think we, each of us here," he motioned at his fellow priests, "are fairly well trained in recognizing good from evil. That's why we chose this profession. To stop evil and help people to avoid it through their love of God and through our faith. What more is there to—"

"Good and evil?" the Bishop interrupted. Do you mean to tell me that most people don't know the difference between good and evil but you do?"

"Well, I mean, they may know the difference, but still make the wrong choice and—"

"Why do suppose that is?" the Bishop asked. "If they know the difference, why would they choose evil?"

"I'm, I'm not sure Bishop," the young man faltered.

"Well, I'm not sure either. But you'll be wasting your time if you look for the reason being as simple as knowing what is bad and doing it. No, that will lead to a blind end every time."

He waited a moment, appearing to be deep in thought then said, "I believe it comes down to a matter of choosing what is easy rather than doing what you know to be right. That's where you'll find evil, the easy path."

Walking to a bookcase, he ran his fingers along the spines until he came across the one he wanted. Taking it from the shelf, he opened it to a page he had ear marked some years before.

"Listen to C.S. Lewis, the author of Alice in Wonderland no less," he said as he found the passage he was looking for. "...night after night, feeling whenever my mind lifted even for a second from my work, the steady, unrelenting approach of Him whom I so earnestly desired not to meet. I gave in, and admitted that God was God, and knelt and prayed: perhaps, that night, the most dejected and reluctant convert in all of England. I, too, had no expectations other than rightfully admitting God's existence. Yet over the following several months, I became amazed by his love for me."

"Is there anyone of us who cannot relate to what he is saying? Beautifully put I think. But did you know that Lewis was Anglican?" A couple of pairs of raised eyebrows gave him his answer.

"Tell me," the Bishop cocked his head looking at his students, "and this is a theoretical question; do you think Mr. Lewis will be welcomed into the Kingdom of Heaven?"

The Bishop sat looking from one face to another waiting for a reply.

"Well," one of the young men before him spoke hesitantly, "his love of God is evident. And he did write a classic children's tale. Err, not that that would matter."

His comrades nodded heads in favor of this response.

"Perhaps it does matter," the Bishop answered tentatively. "Perhaps God's criteria are different than ours? Whatever the answer," the Bishop waved his hand to dismiss the question, "it is our job to get people to *listen* harder."

"But Bishop Connor," a gravelly voice asked, "we don't have our own television show, like The 700 Club. We have about one hour a week with people we only see at Mass. The others are either sick or already looking for support of their faith. And even working with these people will be challenging. How do we get people to listen harder when they won't bother to heed what they already hear?"

"That's a good question and I'm glad you asked it for one very specific reason," the Bishop said. "The reason being, I want you to come back and tell me when you learn it!"

They all smiled at that response as Connor looked again at the book he held.

"You know, it is said that Gandhi read the Bible most everyday and when asked why he didn't become a Christian he reportedly replied, "I would have, if only I ever met one."

Bishop Connor watched as they nodded their heads, but was unsure as to whether they agreed with this statement or they were simply agreeing so as to move off an uncomfortable subject regarding their own faith.

As he was about to resume a hand was reluctantly raised looking for permission to speak.

"Yes, Cameron?" The Bishop asked. Cameron Maloney was a short man who had worked as a high school teacher before entering seminary. His short stature, blond hair and light complexion made him look more like a high school student himself, the Bishop thought.

"I have been thinking about Sarah's father. You remember? The story you told us when we first arrived about her mother forcing her to have an abortion?"

"Yes, of course. Go on."

"You mentioned that Sarah's father left the mother after they lost their child. Well, was anything done, by the parish priest I mean, to help them get back together?" Cameron looked shyly about him hoping someone would support him who had the same interest. His associates simply looked at him and turned their attention back to Bishop O'Connor.

"I'm not sure," the Bishop answered. "Perhaps I should have asked, eh? But let me tell you a story. A poor family consisting of a father, his son, and the mother's father lived together in what was little more than a shack with a work shed connected to it. The mother and grandmother had died some years before and the grandfather, even poorer than his son-in-law, came to live with them. They each had a wooden bowl that was used during breakfast, lunch and dinner. One evening during supper, the grandfather accidently dropped his bowl onto the floor where it cracked. It was no longer any good for holding soups and would likely break when washed again.

"The son-in-law cursed the old man and told his son to follow him to the shed where he started to make a new bowl.

"Grandpa sure does shake a lot dad," the son said.

"That's cause he's old and not able to hold things steady," the father answered. "But this is the third bowl I've had to make for him this year and I'm getting tired of it."

The boy thought a moment and said, "Well, make this one a strong bowl dad. One that won't crack when it's dropped. That way, I won't have to make so many when you get old."

A few of his students smiled and nodded their heads while the others cocked theirs trying to grasp the meaning.

"My point being," the Bishop said, "who will be there to take care of Sarah's father now that he's left his wife? We mention 'for better or worse' and 'till death do us part' during the ceremony, but those words seem to have lost their meaning. Sometimes people simply need to be reminded while others..." The Bishop let the sentence hang not sure how to finish. Accepting that he was unable to, he flicked his hand imitating that they could draw their own conclusions.

"Now," the Bishop said in an abrupt change of subject, "let's spend a moment talking about the Brackton vs. Fitzpatrick case. I assume you are all familiar with it?"

More nods followed only more enthusiastic this time.

"We have an ardent supporter of our Church whose son was involved in a car accident that brought an unborn baby to premature birth resulting in the child's death. As far I know, the Congressman's son is a good man who simply exercised poor judgment in driving that morning. And keep in mind this is the same congressman who is sponsoring the "Faith for Life" Bill. It's an answer to the Church's long sought prayers, in my opinion. With that in mind, to which party do we offer most prayers and support for; the bereaved mother, the dead infant, or the ardent Church supporter?"

A hand shot up, belonging to the same young man who answered earlier.

"Very good!" the bishop said. "I can already see your new assignment will offer us lively discussion for tomorrow night. Give it deep thought as I plan to question each of you on it.

"Now next week, I have a special treat for you. I like to call it Open Forum Night. You get to ask any questions regarding any subject, but with a twist. We'll have a very special guest participating."

The men's eyes widen thinking that perhaps Cardinal Monroe or Arch Bishop Pollock would be joining them.

"As for the statement you were somehow able to agree upon as a reason for no God? Let's say a prayer for those children, of all faiths, now."

Father Canalli bowed his head with the others, but his mind was far from the prayer being led by Bishop Connor. Instead, he concentrated on the latest call from Archbishop Pollock.

"Should this Fitzpatrick case go to trial I am depending on you, Father, to see that Bishop Connor is not seen connected to it in any way. In any way," the Archbishop repeated. "Am I making myself sufficiently clear? The Cardinal and I are depending on you. Are you aware that careers in the Church, as with the private sector are not that much different, Father? They rise or fall on successfully following the orders of their superiors." Then there was a click in his ear and the line went dead. It was as if he received a call from a blackmailer demanding a ransom. His future and his relationship with his superiors depended on possibly undermining the wishes of his boss.

FIFTEEN

Mike was sitting on a bench at the Boston Commons watching as the pigeons landed nearby and circled him, hoping for a hand out. He watched and wondered how his life could have changed so drastically. He was facing charges of homicide and would be tried in a court. Unbelievable, but true. It was while he thinking these thoughts when Ann Cranston, his recent girlfriend, sat next to him on the bench.

"Hey you," she smiled. She leaned over and kissed him on the cheek.

Mike looked at her and offered a weak smile. They sat looking at each other, waiting for the other to speak. Finally, Ann said, "You screwed up big time, huh, Mikey?" She laughed to show she meant the comment to be light.

Mike grinned and nodded.

"If you're not going to speak, this is going to be really awkward," Ann said.

"Sorry," Mike offered. "I'm not sure what to say. You broke up with me and now you wanted to meet with me. Change your mind?"

"Oh Mike, it's not that simple."

"You hungry?" Mike changed the subject. "Want to get some lunch?"

"Sure. Let's walk over to Cheers and get a big margarita, too!" Ann suggested.

"No drinking for me. But I still need to eat. "

Standing together, she hooked her arm in his as they walked towards the bar made famous by the television sitcom.

"Did I tell you Bishop Connor came to my house?" Mike asked.

"The Bishop came to your house! Did you ask for an exorcism or something?" Ann joked.

"My dad is sponsoring that "Faith for Life" bill and the church is really happy about it. I think they're afraid he'll drop his efforts to get it before the House for a vote 'cause of my accident, so there trying to give us extra support. I wouldn't say that to dad, though."

They stopped at the intersection to wait for the pedestrian light to signal them it was okay to cross. Directly across from them was the State House; its gold dome shining in the sun. Once across Beacon Street they ambled along towards their destination in no hurry and with little to say.

"You still volunteering at the clinic? Or did you have to stop that? Because of the accident and the news people and all that?" Ann asked, hoping to introduce a topic they could talk about.

"Still there," Mike answered.

"You never did tell me why you do that," she said.

"You never asked."

"Well I'm asking now you creep!" She tugged with her arm, still locked in his.

"I used to do it out of a sense of debt that I felt I owed to my friend, Jimmy."

Jessica felt a tug at her heart with that comment, remembering how she was attracted to Mike from the start. It was more than his always being honest with her about his dreams for their, but his willingness to expose himself to ridicule for following his heart.

"His dad was my coach in Little League and I practically lived at their house," he continued. "We were both twelve years old when Jimmy was diagnosed with cancer. So instead of shagging baseballs, I'd go with them to the clinic to keep Bobby company while he was getting his chemo. They'd put a needle in his arm connected to a bag with the medications in them, and we'd sit there and play Monopoly or Risk. He didn't get sick to his stomach until later in the day.

"Some days there'd be grownups in the room getting treatments right along with Jimmy, and some days there'd be kids about our age. They'd be there with their mother or father or both. They'd sit there and talk or read a paper while they waited for the bag of chemicals to empty. It was pretty unnerving for me to be playing a game with Jimmy while the other kids sat there and watched.

"He died, but I never forgot about him. Then one day, my senior year in high school, I ran into his father coming out of the library, a stack of books in his arms. He asked what I was doing now and where I planned to go to college. You know, the good to see you what have you been up to chatter. But when I glanced at the titles on the books he was holding, they all were about cancer. He noticed my look and explained that his wife was recently diagnosed and he was trying to get up to speed on any advancements made since Jimmy..." Mike stopped to wipe his eye with the back of his hand.

"He broke down and cried. He dropped the books and held me in his arms and broke down. Right there on the library steps. "

"That must have been awful!" Ann said.

"Yeah, it was. But it got me thinking about Jimmy and how we used to play games during his chemo treatments, and how some people, especially the kids, just had to sit there. I decided to offer my time to them. It depressed, me but I did it. These days it's turned out to be the best day of the week for me. One of the patients, a lady about thirty-five or so, said she read about the accident in the papers and how I'm going to be prosecuted. You know what she said to me?"

Ann shook her head.

"She said, want to trade places?"

"Our breakup came at a bad time for you, didn't it?" she said.

"Ya think?"

"I'm sorry. I just need some space," she replied. "To tell the truth, I'm glad I told you before the accident happened. It would have been too hard for me to do it now."

"I'm glad it worked out for you," Mike rolled his eyes. Then, "Look, I'm sorry. I know you did what you felt was best for you. I don't mean to be sore."

"It's like I told you, Mike," she said, "I still love you but…I don't know, you know?"

"No, but it doesn't matter now does it?" Mike shrugged. "What did your parents have to say about the accident? Did you tell them about us?"

"Daddy shook his head and mom called your mother. Didn't she tell you?"

"No. Maybe. I don't remember."

"And yes, I told them we decided to see other people," she offered.

"You mean, you decided we'd see other people."

"Yeah," she nodded. "Look, Mike, we're young, still free, and there's a lot of life ahead of us. If we're meant to be together, a little separation won't stop that."

"When you first said that, I believed it. But now… I may be facing jail time, Ann. I may have to go to prison!"

They reached the corner of Beacon and Charles Streets and lingered there even when the signal to cross safely appeared. Both had lost their appetites.

"Come on," Ann said while tugging him up Charles Street. "Let's walk over to the Esplanade."

Ann tightened her arm around his as they continued their walk through the shadowed canyon made from the tall buildings on either side.

Across town near the theater district, Brad Sullivan was doing a stroll of his own as he paced up and down the sidewalk a block away from the Exeter Hotel. His lunch with the CEO of Yankee Glass went better than expected as he all but got a sizable check handed to him.

"Put down the ideas you spoke of today and send them to me," the CEO requested as he signed for lunch. "I'll brief the board on our talks, but can pretty much tell you they'll do as I ask. If your agenda in Congress is to lighten the tax-code businesses in this state are awash in, you'll be able to count on a lot of future support as well."

What planet did that guy live on? Sullivan thought. Without the corporate taxes now in place, there would be no funding for more than half the projects in existence, let alone those he had in mind. But getting the money was the first and most important thing. Once you reached your goal, it was awfully hard to lose it. He had confidence the lunches his manager, Frank Ambrasio, had scheduled for him with several other business leaders in his district would go as well. What had him pacing and on edge now was Jessica Brackton, waiting for him in room 314, just around the corner.

He wondered how she could have managed to book not only a room, but a specific room. Probably said it was their anniversary or something and room 314 held a special meaning for them. Or maybe she simply offered reservations more money.

He was to meet her at the Exeter Hotel at 1:30, only moments from now, he realized as he checked his watch again. If he decided to meet her, there would be nothing carnal about it, he swore. But she and her husband represented a lot of money. Money, he was certain, he had put in jeopardy of ever seeing again by his affair with her. To continue to meet with her would only be adding fuel to a fire that had already burnt out. He suddenly confronted the reality that the source of his campaign funds and the high level contacts that John Brackton represented was what needed to be protected and nurtured. "What was I thinking?" He spoke aloud.

He began to consider that Jessica's accident was a blessing in disguise, a chance that would allow him to concentrate on his political future and not clandestine meetings. What's more, he reasoned, the accident had revealed her to be unstable. No, he couldn't risk getting close to her again. If she had an unstable mind, she might willingly expose them as lovers. The act, he feared, of unrequited love or something. Walking towards a taxi waiting at the corner for a fare, he decided that she would just have to accept his reluctance to meet her for what it was; the end of their affair.

Walking into his State House office he was met with Frank Ambrasio seated behind his desk with a phone to his ear.

"He just walked in," Ambrasio said into the phone. "I'll get back to you. No, no, I promise. Gimme twenty minutes."

Hanging up the telephone, Ambrasio offered a big smile to Sullivan, but didn't relent to him his chair. Sullivan reluctantly took one of the two guest chairs placed facing his desk.

"Good news, Bradford boy, but first you. How was lunch with the glass boss?" Ambrasio asked.

"Great," Sullivan answered with little enthusiasm in his voice. His decision to ignore his meeting with Jessica was gnawing at him.

"How great? What's a matter?"

"Nothing. It went great," Sullivan offered with greater emotion. "I told him what you suggested and he bought it. He wants me to put my ideas in writing so he can present it the board. I can expect a check in a week, two at the most."

"Excellent!" Ambrasio said. "Don't worry about the talking points. I'll see that he gets them. Now guess who I was just talking to when you walked in."

Sullivan gave his shoulders a shrug.

"CNN, that's who! They want to do an interview with you. A one-on-one national interview! Am I good, or am I good?"

"National? How'd you arrange that?"

"Truth be told, I didn't. They called me. But the point is, you're going to be reaching a lot more constituents than those that reside in the ninth district and that's a fact!"

"They want to interview me, a representative from Massachusetts running for Fitzpatrick's seat, because..." Sullivan paused to think about that.

"Because the Fitzpatrick accident is that big nationally," Ambrasio finished for him. "They'll have that anchor lady, Andrea what's her name, meet you at the intersection where the accident took place. You know where it is? It's around the corner from here."

Sullivan sat up straighter in his chair.

"You think that's a good idea, Frank? I feel like I'm shoveling dirt into the grave of a guy still living."

"And you should be happy for that! He'll walk away just fine from all of this. Maybe his boy will do a little bunk time with cons but you ain't running against him. And if it makes you feel any better, I'll write some lines for you. You know, something that says you're sorry and concerned for the troubles the Congressman's facing, but you're even more concerned for the troubles facing this country. It's time for a change in direction, a change in attitude for the common man, a change in leadership. And...hold on," Ambrasio stood and started walking to the door. "I need to get back to my office and write this stuff down. You meet her at nine tomorrow at the intersection. Get there a little early so they'll have time to throw a little makeup on you. I gotta call CNN back and..." the sound of Ambrasio's voice cut off as the door he exited closed.

Sullivan pushed himself to his feet and flopped down in the chair behind his desk. Staring at the phone, he found himself pushing the four-one-one buttons on the key pad. Once he had the number for the Exeter Hotel he dialed.

"Exeter Hotel, how can I help you?" Asked the voice of an older man.

"Room 314, please."

"Certainly, and the name of the guest?"

"Brack...," Sullivan stopped himself just in time. "Sanford. Barbara Sanford."

"Yes sir, connecting."

Sullivan glanced at his watch and realized it was nearly three o'clock. He waited until the phone rang several times before reluctantly giving up. She obviously checked in and had left by now. They never bothered to check-out in person.

He suddenly had a gut wrenching feeling it was a mistake to not have met with her. If there was to be a blow-up between them, it would be better to know it was coming so evasive actions could be taken. At the least he could have bought some time for himself with her.

He lifted the receiver again and dialed her cell phone number from memory. "You have reached a non-working number…" The robotic voice informed him. He disconnected, wondering if calling her home number was an option.

***

Winter turned to summer without another word from Jessica. During that time, especially as a result of Frank Ambrassio's efforts, his momentum in the polls grew to the point that there was a three way tie for the democratic ticket.

It was uncomfortable, but necessary for him to speak to John Brackton a couple of times or more a month on the phone, explaining his progress and where he was encountering road-blocks. Brackton always knew someone to speak to or to pay-off, Sullivan imagined, to smooth his way. To become powerful, Sullivan theorized, depended on the powerful.

SIXTEEN

Brad and Maggie Sullivan walked up the gangway of the Hy-Line, a ship providing a one hour boat transport service between Hyannis and Nantucket, and headed to the bow of the boat where the first-class section was located. Finding an empty table, they tossed their over-night bags under it and ordered coffee. Brad's whole body seemed to spasm as the boat's whistle, indicating that the ship was leaving dock, startled him. He covered his ears in anticipation of another blast

"Oh, Brad, stop it!" Maggie complained. "You're embarrassing us."

"I have low tolerance for loud noises. You know that," he answered.

Maggie chose to drop the subject and turned to gaze out the window. "Isn't this wonderful, Brad? I told you that there would be special benefits to being a chapter president."

"Ah, yeah, but we're still paying for this visit," he pointed out.

"Well at least we get to go! How many times have we said we should visit Nantucket? Well, now we are. And if we run into a little financial setback, we have the second mortgage to see us through until you become Congressman Sullivan." Maggie smiled at the notion.

"Great, only we'll hardly see each other while we're here," he said. "You have a reception tonight and your meetings tomorrow last most of the day. And why didn't you at least invite spouses to the reception tonight?"

"It's a women's organization, Brad. Not a marriage seminar."

Pulling a brochure from her handbag she began flipping through its pages.

Changing the subject he asked, "What do you know about the place we'll be staying at?"

"The Jared Coffin House," she said finding the page she earmarked earlier. "It was the first three story mansion built on the island. It's like 150 years old, or something. And get this; President Grant stayed there!"

"President Grant! Does it have plumbing?"

Soaring overhead, John Bradford's private jet, a state-of-the-art Gulfstream III, banked to the east headed for Nantucket.

The skies were blue and the winds relatively calm, making for a pleasant voyage by water. Both Maggie and Brad enjoyed watching the seagulls, expertly navigating the winds, sweeping in to snatch crackers held in the air by passengers. And while passing Brant's Point Light, a light house built in 1856, Maggie chided herself for not bringing a camera.

Enduring another blast of the ship's whistle as it pulled into the dock at Nantucket, Brad and Maggie gathered their bags, walked down the gangway, and took their first steps onto the famous whaling island.

Brad surveyed his surroundings and thought, "quaint" while Maggie's first impression was, how primitive!

"According to my guide book, we can walk to the hotel from here," Maggie said. "We just go straight up Broad Street here."

"You want to walk?" Brad asked.

"Come on! Do you see anyone taking taxis?"

Actually, he did see taxis pass them with passengers from their boat, but decided it would be better to just let Maggie call the shots.

Walking towards what appeared to be the town center; Brad was surprised at the number of people about. "This town must live off tourism," he thought. Numerous small shops were lined on both sides of the street offering everything from trinkets to art to ice cream.

"Wow!" Brad exclaimed. "Cobblestone streets. They even look ancient."

"And they're killing me with these high heels! I'll be lucky if I don't sprain an ankle." Maggie said. "You'd think the guide book would warn a person."

A ten to fifteen minute leisurely walk would be the typical time it takes to get from the dock to their hotel. But Maggie used the disability her shoes provided to take advantage of visiting several of the clothing shops they passed along the way. Buying a pair of chic sandals to ease her discomfort, it was more than an hour later they were checking in to their room.

"What are you going to do with your day, Brad?" Maggie asked as she booted up her laptop on the work desk next to their bed.

"Don't worry about me," he answered. "I have my speech to the Kiwanis's Club to work on."

"Well I need a good hour to myself to review my speech for tonight, so why don't you visit that Whaling Museum we passed down the street?"

Rolling his eyes, he patted his pockets for his car keys before realizing they would be on foot throughout the weekend. At the door, he turned to ask if she wanted to catch something to eat together that evening, but he knew the look of concentration Maggie was giving to the computer screen meant 'don't interrupt me or else'.

Retracing his steps on Broad Street, he headed back towards the ocean and the museum. He remembered enjoying museums as a boy, but since starting his law practice and eventual run for a representative seat, he had little time to contemplate the past. And, with his current effort to unseat Fitzpatrick's congressional seat, free time was more of a concept than an actual experience. It was one of the reasons that he agreed to accompany his wife this weekend. Between their schedules, they didn't get to say more than good morning and good night, with little to no physical interaction in between. The one person who could have stopped him from coming, besides Maggie, was his campaign manager, Frank Ambrasio and he nearly did.

"Whataya mean you're going away for the weekend?" Ambrasio asked.

"I need some time to myself, Frank. Between the speeches and the interviews, I'm beginning to lose track of what day it is. I'm losing weight and…hell! I thought I was going to pass out during the television debate Wednesday. My opponents were smelling blood. I could almost taste it myself. Only I was tasting my own blood!"

"What are ya talking about? You killed 'em. The polls will be out tomorrow and I'm telling ya, you're gonna be declared the winner."

"I stumbled on more than one issue, Frank. Let's look at this honestly. Taxes to support abortion? I didn't know if I was nodding yes while saying no or vice versa. I need a break."

"Hmmmm," Ambrasio mulled it over a moment and said, "Maybe a couple of days away would be good for us. It'll give the Fitzpatrick people something to worry about, you being out-of-sight a couple of days."

And with that, Sullivan left his office at noon and headed home to pack.

Most of his time at the museum was spent staring at the skeleton of the sperm whale that was suspended from the ceiling. Once he grew tired of that, he walked out of the door and headed for Main Street.

Traffic was heavy for an island, he thought, with delivery trucks coming off of the boat while others queued up to get back on for the return trip to Hyannis. Motor bikes or scooters zipped past him in both directions making the air hum with the sound of their motors.

Stopping at a corner paper store to look for a magazine, he stood frozen at the doorframe as he watched Debra and John Brackton come out of the bank a block further up the street, and walk towards a book store located at the corner of Main and Orange Streets. He watched as they passed the bookstore and continued down Orange Street.

What the hell? He thought, as he moved up the street in their direction to see where they would go. Just as he reached the bank and looked across Main Street and down Orange, he saw them walk up the steps of a large white house where John Brackton inserted a key into the door and opened it for his wife.

"They must have a place here," Sullivan realized. "Damn! This is what comes of trying to skip a couple of days of work. I'm stuck on an island with the last person I want to see or run in to."

Turning back to the paper store, he loaded up on several magazines, realizing he would be a prisoner in his room until the boat left Sunday morning. But when the next morning came and Maggie had left for her meeting, he realized he was unable to stay put.

"What activity is available that will help pass the time with little worry of running into Brackton," he mused. Flipping through the brochures that Maggie had left on the nightstand, the answer came to him; real estate. Pulling his baseball cap low on his head and donning sun glasses, he headed back towards Main Street to find a real estate agent willing to take him on a tour of available homes. He was in luck.

"My wife and I just love this place," he said enthusiastically, "and she asked me to take a look at what's available. You got some time for me?" he asked.

"Certainly do, Mr...?"

"Sullivan. Brad Sullivan."

"Well my name is Cliff Obanyon," the agent said as he shook Sullivan's hand and offered him a seat. "What kind of price range did you have in mind?"

That question had caught him off guard, but realizing that this was island real estate he assumed it would be pricey, so he offered a price that fell into his current residency's range, feeling it would be enough to peak the agent's interests.

"Ah, that may be a problem, Brad," the agent said. "Most places on the island start at one million dollars. Not all of them mind you, but I want to be open with you upfront."

Thinking quickly, Sullivan countered with, "I suspected as much, Cliff, but I'm just so damned uncomfortable mentioning an interest in spending that much right off the get go. So let me amend my estimate and let's say, for starters anyway, that anything under one and a half million would be do-able."

Agent Obanyon smiled at this and pulled from his desk drawer a dozen or more pieces of paper describing the properties available. Flipping through several, he stopped and handed the sheet to Sullivan. "Now here's one that recently came on the market. It's over on Cliff Road. Are you familiar with that side of the island? Not too far from here."

"We're still trying to get a handle on street names, let alone what 'sides' the island has. Any chance we can take a look?"

And with that, Sullivan left the office with Obanyon and jumped into the agent's jeep. After viewing the house on Cliff Road they drove to 'Sconset' where he was shown a small cottage the worth of his current home, and then onto Madaket where for a mere two point five million he could purchase a slightly bigger cottage. And that, he was told, was because the sellers were motivated.

By mid day they were back on Main Street where Sullivan assured Obanyon he would be back in a couple of days with his wife in tow.

Heading back to his room he couldn't help but think of how much money the residents of this island represented. And most of them, he learned during his tour with Obanyon, where only part-timers. Many of the million dollar plus homes were visited only a couple of weeks a year by their owners.

Maybe he was over reaching with this run for congress. Hell, even Fitzpatrick could afford a second home here. Whenever he thought of the money he had already invested in this race, he had to change his thoughts quickly. Even with Ambrasio's fund raising skills, which were phenomenal in Sullivan's opinion, and along with the funds that John Brackton was funneling to them through unknown third parties, he and Maggie were up to their eyeballs in debt. He made the decision to use the money available to him through their second mortgage loan without consulting Maggie. He had Ambrasio's confidence that he would win to thank for that. With interest rates rising, he could barely keep up with the monthly payments. They were living paycheck to paycheck for the first time and this 'weekend getaway' wasn't helping. Losing this race would nearly finish them financially. No, he corrected himself, not nearly, but thoroughly finish them.

Reaching his room, he fell onto the bed only to feel the vibration of his cell phone in his pants pocket. Looking at the screen, he saw it was Ambrasio.

Opening the cell's cover he spoke more sternly then he had intended, "Frank! I'm supposed to be on vacation, remember?"

"Yeah, yeah," Ambrasio answered. "But I thought you might like to know the latest polls, and I mean all of them, have you in the lead! It was that TV debate. Tell you the truth, I couldn't tell from your answer if you supported tax payer supported abortion or not, but neither could the audience. Half of them that want it are quoted as saying you support it and the other half are for you because of your stance against it. What a country! Rumor has it that one of your opponent's is calling a press conference later to make his withdrawal official. The other one can't be found for comment. But I have it on good word that he and his manager are meeting with his banker right now. After that debate he's gonna have trouble getting funds. He's nearly broke buddy! He couldn't get another dime from his own mother!"

So, I'm not the only one drained to the pocket lining, Sullivan realized. The thought of his opponent's financial woes did nothing to relieve his own tension. But he didn't want to let Ambrasio know just how badly he needed money, too.

"So out of curiosity Frank," Sullivan asked, "how much funds are in the war chest?"

"You let me worry about that! You know what the Campbell Soup founder said when he was asked why he kept spending money on advertising when he already had the market cornered? He said, 'you don't turn an airplane engine off once you're in the air'! Classic! So if you can afford a few bucks in support of your own campaign, we'll keep on flying!"

Sullivan wanted to explode but kept his emotions in check. The last check he wrote at Ambrasio's request was the last check he would be able to write.

"Hey!" Ambrasio added before terminating the call. "Am I good or am I good?"

Leaving the harbor for their return home Maggie and Brad stood at the railing mesmerized by the view of the island from sea. The church steeples, the grand old houses, once the homes for whaling captains, and the masts from the many sail boats that lined the piers provided a tranquility they both had missed when arriving.

"It would be nice to live here, wouldn't it, Brad?" Maggie murmured.

"Yeah," he answered, "It would be nice to have a penthouse in Times Square and a little get-away spot in Bermuda too."

Maggie turned to face him. "What's got into you?"

Brad shook his head trying to dismiss the financial debt he was in, they both were in he corrected himself, and turned his thoughts of the life they would have once he was in office.

"Sorry," he said. "It's the stress talking. Do you have any idea what one those homes cost? I spoke to a realtor while you were at your meeting."

"Really?" she asked. She consciously raised her voice to be heard over the ship's speakers as the captain made an announcement concerning the upcoming blast from the ship's horn. "That can't be true for the whole island," she continued. Didn't you notice all of the workers here? Waitresses, fish and lobstermen, hotel employees; they must live somewhere."

Before Brad could answer her both of their cell phones alerted them to incoming calls.

"Carrie!" Maggie squealed like a high school girl. "It *is* magical here and we've had a memorable trip."

Looking at his cell phone's caller ID Brad saw the name "Ambrasio" and walked toward one the deck chairs to provide distance from Maggie. Just as he opened the cover to take the call the ship's horn gave a blast that startled him so thoroughly the hand holding his cell phone shot into the air. He watched in fascination and fear as his cell bounced off of the deck's railing and fell over the side of the ship. It was indeed a memorable trip, he thought, as he lifted his eyes to see a private jet, a Gulfstream III, heading towards the mainland.

SEVENTEEN

Stan Ross had been unaware of just how many hours there were in a day before teaming with Kim Marston. He still arrived at his office at eight in the morning, but these days, instead of heading to his home between five and six in the evening, he was ordering dinner in and able to catch only the last portion of The Tonight Show before retiring. Working long hours, seven days a week, was not what he envisioned when he volunteered to help the Congressman. But if a reason for sacrifice was necessary, he need only observe Matson.

She was already deep into her work by the time Stan arrived and was often the one to turn out the lights when she left, whenever that was, Ross mused. Once a trial was deemed warranted as a result of the hearing, a foregone conclusion in Matson's opinion, they turned their attention to the jury pool. Ross was responsible for combing through each of the questionnaires that Matson had contracted a specialist in jury pool selection to prepare. His job was to separate those that would be unacceptable to one side or the other. Of the five hundred applicants making up the two piles, the ones that represented the best candidates to support their side were noticeably smaller.

"How can that be?" Ross asked. "I'd of thought maybe a ten to twenty percent difference, but the prosecutor will have a cake walk in jury selection."

"Oh no he won't," Matson responded. "First of all, people lie. There are some people who would say anything to be selected to a jury for a trial of this importance. What you've accomplished so far, Stan, is simply a preliminary exercise. The real work starts now."

"How so? What's left to do other than make a list of those favoring our side and work to get them seated past O'Brien's objections?"

"Uh uh," Matson objected. "O'Brien had his own questionnaire approved by the courts and he will be facing the same problem we are regarding who to believe. What we have to do now, or more accurately put, what you have to do now is start investigating the potential juror's one by one; both piles."

"You're kidding, right? How would I even begin to do that?"

"Get online and check their credit reports, value of their homes, religious and political affiliation, and anything else you can find out about them. There's a bunch of online services that are available to do that, for a price. And once you document everything, you can learn about them we'll send you out to buddy-up to their friends, neighbors and co-workers."

Ross ran his hand through his unkempt hair and sighed audibly. Then he smiled.

"You regretting that you volunteered for this?" Matson asked.

"No way! I just remembered why I chose to become a tax lawyer instead of concentrating on criminal law."

"If it's any consolation Stan, I envy you more each day."

It was a week before Christmas when Sailor's in-depth piece on Fitzpatrick's "Faith for Life" bill was published in The Hub. He made reference, in third person, how many in congress thought the bill called for draconian measures against doctors and that it would set civilization back fifty years. His best work came from his interviews with Maggie Sullivan, Regional President of NOW, and Archbishop Pollock of Boston.

A lifetime democrat himself, Maggie gave Sailor pause when it came to his pledge to always vote straight party line. She was hungry for power and attention and found the support she needed to massage those needs, not only with her role in NOW, but with her husband leading in the polls to replace Fitzpatrick in Congress. Here was a woman, he thought, of the Hillary Clinton vain. "You may not have elected me, but I'm here to rule through my husband's power."

It was shameful, he thought, how the media, all but him of course, ignored Hillary's run for the presidency while giving her democratic opponent a free ride. That woman had spunk, he realized, and if the elections were to be held again today, she'd be a shoe-in. The press had power, he always knew, but what he came to realize recently was that the press was the power. Was it always like that? He asked himself. He couldn't be sure, but it didn't matter. The fact of the matter was that what the media wanted people to believe, is what they told them to believe. And he was proud to be part of that.

"The Judeo-Christian religions have always supported the right to life," he quoted Archbishop Pollock. "From apostolic times, the Christian tradition *overwhelmingly* held that abortion was grievously evil. In the absence of modern medical knowledge, some of the Early Fathers held that abortion was homicide; others that it was tantamount to homicide; and various scholars theorized about when and how the unborn child might be animated or 'ensouled.' But *none* diminished the unique evil of abortion as an attack on life itself, and the early Church closely associated abortion with infanticide. In short, *from the beginning*, the believing Christian community held that abortion was always, gravely wrong."

"NOW has always had one mandate from its conception: women's rights," he quoted Maggie Sullivan. "In fact, I believe the foundation was started not only as a protection against a man ruled world, but from the man ruled church as well. What have women gained? We finally get our Supreme Court to agree to our grievances and make lawful what we know in our hearts to be right, but the leaders of our church stubbornly refuse to accept. Do you know that some Cardinal's are on record as saying that politicians that support a woman's right to choose should not take part in the sacraments? Can you imagine that?"

Sailor, a Catholic himself, understood why the Cardinals made such statements as a way of defending their personal belief system. His own system called for less drastic measures and tended to support whatever he believed to be right while adhering to what he believed the Church had right. Maggie Sullivan made a good point, he thought, along the same lines.

"Can you imagine the problems this country would be faced with today had women continued to listen to Church teachings and spurned contraception?" she asked. "We don't have enough jobs for those willing to work today, or enough food and shelter for those that go without. Now multiply that number by thousands, hundreds of thousands, and think about that!"

Sailor did think about that and came away with a nagging doubt that she might be wrong. After all, having "safe" sex didn't necessarily mean a child wouldn't be produced. It simply meant you needn't be as a careful in preventing that outcome. The world seemed to amble along fairly well prior to women's contraceptives, but as far as he was concerned, her comments, right or wrong, represented a national organization. But this woman's presentation of facts was allowing no middle ground.

"Certainly you can find some things you can agree with the Church on?" Sailor asked as a way to prod Maggie towards a more conciliatory close to the interview.

"Well, I do agree on the sanctity of marriage," she conceded. "But I'm not sure they were the ones to figure that out! A successful marriage has always been tantamount to the success or failure of a country. Every bit as important as the laws they pass to ensure fairness.

"I can promise you this much, Jeff," Maggie offered her own prepared closing statement to the interview, "when my husband gets to Congress, the women in this country will have a strong advocate fighting for *them*."

His piece in The Hub was met with praise and won him the Regional Award for News Excellence. He spent January and February before the cameras of the national news networks as the local "expert" on the upcoming trial and even entertained an offer to join CNL Cable NEWS as their reporter at large. But Sailor knew bigger offers would be coming and he only needed patience and continued air time to receive them. No matter how this trial ended for Fitzpatrick, there would be months ahead of reporting on the aftermath. Someone lost, while someone won, and life went on for each of them.

It was the last week of March, two weeks before Holy Week on the Christian calendar, and a little more than a year since the accident, that the trial began.

EIGHTEEN

As was expected, the court was packed with spectators. More than half the rows were filled with the media representing radio, print, cable, and TV. No camera's were aloud in the courtroom, but those correspondents not writing about the trial would be expected to provide live updates during breaks in the proceedings.

Jack O'Brien sat in his new Brooks Brother suit and silk tie, His silver hair shined like it had been buffed, rather than brushed. His mind kept jumping from the case before him to the Beacon Hill townhouse he was considering purchasing so he could live closer to the power and money of Boston's elite.

He'd thoroughly reviewed the profiles of the defendant and his family. He knew each of the juror's names, their religions, and their political party. Fitzpatrick's attorney was aggressive during the selection process and he had to admire her arguments to allow, or disallow, some of the jurors. But this was a slam dunk case that a first year law student could win. He glanced at Kim Matson as he thought this. He did his research on her, too, and found her court win record to be very impressive. He concluded the only reason she would associate herself with this case is for the notoriety. O'Brien had quietly pumped an impressive amount of money into public opinion polls, jury selection consultants, and negative publicity regarding the anti-abortionists stance. All of which was tricky to manipulate as a public servant, but with Brackton's money, anything was possible. Better yet, some things came free. Even as he sat here internally reviewing his opening statement, he could almost hear the chants of the NOW and MADD protestors circling on the sidewalk outside.

Beside him sat one of the most beautiful clients he ever had, and if the glances that the male jury members were giving her were any indication of who they would favor, well, easy money. And some of the lady juror's were just as attentive to Mr. Brackton. Yes, the dream couple, he absently nodded in agreement. The kind you only read about in novels.

At the other table sat Michael Fitzpatrick. Tall, dark hair trimmed to the collar, fit and good looking.

Stan Ross was leaning over the rail that separated the spectators from the actual court proceedings, speaking to Congressman Fitzpatrick and his wife. From his mannerisms, all could see that he was telling him not to worry.

Kim Matson had her shoulder length jet black hair pulled back in a ponytail. With one hand resting on her forehead, she reviewed the papers before her. She wore dark framed glasses which helped her conceal any expressions her eyes might reveal while reviewing her notes. . . She went over every note of every interview dozens of times, but felt she was missing something. A really big something. She was certain as she could be that Michael would have passed the breathalyzer test. It would have been a big help, but that was something she had to do without. The notes she kept returning to were the ones taken during her interview with Mrs. Brackton. She awoke each morning for the past week with those notes still lying on her bed. It wasn't until this morning that she began to realize her unease had more to do with the way Brackton answered her questions than what she had said.

She studied the notes from that interview again. She had already highlighted those questions and responses she deemed most important and concentrated on those entries. Only this time, she was visualizing Brackton's facial expressions and mannerisms as she answered. She willed her mind to return to Stan Ross' office where she met with Jessica Brackton and her family attorney Hank Ryman.

"Will you be with Mr. and Mrs. Brackton throughout the trial, Mr. Ryman?" Matson asked. It was uncommon to have a personal attorney on-hand during the trial when the State was prosecuting on your behalf.

"I will be available to the Brackton's throughout the trial," was all that Ryman provided.

Turning her attention to Mrs. Brackton, she asked if she were comfortable and ready to begin.

"Yes, I'm ready. But I want you to know that it's not my wish to press—"

"Stop there, Mrs. Brackton!" Her attorney interrupted. "That's an argument between you and your husband. Ms. Matson needn't be made party to it."

Brackton lowered her gaze and nodded once.

Matson thought she was about to say she didn't wish to press charges and filed it away in her mind for future reference.

"How did you spend the morning prior to the accident?" Matson asked.

"Why is that relevant?" Ryman countered.

"I am trying to help Mrs. Brackton to be at ease," Matson said.

Ryman thought about it a moment and nodded his consent.

"Nothing special," Brackton answered. "My husband was coming home from his office in New York that Saturday and I had an appointment at Hassam's with my hair dresser. We had plans to eat out that evening."

"Is that Hassam's in Brookline," Matson asked.

"Yes, do you know it?" Brackton brightened at them having a mutual acquaintance.

"I've heard of it," Matson answered. "He had a write up in Boston Magazine last month."

She continued, "Does he normally come home on Saturday's?"

"No, not usually," she said while seemingly to contemplate her answer. Her shoulders seemed to slacken and her gaze became distant.

Matson waited for her attention to return, but when Brackton appeared to be lost in a dream she asked, "Mrs. Brackton?"

Brackton looked back at her and gave a slight shake of her head. "I'm sorry. What did you ask?"

"You said not usually. When does he normally return from New York?" Matson asked this to get Brackton's concentration back on the interview. She must be going through a very tough time and there was no reason, in Matson's opinion, to make her remembering that day any more difficult than it was.

"He normally returns Friday nights," Brackton answered. "But in the winter, when the weather's bad, it's sometimes easier to wait until the next morning." And then she added, "There was an icy rain that night. I suppose they had ice in New York, too."

Matson made an 'icy rain' entry into the notebook. Even though she was taping this interview, with O'Brien's and Matson's permission, there were times you needed to capture ideas as well as the words being spoken.

"You said he flew home that morning?"

"No," Brackton replied. "He normally flies home the next morning when weather is bad, which it apparently was, but he delayed his return to visit with our tax attorney. He wasn't due to arrive until six that evening."

"Can you tell me what you did, where you went, the week leading up to the accident?"

"Wait a minute!" Ryman sat forward in his chair. "That question has no bearing on the accident itself."

"Then you shouldn't mind her answering it," Matson said. "I know this question may seem a little odd of me to ask, Mrs. Brackton, but sometimes being able to relate to activities and events prior to an accident helps to sharpen the recollection of an incident."

Mrs. Brackton turned to face her attorney with a look of apprehension, Matson recalled. At the time she wrote it off as Brackton just being nervous, but now she wondered what other reason there could be that would make that question cause unease.

"I suppose it's okay, but let's try to get on track here," Ryman said.

"Mrs. Brackton?" Matson prompted.

"On Monday, I dropped off John's suits at the cleaners and had lunch at my tennis club." Brackton hesitated apparently trying to recall her week.

"On Wednesday, I attended a meeting of the Ladies Auxiliary at my church."

"Which church is that, Mrs. Brackton?" asked Matson.

"If that's some back door attempt to base this case on religious grounds—" Ryman stated.

"It's an attempt, Mr. Ryman, to ask what church auxiliary she was referring to not, what religion."

"United Congregationalist," Brackton offered.

"Thank you," Matson said. "Please go on."

"I met with a designer, at my home, on Thursday. We're considering having our guest room redone."

In anticipation of their baby, Matson thought, but decided not to ask.

"And on Friday I played tennis with Betty Connors, a friend from college who was visiting her son here in Boston. He attends Boston University."

"And on Tuesday?" Matson asked.

"What about Tuesday?" Brackton looked puzzled.

"You didn't say what you did on Tuesday of that week."

Jessica Brackton's posture stiffened as though she was about to refuse to answer that when her attorney spoke for her.

"Okay," Ryman interjected. "That's enough of memory lane."

"Very well," Matson conceded. "Let's talk about the morning of the accident."

"Was Phillips Street your normal route to Hassam's?"

"Yes, it allows me to avoid the traffic on Cambridge Street."

"And how were the streets that morning?"

"Not crowded or anything," Brackton said, obviously not sure what Matson meant by her question.

"That's good, "Matson smiled, "but how did you find driving that morning? You mentioned an icy rain had fallen."

"Oh. I really didn't notice. John had new tires put on the Mercedes just a week earlier. They're a much heavier vehicle than many people imagine."

Matson assumed she offered that statement for her benefit seeing where she was one of the many people unable to afford a Mercedes.

"Did you notice the streets being slick or any patches of ice on them?"

"No, but like I said, I really didn't notice."

Matson came back to the present and removed her glasses. She turned to look at the clock hanging on the back wall above the doors to the court room. Ten-fifteen. She hoped the judge wasn't trying to be fashionably late, but had a legitimate reason for being tardy. Just then, the judge's chamber door opened and the Court Clerk stood and addressed the spectators.

"Hear ye, hear ye, this Honorable Division of the General Sessions Criminal Courts, is now open for the transaction of business pursuant to adjournment. All persons having business with the Court, draw near, give attention, and ye shall be heard. The Honorable Judge Anthony Moretti presiding. Be seated, please. No talking in the courtroom."

Judge Anthony Moretti sat holding papers pertaining to the current case while he peered over his spectacles to scan the courtroom. Glancing back at his papers he memorized the names of the plaintiff attorneys as well as the defendants. He couldn't help but notice the beautiful blond sitting at the plaintiff's table and her likeness to Grace Kelly. Turning to look at the defendant, he saw a young man that was obviously a Fitzpatrick, and on either side of him sat a curly-haired, Kramer-like fellow on his left, and an Oriental woman on his right.

The judge picked up his gavel and rapped it twice to stop the murmuring and get everyone's attention.

"A few ground rules before we start," he said while scanning the faces. "This court will not tolerate unruliness in any form or manner. There are rumors circulating that I have placed reporters, spectators and lawyers in custody during a trial for disregarding my instructions. These particular rumors, it saddens me to say, are true.

"Woe to the person who's cell phone rings, who speaks above a whisper to their neighbor, who pulls out a bagel, sandwich, cookie or interrupts these proceedings with anything but a life threatening situation."

Turning his attention to where the attorneys sat he asked, "Are you ready with your opening statement Mr. O'Brien?"

"I am your honor." O'Brien made a show of arranging some papers that were laid out in front of him before stepping forward of his seat.

"Thank you, Judge." O'Brien said and turned his attention to the jury. "Good morning. Over the years society has seen the damage that driving while under the influence of alcohol can wreck on lives and property. As a result, laws have been enacted to protest us against those individuals who choose to ignore the consequences of deliberately ignoring the safety of others. Those laws insure that individuals have certain rights to protection as basic as life, liberty and the pursuit of happiness. The facts of this case will show that all three of these rights we uphold as the dearest to the American way of life, were lost to the Brackton's by Michael Fitzpatrick's disregard of the law. That is what this whole case is about.

"The facts of this case are actually very simple. The evidence will show that on February fifteenth of the year 2008, Michael Fitzpatrick, while under the influence of alcohol, drove his expensive, foreign sports car into Jessica Brackton's vehicle, resulting in severe bodily damage to her person and her vehicle. More importantly, it took from the Brackton's their son, Taylor. Taylor was to be their first child." O'Brien paused while he slightly lifted his head and slowly gave it a shake to indicate how unfathomable this was.

"You will hear from Michael's friends, who he partied with the night before the accident and, indeed, shared a parting shot of liquor with moments prior to the accident.

"You will hear from the officers who responded to the accident as to the appearance of Michael Fitzpatrick and his refusal to take a breathalyzer test. And, and" he repeated to make sure he had their attention. "You will hear from an expert on religions regarding the sanctity of life as it exists in the womb.

"Now the attorneys for Mr. Fitzpatrick will try to paint a different picture for you. That Michael was not impaired the day of the accident, that he is a 'giver' that spends his Sunday's as a volunteer at the Cancer Center, and, perhaps, that he is being held to a higher standard simply because he is the son of a congressman.

"Do not be fooled! The simple fact of this case is that Michael Fitzpatrick knowingly chose to operate a vehicle in dangerous conditions while impaired due to his intake of alcohol. And that his decision to do so, his obvious lack of responsibility to others, led to the death of what was to be a first born child of one of the oldest, most respected family names in New England.

"Thank You."

O'Brien turned to his seat and waited for his opponent to take the floor. He knew this wasn't his best opening statement and, in fact, was undoubtedly his shortest. But like a poker player holding pockets aces, he didn't want to overplay his hand on the opening bet. He felt fairly certain he nailed the defense position and that they would try to convince the jury Fitzpatrick was being crucified. It was time to find out.

"Good morning ladies and gentlemen," Matson addressed the jurors. "I must concede to you that Mr. O'Brien is right. But on only one point, that the facts of this case are simple. My client, Michael Fitzpatrick, is being unfairly prosecuted due to his relationship to his father. It saddens me to have to point out to Mr. O'Brien, an attorney with a national reputation, that refusal to take a breathalyzer is in no way proof of guilt.

"According to Mr. O'Brien, he will produce witnesses who will speak of Michael's appearance, friends of Michael, who shared a shot of bourbon with him the morning of the accident. One drink. I don't know of any twenty-two year old who gets drunk after one drink.

"The law uses a French term to explain what happened that morning.

It's force majeure. It means superior or overwhelming force. An act of God. And while the result of that accident, that neither you nor I could have avoided was tragic, it was not one of negligence nor over indulgence. It was, sadly and as unconceivable as it may seem to us, an act of God.

"The law is about fairness, not retribution. Is it fair that the Brackton's lost their unborn baby?" Matson empathized the word 'unborn'. "Certainly not."

"Is it fair that Michael, a Harvard student who gives up his Sunday's, a day of rest for most of us, to volunteer his time at the cancer center, to be the one driving downhill that morning on a street covered in black ice? That's right. Black ice. If any of you have had the misfortune of encountering this phenomenon while driving, you know I am right when I use the word unfair. Black ice," she repeated. "You can feel it, but you can't see it.

"We will have a meteorologist appear here to speak about the weather that morning, as well as a university professor to explain the phenomenon known as black ice.

"Mr. O'Brien will attempt to fool you by presenting witnesses whose testimony will add up to nothing more than hearsay. There'll be no facts presented, mind you, that can, or should lead to a conviction. Just a series of events that led to Michael being unjustly tried for an accident that could not be avoided. Force majeure; God's will.

"Thank you."

Upon Matson returning to her seat Judge Moretti addressed the jurors.

"We will suspend proceedings until Monday morning when we can all look forward to fresh week and a lot of work before us. Keep in mind that you are not to discuss this case with anyone, not a family member nor even each other.

"This court is in recess and will return this Monday morning at 10AM."

"All rise!" Came from the clerk.

Jack O'Brien stood smiling as the judge made for his chambers. His opponent's defense rested on a meteorologist and a university professor? Oh, life could be sweet!

NINETEEN

Matson and Ross sat in his office in Medfield the following morning. They both looked haggard from lack of sleep and a feeling of foreboding doom.

Stan tried to put a better face on the situation. "You were right, Kim. O'Brien has only speculation to go on. Nothing in the way of proof."

"I was wrong about one thing, Stan." She answered. "The law is about retribution, not fairness. Someone's been wronged and someone has to pay."

"Actually, Kim," Ross was smiling at her. "That would make two wrongs. Force majeure is a contractual term."

"We know that, but hopefully the jurors don't," and added a wink.

They busied themselves with their laptops for several minutes until Matson spoke again.

"You know, Stan, my mind keeps going back to my interview with Mrs. Brackton. There's nothing that jumps out at me, but maybe you could take another look at my notes?"

"Sure. Hold on." Stan hit a few keystrokes on his computer. "Here they are."

Matson sat quietly as Stan's eyes read the words on the screen before him, occasionally hitting the 'page down' button to move to the next page. After several minutes he leaned back in his chair and studied the ceiling above him.

"Nothing there, huh?" Matson asked.

"Not really," he answered. "But there is one thing that remains a mystery."

"Yeah?"

"She never did tell you what she did or where she went on Tuesday of that week."

"It was days before the accident, Stan," Matson stated. "It doesn't matter."

"We don't know that," Stan lowered his gaze to look at her. "But we can find out."

"How?" Matson asked. Skeptical they would be allowed to get anywhere near Brackton before she took the stand. It was not something she had in her plans anyway.

"She drove a 2008 Mercedes, for cry eye! Donuts to dollars that baby had the latest navigation system in it. Hell, it probably came standard with the car."

"And?" Matson had no idea why that would matter.

"We can get a court order and impound that sucker. It'll tell us everywhere she went, how long it took her to get there, the routes she took, even how long she parked."

Matson tilted her head to the side and lifted her eyebrows to indicate a 'so what' attitude.

"Look," Stan said. "We can use all of the information we can get our hands on. Besides, I'm a business slash tax attorney who always wanted to have a reason to get something impounded."

"But that car was totaled, Stan," Matson pointed out. "I'm sure it's been crushed, burnt, made into toasters or something by now."

"Of course it has," Ross answered. "But no scrap metal dealer worth his salt would crush a perfectly good, state of the art, GPS system. I just have to find it."

"Can't argue with that logic, counselor."

By Sunday evening Stan had still not returned to the office. Matson assumed he was still tracking down the GPS system that was installed in Brackton's car. Matson spent the afternoon meeting with the meteorologist who agreed to testify on her behalf. She returned to her hotel room, ordered room service of pizza and coke, and went to bed, drifting off to visions of Jack O'Brien having an accident of his own that would delay the trial.

The next morning, as expected, the court room was full of reporters and those with enough influence to be assured a seat. Two of those spectators were Representative Bradford Sullivan and his wife, Maggie. Sullivan could not have imagined in his craziest dream that he would be attending a trial, or any other event, that would place his former lover with his wife in the same room. Yet here he was.

Having no great love of Fitzpatrick, the media had taken hold of Sullivan's candidacy for congress. On another front, and one important to his opposition of Fitzpatrick, the media had been concentrating on the riff that had been developing between the Catholic Church and Catholic politicians in favor of pro-choice. There were some days he had to wonder if he was running against Bishop Connor or Fitzpatrick. It seemed like a day didn't go by that the Bishop wasn't being quoted by the local media on the Church's stance regarding abortion. Sullivan had been forced on several occasions to announce an opposing view in order to win the favor of his constituency. The Pope may be infallible, but dead wrong on this topic, he thought. The Hub, the largest and most widely read daily in the state, knew when it had a good story and they ran with it.

It was Frank Ambrasio, his campaign manager that insisted he attend the trial.

"It'll show you have compassion," Ambrasio said, "for both sides.

When the press asks you what you're doing there, you tell them you're concerned for your opponent's family as well as the tragedy that has befallen the Brackton's. It's free press, Brad, and it's good press, for you."

"But my wife has arranged for protestors to be there, for God's sake," he argued. "How's that going to look?"

"Like a free publicity jackpot!" Ambrasio answered. "What better person to support your views on the right for a woman to choose? And it's going to put your mug on the front page of the Hub and every TV news program in the country. We're talking about the chance for national exposure here, Brad. You don't turn your back on that."

His appearance in the court room caused such a stir amongst the attending reporters that when Jessica Brackton turned to see what the commotion was about, their eyes met. Her bewildered expression suddenly morphed into one of disbelief as Sullivan quickly turned his attention to finding a seat near the rear of the court. Maggie Sullivan noticed Jessica Brackton's expression and mistook it for one of gratitude that they came. She gave Brackton a brief wave and pulled on her husband's arm while ushering him to a seat closer to the proceedings.

"Maybe we can get your picture with Mr. and Mrs. Brackton," Maggie whispered. "She's obviously happy to see us here."

Sullivan took a seat in the second row, next to his wife and directly behind the Brackton's. Facing straight ahead, his heart pounding, he willed with all of his strength that Jessica Brackton not turn her head to face him.

"Hear ye! Hear ye!" the court clerk recited the time worn statement that announced the start of the trial proceedings.

Judge Moretti stared out at the crowd seated beyond the attorney's tables and took a breath before speaking.

"I won't bother to repeat myself as to how I expect the spectators here to conduct themselves at all times. Suffice it to say that this courthouse has sufficient holding pens." Turning to O'Brien he said, "You may call your first witness."

"Thank you, your honor," O'Brien replied while standing. "We would like to begin by calling Doctor Hayes to the stand."

One of the court officers standing near the doors to the courtroom opened them and spoke loud enough for everyone to hear. "Doctor Hayes?"

Walking through the doors to the court and down the aisle to the witness stand, Doctor Hayes looked young enough to be a first year college student. Wavy black hair, a bit unruly and overlong gave the impression of a soap opera star more than a resident doctor at Mass General.

Upon raising his right hand and promising to the oath all courtrooms insist be administered, he sat, back straight and hands in his lap. Matson glanced at the jury and noticed how intently the women were gazing at him. She determined to get him out of the courtroom as soon as possible. The last thing she needed was for jurors to be falling in love with a prosecutor's witness.

"Doctor Hayes," O'Brien said. "Would you please tell the court something about your background?"

Hayes cleared his throat and spoke.

"I graduated from Tufts Medical School with advanced training in medical trauma and am employed at Massachusetts General Hospital."

"What do you mean by having advanced training in medical trauma?" O'Brien asked. "Aren't all doctors trained to address trauma?"

"Well, yes. But in a hospital the size of Mass General and with the number of emergency room visits we attend to in the course of a day, it's important to be more than just familiar with the damages we address from one patient to the next."

O'Brien slowly shook his head as he looked at the floor before him in an effort to show he was having trouble trying to grasp what he was told.

"You mean you may be treating a broken arm one moment, and the next patient has appendicitis?"

The doctor smiled and said, "Something like that. And in fact I experienced that very scenario last week. But it's more than that. A severe car accident may involve several people with multiple fractures or worse."

"By worse," O'Brien asked, "do you mean someone who's been in a car accident might have extenuating medical risks prior to the accident?"

"Yes. Exactly."

"Would a pregnancy be considered an extenuating medical risk?"

"Objection, your honor," Matson came to her feet. "If the counselor wishes to lead the witness perhaps we should all be given a script to save time."

"Counselor?" the judge asked turning his attention to O'Brien. It was obvious he agreed with Matson.

"I'm sorry, your honor," O'Brien said.

Facing Doctor Hayes he asked, "What were the circumstances under which you met Mrs. Brackton?"

Doctor Hayes thought a moment before answering.

"She was brought to the emergency room by ambulance, having experienced lacerations to the face and heavy bleeding from her uterus as a result of a car accident."

"And based upon your examination of her, what did you find?" O'Brien asked.

"What did I find?" Hayes repeated obviously confused by the

question. "Oh! You're referring to her pregnancy," he answered, appearing to be pleased with himself. Then, assuming a more professional tone he continued. "Mrs. Brackton was in her first trimester of pregnancy and lost the fetus due to the trauma she experienced in the accident."

O'Brien was pleased that the doctor volunteered this information without the need for further direction on his part.

"Did Mrs. Brackton receive any visitors that day?" O'Brien asked.

"Objection!" Matson said. "Are we believe that Doctor Hayes had such a slow day that he monitored who visited Mrs. Matson?"

"I'll withdraw the question," O'Brien said.

"Doctor Hayes, did anyone visit *you* the day of the accident in regards to Mrs. Brackton?"

"Yes, I was told that Congressman Fitzpatrick wanted to speak with me in the visitors lounge.

"And did you meet with him?"

"Yes, I did," he answered.

"Tell me doctor," O'Brien said. "Is it a normal occurrence to be asked to speak with the father of the person responsible for causing harm?"

"Objection!"

"Sustained," the judge said.

"Let me rephrase the question," O'Brien said. "Are you normally asked to speak with the parents of someone responsible for an accident—?"

"Objection!" Matson jumped to her feet. "Your honor, are we to assume my client is already guilty?"

"I withdraw the question," O'Brien said knowing he made his point to the jury.

He thanked the doctor and announced, "No more questions your honor."

"Do you wish to cross examine counselor?" the judge asked Matson.

"Yes, your honor," Matson replied and walked to the witness stand to address Doctor Hayes.

"Doctor Hayes," Matson began. "You stated that Mrs. Brackton lost the fetus due to the accident?"

"That's correct," he replied.

"Is it possible she may have lost the fetus due to another reason?"

"It's possible, but under the circumstances—"

"Isn't it possible, doctor," Matson interrupted, "that she may have been experiencing a miscarriage just prior to the accident?"

"Well, yes. But—"

"Or perhaps the miscarriage, as unfortunate as it was, began exactly at the hour nature intended it to and the accident had nothing to do with it."

"Objection, your honor! Speculation."

"I can't be certain what nature—"

"Sustained. You needn't answer, Doctor," the judge said.

"In fact, doctor," Matson continued, "you can't say with any certainty at all that Mrs. Brackton's pregnancy was aborted as a result of the car accident can you? "

The doctor stared at her open-mouthed and was about to refute her argument when Matson turned to her seat and stated, "No more questions, your honor."

The remainder of the day consisted of continued objections followed by rephrased questions for witnesses that attested to the good will and character of Mrs. Jessica Billington-Brackton.

TWENTY

That evening, upon returning from the court, there was a Fed-Ex package waiting for Stan Ross on the floor outside his office door. It was apparently signed for by the hair dresser who operated his business just below Stan's office.

"Great guy, that Andre," Stan said as he flopped into his chair and began opening the box. "Although I doubt that Andre's his real name."

Matson took her seat at the folding card table that served as her desk. She was too lost in thought reviewing that day's witnesses to pay attention to what Stan was saying. After the doctor's damaging testimony, O'Brien had spent the day building Brackton's reputation to one approaching sainthood. She had every reason to believe the prosecutor would rest his case by tomorrow's end and it would be left up to her to save Michael from the jaws of revenge.

"Hello," Stan said looking into the box now that he had the lids folded back. Reaching in he pulled out a package enveloped in bubble wrap. Peeling away the wrap he uncovered his prize, the GPS Navigator from Jessica Brackton's wrecked Mercedes.

He looked up to see Matson wearing a "what's that" expression.

"This is going to tell us where Mrs. Brackton spent her day on that 'missing' Tuesday," he said.

"I didn't know you found it," Matson said.

"The power of a court order, counselor. It opened a lot of doors, I can tell you. I spent all of yesterday learning how to get at the information hidden inside and acquiring the software and hardware attachments I need to get at it. Not an easy thing to accomplish on a Sunday, I can tell you. Anywho...." Stan busied himself taken wires hanging from various attachments and plugging them into his PC and the GPS device.

The evening in Stan's office was one of quiet concentration broken only when the Chinese food they ordered arrived. Filling their plates in silence, they returned to their respective desks without breaking stride in the thoughts that had been occupying them.

With her review of the next day's witnesses and the probable questions she'd expect to come from the prosecutor complete, Matson turned her attention to what she would ask during her cross-examination. It was nearing ten o'clock in the evening when Stan, studying his monitor muttered, "That's interesting." He jotted down an address and returned his attention to the screen.

Typing in the WEB address for Google, he selected maps and clicked on 'street view'. Typing in the address from his pad he sat back and said quietly, "I thought so. What the hell would she be doing there?"

Ross picked up that morning's newspaper, ripped out the page he was looking for and folded neatly into his top shirt pocket. Grabbing his sports jacket and picking up the legal pad with the address on it, he walked past Matson saying, "I'll be back later tonight."

"Later tonight?" Matson asked in disbelief. "It's already after ten." But Stan had already closed the door behind him.

Checking the address once more, he stepped from his car and walked towards the entrance of the Exeter Hotel. It was late, nearly midnight, he guessed, as he walked through the glass doors and approached the front desk. The front desk receptionist was a middle aged, grey haired man wearing a faded red vest with a patch stating, "Exeter Hotel" sewn into it. Over the top of that was pinned a name tag with the words "Flaherty/Manager" embossed on it.

"Be needing a room, sir?" he asked with what was an unmistaken Irish accent.

"No, thank you, Mr. Flaherty," Ross said smiling at him. "Just came to ask a question or two of you." Reaching into his shirt pocket he pulled out the ripped page of The Hub newspaper and, unfolding it, laid it on the front desk. It was a picture of Jessica Brackton standing beside her husband outside of their Beacon Hill brownstone.

"Recognize this woman?" Ross asked, pointing at Jessica Brackton.

"Sorry sir," the manager shook his head. "They'd be having my job if I spoke of those who stayed here."

"Well, this would stay between me and you," Ross said as he placed his hand on the counter exposing just enough of the fifty dollar bill he held there to be seen by Flaherty.

"Well now," the manager said while rubbing his grizzled grin and peering at the corner of the bill. "I suppose it would be depending on the questions being asked, now wouldn't it."

"True enough," Ross agreed. "Better yet, if you recognize this lady as someone who has stayed here recently, just nod your head."

Flaherty nodded once, reached across and snatched the bill from under Ross' hand.

"Was she with someone?" Ross asked.

The manager twisted his head answering, "Now that might be a question which could find me in hot water."

In response, Ross pulled his wallet from his back pocket and exposed a hundred dollar bill to the manager whose eyes widened noticeably.

"To earn this," he said, "I need a few more answers from you." Without waiting for consent he asked, "Was she with the man in this picture she's standing beside? A nod yes or no, will do."

The manager shook his head to indicate she was not with the man in the photo.

"Was she with another man?"

He nodded and asked, "You'd be the husband, is that it now?"

"No, nothing like that," Ross answered as he handed the bill to the man.

"How long did they stay here? One night?" He asked.

Shaking his head as if in thought he answered, "My memory isn't as good as it once was and my brain isn't as sharp as young man's."

"Look," Ross said, "You've earned a good wage from me without having to utter a word about your guests. I wouldn't want to have to serve you this but I will if you make me." Ross pulled from his inside sports jacket pocket the warrant he had drawn for the GPS system. He was gambling the man would take it on sight as something more directly related to his visit.

"You're the law, are you?" the man stated more than asked, looking more frightened than he should have. Ross figured he was here in the States illegally. Probably came to visit a relative and decided to stay.

"I notice things of course, but being the manager here is a twenty-four hour a day job. Some days I'm here at the desk and others I'm fixing a leak. The Haitian's they hire to help me? I could get more out of one those seeing-eye dogs. Have the dog show guests to their room, is what I'd prefer. But I did happen to be upfront here when her highness there registered," he said nodding towards the clipping on the desk. "A little while after that comes a man saying he's her husband and asking for his wife's room number. A couple hours later, the room's empty. They use the TV to check out. I ain't never seen them leave, just check in."

"I want to be perfectly clear about this," Ross said. "You registered Mrs. Brackton yourself on at least one occasion?"

"Wouldn't know," the manager answered with a bewildered look on his face.

"Mrs. Brackton," Ross repeated while pointing at her picture. "You just told me you registered her for a room here."

"Now that lady I registered," the manager said. "But she was no Mrs. Brackton. Hold on a minute. It was last February was the last I saw her, or was it March?" The manager flipped through his registry book, one that still required a visitor to sign his name into, and stopped when he reached the end of February.

"Here she is in her own writing," the manager said with satisfaction as he spun the register towards Ross. Half way down the page the old man's rheumatoid finger was pointing at the name Barbara Stanford."

"You're sure this was the same woman in the picture?" Ross asked.

"Unless she has a twin, like my nieces Doreen and Corinne, cutest things you'd likely to see..."

"Can you describe the man she met with?"

"Describe him?" the old man's eyebrows rose on his face like he couldn't believe the question. "I fooken know 'im!"

After several moments explaining what he knew of the man who met 'Barbara Sanford', Ross elatedly handed the manager the last bill in his wallet and headed directly back to his office.

TWENTY-ONE

Kim Matson was leaning over the court railing reassuring the congressman that it was too soon to be overly worried, and that he and his wife were doing the best they could be expected to do by just being there. Her real concern was for Stan Ross at that moment as he had not shown himself this morning.

O'Brien stood at his seat and stated that he would like to call Tim Jenkins as his first witness of the new day.

Tim strode down the aisle and stood in the witness box to take the oath. He was wearing a light brown three-piece suit that complemented his freshly cut red hair. Michael had never seen Tim looking so polished and couldn't help but stare at his old friend. Upon stating the words, "I do", he sat down and gave Michael a wink as a way of support.

Neither O'Brien nor the jury missed it, but O'Brien was going to make sure.

"Who did you just wink at?" O'Brien asked Tim.

"Michael," Tim answered.

"Do you always wink at other men or was it a signal of some kind? You are under oath, I'll remind you. I know you are visiting here from the U.K., so perhaps I should mention that we take that oath seriously here."

"I don't take oaths lightly myself," Tim smiled while answering in what was an apparent British accent. He was the son of a British Lord, although O'Brien wasn't going to volunteer that fact to the jurors, several of whom smiled at the innocence Tim was displaying. Realizing that his point was made and that he may be pushing too hard, O'Brien changed tack asking Tim where he lived, where he went to school, and how well he knew Michael Fitzpatrick.

"We've been buds for three or four years now," Tim answered.

"And when you get together it normally involves a drink or two, doesn't it?" O'Brien asked.

Tim rolled his eyes up, thought a moment and answered, "Yah. Sometimes a good deal more," he said facing the jury. "Seeing where I'm under oath an all."

The spectators and a few of the jurors laughed aloud and the judge slammed his gavel to stop it.

O'Brien was pleased with Tim's answer as he recognized it as an opening to prove that Michael was more than a casual drinker. It would also give O'Brien pleasure in squashing this Limey and wiping that grin from his face.

"A good deal more, you say." O'Brien was smiling at Tim, trying to show his questions were innocent. "Like what? Three or four drinks? Maybe a couple of beers to wash the liquor down? I bet getting through Harvard, all that studying, all those tests, can really build a thirst, huh?"

"Absolutely," Tim answered. "That's the very thing I tell my father. A guy needs a little release now and then, you know?"

"Absolutely," O'Brien mimicked. "So what is it? Three, four or more drinks? A few times a week, huh?"

"That's about right," Tim nodded. "Unless it's finals week," he suddenly added. "I normally need real relaxing after finals."

Perfect, O'Brien thought. I've got him now.

"You and Michael, right?"

"I wouldn't know," Tim answered.

"What do you mean, you wouldn't know? You just stated you have three or more drinks a couple times of week with Michael."

"No I didn't," Tim replied. "I said *I* have two or three drinks a few times a week."

The spectators laughed again, but the judge was ready and banged his gavel.

Feeling his face beginning to turn red, O'Brien walked back to his table to flip through a legal pad. He concentrated on his breathing and when he felt sufficiently in control of his emotions, he looked up at Tim.

"On the night of February fourteenth of last year, Michael spent the night at your apartment, didn't he?"

"Yes."

"And you drank alcohol with Michael that night, didn't you,"

"Yes."

"How much would you say Michael drank?"

"A few beers, I suppose," Tim offered.

"By a few beers you mean six or seven, don't you?"

"That's possible."

"And bourbon? How many shots or mixed drinks did the two of you consume?"

"Not a one," Tim answered confidently.

"So, Michael had several beers, possibly more that night." O'Brien paused to give the jury a chance to think about that.

"In fact, so much beer that he was unable to drive home safely and you insisted he sleep on your couch. Isn't that right?"

"He slept on my couch because I offered it to him. No one insisted."

"Let's move on to the next morning," O'Brien said. "Describe for us what took place when your friend Steve dropped by."

"Steve came by to borrow my ski poles."

"And what happened then?"

"I told him in no uncertain terms he bloody well better not lose them."

The judge made a motion to pick up his gavel which was enough to keep the spectators from laughing aloud.

Exasperated, O'Brien asked him a direct question.

"How many shots did the three of you share that morning?"

"Only one. You see, Mike's girlfriend had just broken—"

"What time was that?" O'Brien interrupted.

"About eight, I think."

"So after a night where Michael Fitzpatrick drank so heavily he had to sleep on your couch, you start the next day by drinking a shot of bourbon at 8 o'clock in the morning."

"Yes, but you should understand that—"

"No more questions, your honor."

"Ms. Matson?" the judge asked.

Matson walked over to Tim and stood so that she could address him while facing the jury.

"Do you recall what time Michael went to sleep that night?"

"About eleven, I guess."

"So after eight hours or more of sleep he shared one shot with you and your friend Jim?"

"That's correct," Tim was nodding.

"Is that a common occurrence?"

"No, no. You see, Mike's girlfriend had just broken off with him and he was upset. In fact, I more or less forced it on him."

"Would you describe Mike as being drunk that morning?" Matson asked.

"Objection, your honor," O'Brien said. "Whatever Mr. Jenkins thought of Fitzpatrick's sobriety is speculation at best."

"Sustained," Judge Moretti said.

"Was Mike stuttering that morning, throwing up, weaving when he stood?" she asked.

"He was right as a constable, ma'am," Tim answered.

"Thank you, Tim. No more questions your honor."

As Tim left the witness box he winked again at Michael, causing several jurors to smile.

"Your next witness, Mr. O'Brien?" the judge asked.

"Yes, your honor. We call Steve Bryant."

"Your honor," Matson rose from her chair. "I believe it is Mr. O'Brien's plan to call not only Steve Bryant, but Tim Jenkins' girlfriend to the stand for no other reason than to prove by their testimony that Michael drank several beers the night before the accident and a shot of bourbon the following morning. The defense is willing to concede this point to him *if* Mr. O'Brien will concede the fact that Michael Fitzpatrick, after having several hours of sound sleep, was not drunk when he awoke."

"Mr. O'Brien?" the judge asked.

Clever girl, O'Brien thought. By conceding to him, she was taking away additional sworn testimony all pointing to the fact Fitzpatrick drank heavily that night. On the other hand, if he denied her request to concede Michael was not drunk that morning, he would only be doing exactly what Matson told the jurors he would do, which would appear to them to be a waste of their time. He decided that his point was sufficiently made. By her own admission, her client drank heavily the night before and started his next morning with a shot of bourbon. Overplaying a winning hand could cause more damage than good, he knew, and he had enough trial experience to not fall into that trap. Besides, he thought, there was a fine line between being drunk and being impaired. As long as she was willing to admit to the jury that her client had drank a shot of bourbon just prior to the accident would leave plenty of doubt in the jurors' minds as to just how impaired he was. And that doubt he had every reason to believe was about to be quashed when he called his next witness.

"Yes, your honor," O'Brien answered. "We are willing to concede that Fitzpatrick was not drunk when he awoke."

O'Brien's statement surprised John Brackton who leaned across his wife to speak into O'Brien's ear.

After a few moments of whispered conversation between the two, the judge spoke.

"It is nearing eleven-thirty. This court will stand in recess for lunch and resume at one pm this afternoon."

"All rise!"

TWENTY-TWO

During the lunch break Matson called Ross' office and had to settle for leaving a voice mail. She decided she would present Stan with a gift of a cell phone. Being out of contact with her co-attorney slash investigator was no way to conduct a trial.

The court resumed the proceedings, as promised, at exactly one o'clock.

"The state calls Officer John Doyle, your honor," O'Brien said. He planned this next witness to be his last one. More importantly, the most damaging one.

"Would you state your name, department, and number of years on the force, officer?" O'Brien asked.

"Officer John Doyle, sir, traffic department with twelve years on the force and preparing for the sergeants exam this spring."

"Sergeant, you say? Very good, officer," O'Brien nodded. "It's important that the department promote men with your experience." O'Brien paused and stepped back so the jurors could have an unobstructed view of this witness in uniform.

"How many times, would you say that you've had to pull over drunk drivers?"

"Objection, your honor." Matson said. "The counselor has already agreed to Michael not being drunk that morning."

"With all due respect, your honor, I agreed that Michael was not drunk when he awoke that morning. But be that as it may, let me rephrase the question." Turning back to the witness he asked, "How often, would you say, that you've responded to an accident scene where alcohol has been involved?"

"Objection!" Matson shot to her feet.

"Overruled," the judge shot back at her. "He's not asking how many times he's responded to an accident that your client has been in."

"But by referring to alcohol, your honor—"

"Overruled," the judge interrupted. "Sit down, counselor."

"Officer?" O'Brien asked.

"I, I..." Doyle was shaken his head. "I'm sorry sir, but with twelve years in the traffic department there's just too many times to be able put a number to it."

"Perfectly understandable, officer," O'Brien agreed. "Would you say you are called to such an accident once or twice a week?"

"At least once or twice during weeknights, sir. But the weekends are the worst. When the sporting events let out and when the bars and clubs close, it's constant."

"By constant you mean there are many accidents that are the result of people driving while impaired?"

"Yes, sir," Doyle answered. "Almost all of them, in my experience."

"And day after day, night after night, for twelve years is quite a lot of experience we're talking about here," O'Brien responded more for the jury's benefit.

"Let's go back to the morning of February fifteenth. Can you tell us what happened?"

"Yes sir," Doyle said. "I responded to a call from dispatch that there was a car accident on Anderson Street. That's on Beacon Hill," he added.

"And what did you find when you got there?" O'Brien asked.

"An Alfa Romero Spider had impacted a Mercedes Benz at the intersection of Anderson Street and Phillips. The EMT's were already there so I asked the driver of the Alfa Romero to join me in my squad car to get a statement."

"Do you see the driver of the Alfa Romero here in the courtroom"?

"Yes sir," Doyle answered and pointed at Michael who was looking at the legal pad on the desk in front of him. A pen lay limp in his fingers.

"Let the record show the officer pointed at the defendant," O'Brien instructed the court recorder.

"Please go on, officer."

"I asked Mr. Fitzpatrick if he had been drinking."

"Is that a standard question, officer?" O'Brien seemed surprised.

"Only when it appears a driver has had alcohol."

"And did Michael Fitzpatrick, in your many years of experience with this, appear to have been drinking?"

"His eyes were bloodshot, pants all wrinkled and his hair uncombed so, yes, I felt justified in asking him if he had been drinking."

"And what happened next?"

"I told him I was going to give him a breathalyzer test and he refused it."

"In your many years of experience officer, why does someone normally refuse a breathalyzer test?"

"Objection, your honor," Matson said. "Is Mr. Doyle a psychologist as well as a police officer?"

"I'll rephrase your honor. What reason did Michael Fitzpatrick give you for refusing to take the test?"

"He said that he didn't think it would be in his best interests," Doyle replied.

"Well I'm no psychologist either," O'Brien said facing the jury, "but it seems to me that a test that would determine that his alcohol level was below the legal limit would be decidedly in his favor. Wouldn't you agree, officer?"

"Objection!"

"Sustained."

"No further questions, your honor."

"Mr. Doyle," Matson strode towards the witness box. "How did you find the condition of the streets that morning?"

"They were fine in my opinion," Doyle said.

"Are you familiar with black ice? When the roads are covered with a very thin sheet of ice? So thin that seeing it is—"

"I know what black ice is," Doyle said curtly. "There wasn't any that I could see."

"That's the point, isn't it, officer?" she asked. "You can't see black ice. But never mind that for now," Matson gave a wave of her hand.

"You say you based your decision to have Mike take the breathalyzer because his pants were wrinkled? His hair was uncombed? There are several spectators here this morning that would require a breathalyzer test using your guidelines."

Quiet giggles came from the spectators section.

"Yes, but I smelled alcohol on his breath too."

"Is that information you just remembered to offer?" Matson asked incredulously. She was aware of his smelling alcohol on Michael that morning but he overlooked mentioning it while being questioned by O'Brien. Stealing a glance at O'Brien she could see he was inwardly chastising himself for his oversight. 'Being over-confident of your case will often result in your worst performance,' the words of his old law professor echoed through his mind.

"Yes it is," he answered uneasily. "I smelled alcohol. He admitted to having a drink."

"Did you check his car for open containers?"

"Yes. Well, no. The other officer on the scene did that."

"And were any found?"

"No."

"Then the alcohol you say you smelled could have come from cough medicine?"

"Unlikely."

"Or after shave?" she asked.

"It didn't smell like—"

"Are you aware of the alcohol content of some aftershaves?"

"I know they contain some alcohol but if that's the case then why—"

"I assume you were given proper training on administering a test using a breathalyzer?

"Of course, I have a certificate."

"Then being certified, you should know that breathalyzers also detect alcohol found in a person's mouth and assume that it is coming from air deep in the lungs. Of course the problem with this is that it could be detecting alcohol found in mints, cough syrup and a number of other things besides ethyl alcohol, skewing the test results. Isn't that true?"

"It's possible," Doyle conceded while shifting in his chair.

"In your many years of experience," Matson checked her note pad at this point, "twelve years to be exact, have you ever heard of a breathalyzer given a false positive reading?"

"I've heard of that happening but I never—"

"But that would never be the case with the breathalyzer unit you use? Is that what you wanted to say? No more questions your honor."

"Mr. O'Brien?" Judge Moretti asked as officer Doyle walked towards the exit.

"We have one more witness your honor, but she will not be available until tomorrow."

"That being the case," the judge said, "we stand in recess until tomorrow afternoon at two o'clock. Even judges have to adjust their schedules to obtain a dentist appointment."

"All rise!"

Outside of the courtroom is where the local TV and national cable networks were camped. While they had a productive day filming and interviewing the crowd that had gathered, they were able to intersperse normal programming with "breaking news" as their compatriots seated in the courtroom came out to provide up to the minute details of the proceedings. It was into this firestorm that Brad and Maggie Sullivan exited.

"Representative Sullivan? Representative Sullivan?" came from the mouths of several second tier news reporters as microphones were shoved near their faces.

"With your challenge to Congressman Fitzpatrick's seat this fall it seems odd you'd be here."

"Odd?" Sullivan repeated. "Not at all. I am concerned for the Congressman's son as I am for the tragic loss of the Brackton's. Here in Massachusetts we may have squabbles amongst one another, but when it comes to family, we are one."

And so the questions went until they were seated, windows closed, in their car.

TWENTY-THREE

Bishop Connor was sitting in the living room with his novitiates answering their questions the best he could. He referred to this as 'open forum night' where no question was considered out of order. Next to where the Bishop sat was another chair, a recliner that normally stayed in Father Canelli's room.

As soon as the priests took their normal places sitting on the rug, they exchanged glances, hoping someone knew the reason for the empty chair. Father Canelli usually stayed leaning against the door between the living room and dining room as though he needed to be available to scoot away at a moment's notice.

"And so you might ask yourself this question," Bishop Connor was saying when Father Canelli walked into the room escorting an old, gray haired man wearing a wide brimmed black hat.

"Ah, Rabbi Casltewitz!" Bishop Connor exclaimed as he rose from his chair and hugged his friend. "I want to start by thanking you for taking the time to visit us this evening."

"Always a pleasure, Bishop," the Rabbi replied. "But tell me, are we to continue the evening using titles Seamus or were you trying to elicit a shock from your new friends?" Looking at the men that stood near him he smiled. "If so, I think you've accomplished it."

"Gentleman," Bishop Connor said while looking at the priests, "This is Rabbi Jakob Castlewitz. Rabbi Castlewitz to each of you," he intoned providing them with sufficient warning. "Jakob is an old dear friend of mine."

"Old, yes?" The Rabbi said.

"I've asked the Rabbi to join us at our Open Forum Night so that you'll have a chance to broaden your knowledge by answers provided by a leading authority," the Bishop said.

"Leading authority?" the Rabbi repeated. "I've never led authorities anywhere!"

Laughing, the priests introduced themselves. Once the handshaking was complete, they took their seats on the floor as Bishop Connor led his friend to the recliner.

"Rabbi Castlewitz is the author of several well read books concerning Jews and the world we find ourselves living in today."

"Actually, Seamus, the topics are about the world we Jews find ourselves living in today."

Ignoring his friend he continued, "Some of you may be familiar with one of his earlier works, "Jesus was a Jew."

The priests gave each other a side glance.

"I thought not," the Bishop said. "And that is why I have purchased a copy for each of you. You'll find them on your beds tonight. Won't they Father Canelli?"

"I'm on my way, Bishop," Canelli answered.

"Wait! Wait!" the Rabbi said. "I like this man's company, Seamus. He drives slowly and talks of Italy like he left there yesterday. Let him stay with us a while won't you?"

"Yes, of course. Plenty of time later, Father," Connor said as Father Canelli rested his frame once again on the door jamb.

"Who wants to start?" Bishop Connor asked while rubbing his hands together. He was obviously excited for his men to meet the Rabbi.

Blank stares were all that met him.

"Excuse me, Seamus," the Rabbi said. "Perhaps it would be better for me to start?"

"Of course, Jakob," the Bishop granted.

"Who of you here hate me for killing your Christ?"

Again the heads swiveled toward one another.

"Yes, you heard me correctly. You might like to know that I wanted to add a subtitle to the book, Jesus was a Jew". It was to be "Ha Ha". But my publisher forbids it."

Silence.

"Okay then," he said. "Who here will deny to me that the Jews are God's chosen people?"

Blank stares and silence.

"They're well mannered, Seamus," the Rabbi said to Connor. "Perhaps we should play pinochle, eh? We could break up into teams."

"Men," Bishop Connor spoke. "If necessary I will start calling out your names. The Rabbi has come here tonight to answer your questions as he has willingly done for the past several Open Forum Nights."

"Let me try a different start, Seamus," the Rabbi suggested. But then a tentative hand was raised.

"A victim?" the Rabbi smiled raising his eyebrows.

"Jews were chosen because they were the only people at that time that recognized God as, well, being God."

"Very good!" the Rabbi exclaimed. "But wrong. As Deuteronomy points out, God chose the Jews "not because you are big, indeed you are of the smallest nations" but because we are the offspring of the first ethical monotheist, Abraham. That is all. The only reason. It does not confer privilege or superiority, only obligation and," he sighed, "suffering."

The class of priests sat motionless, their total attention upon him.

"So, we were chosen. But chosen to do what? I'll tell you", he said before another hand could be raised. "We were chosen to make humanity aware of the Supreme Moral Being. God! Does anyone wish to tell me we did a poor job?

"The Commandments we live by are found in the Old Testament, not the New. Yes, we did our job and yet we are persecuted to this day. Can anyone see privilege in that? Superiority?"

"Why is it then," a student asked, "that God has not shown you greater favor?"

"Because, like you, we are men! We grow weak and seek earthly pleasures. Easy women, for some men, any women; we drink in excess; we gamble; we lust after what is not ours to have and then when those choices bring us to our knees, we find God again. Miraculous isn't it? 'Oh God!' we pray, 'Please help us!' And you know what is really miraculous? He does help."

"The Cycle of Baal", Bishop Connor said.

"Cycle of Baal?" the teacher turned priest asked.

"It refers to a cycle where Jews start out with a good relationship with God. Hence, they are given land, goods, and wealth. They get complacent and begin to ignore and forget the poor; after a while they even forget God and replace Him with other gods, like Baal. Soon they're facing trouble and are murdered or exiled. Prophets appear telling them they've grown apart from God and must repent. The people don't want to hear that, of course, so most prophets are killed. Eventually, when things are darkest they cry out to God for deliverance and reconcile their ways with God. And after awhile, it all starts over again."

The Rabbi was slowly nodding his head. "Cycle of Baal or wash and rinse cycle, call it what you will, we, the people chosen by God, have let our God down a number of times."

Looking up he asked, "And what about you? How many of you have 'heard the calling' as you put it, only to take vows, don your priestly garments, and then molest innocent children?"

The priests were startled at the vehemence used to deliver that question. They looked at the Bishop for a response, but he only stared at them as the Rabbi was doing.

"Who do you think makes up the greatest percentage of drug dealers, drunkards, prostitutes, and illiterates? Jews or Christians? Who has a higher divorce rate? Jews or Christians? In every instance you will find the Jews to have fewer instances of drunkenness, divorce, abortion and illiteracy. So it begs the question, is God persecuting us or is it *you*?"

Mouths were open as jaws relaxed. The only comprehensive sound was the Rabbi's voice as even ambient noise, a plane flying overhead, could not enter their consciousness.

"That was a rhetorical question," he said in a softer tone. "I lost my grandparents at Auschwitz. My step-father was interred at Belgrazen and would have died but for war ending just before his life did. I never knew my biological father. He was a University Professor in Germany and when he refused to sign an oath of allegiance to Hitler, as all educators were required to by law, they came to his house, beat him first and then arrested him. My mother was two months pregnant with me and never heard from him again. While he was being beaten our neighbors came to the door to protest and were told to mind their own business or they would be visited next.

"My mother told me that at first, she was very angry with him for not swearing allegiance to that madman. What harm would it cause? But she later realized it would not have mattered. We were Jews and so we were doomed."

"What happened to your mother, Rabbi?" a voice of raw concern asked.

"Ah! A star for that one Seamus! It is the first time I've been asked and now I will tell you. My parents' neighbors you see, the ones who protested, were Italian diplomats. They provided her with false papers that allowed her to get into France where a farmer and his wife, both Catholic's, hid her until the war's end." Rabbi Castlewitz took a moment to look at Father Canelli and Bishop Connor before resuming.

"So you see why I feel some sense of indebtedness to come here?"

"Oh bull!" Bishop Connor said,

"Okay, perhaps it has more to do with Father Canelli's spaghetti. You prepared it kosher, huh?" he asked.

"Of course, Rabbi Castlewitz," Canelli smiled. "I only use the pots you provided me on your first visit."

"Why is it that your people refuse so adamantly to accept our lord, Jesus?" Someone asked.

The Rabbit scratched at his beard a moment and asked. "Do you believe there is one God?"

"Yes, of course. But—"

"So do we!" the Rabbi answered. "Did you know that there are now more Muslims in the world than there are Christians? Not Catholics, mind you, but Christians. Are you also aware that they believe Jesus was the son of God, but Mohammed was one as well and the last one to visit us?"

"Dribble", one of the priests' said.

"Ah, I am beginning to see," the Rabbi responded. "There can only be room for one God and one son. Am I right?"

No one answered, but the look in the eyes of the newly ordained began to show contempt.

"Why is it, do you think, that Martin Luther was able to bring so many people into a new faith?" the Rabbi asked. "You know the reason for it, but prefer to think of it as too old to matter. The Church, your church, was corrupt! Priests were living with women, some even had offspring; you could pay for forgiveness of sins without having to atone; at times you had more than one Pope at the same time fighting each other for control, for power.

"Luther brought the Bible to the common man by having it translated from Latin. You know why the majority of his 95 Thesis were eventually adopted by the Church? Because he was right! Your Church leaders were corrupt! Your Church was foundering and had Luther's demands continued to be ignored, you would have no church today. The Church leaders at that time were zealots whose only desire was to keep their considerable power over their flock while increasing their own power and wealth. This I can understand, they were men. "

Rabbi Castlewitz looked from man to man with an expression that hoped for confrontation. He knew what he said was accurate and he knew they knew it as well.

"I may be a friend to your Church, indeed I want to be, but I am no friend to Martin Luther. His statements that the Jews' homes should be destroyed, their synagogues burned, money confiscated, and liberty curtailed were revived and used in propaganda by the Nazis. I only hope to show you that we Jews did not crucify your Jesus."

"I still don't understand," Dribble, as he was to become known from that night forward, said. "What does Martin Luther and corrupt church leaders from hundreds of years ago have to do with two-thousand years ago?"

"You believe that Jesus was the son of God, correct? And," he continued, "If someone were to challenge that belief, even with guns, you would be ready to stop them. Such heresy could not be allowed to continue?"

"You're damn right, Rabbi!" Dribble said. "Bishop Conner, this is blasphemy! Why are you letting him continue?"

"Son, can't you see?" the Rabbi answered for Connor. "The Jewish people didn't kill Jesus. Jewish zealots did. And zealots are people both our faiths have had extensive experience with."

TWENTY-FOUR

"Are you watching this?" Frank Ambrasio, Sullivan's campaign manager's voice boomed through the ear piece into Sullivan's head.

"I told ya! I told ya! This is a freakin' gold mine of free publicity. Where'd you get that Massachusetts family malarkey? Pull it out of your butt? Did you catch CNN? They played that piece and mentioned your run for Congressman Fitzpatrick's seat. The whole freakin' country saw that!"

"I'm glad, Frank. I'm glad it's over. We need to concentrate on—"

"Over?" Ambrasio yelled. "Over? You have your butt back in front of that courthouse moments before it begins tomorrow. Only moments, you got that? We don't want to look like we're holding a press conference, you see? Just answer a question or two on the ways in. Real natural like."

"I can't do that, Frank," Sullivan said.

"Why?" Ambrasio asked. "What's a matter?"

"It takes up the whole day; I should be out meeting people and—"

"Your meeting the freakin' country, ya bozo! More accurately, the country is meeting Bradford Sullivan, up and coming national politician! And try to think of something like that family thing you used today. It was gold, kid. I'll be in touch."

Sullivan closed the cover of his cell phone as he pictured Jessica Brackton as she looked today. She really did seem affected. She'd lost weight to the point of looking anemic. And when she saw him there, in the courtroom, he thought for a moment she was going to scream. There's got to be a way that would keep him from having to go through that hell again tomorrow.

"You don't have the sound on?" his wife Maggie said when she entered the room holding her cell phone to her air. "Carrie's telling me we're on the CNN! Hold on, Carrie."

Grabbing the remote, Maggie adjusted the volume as CNN went to a commercial.

"Damn!" she said into her cell. "I missed it! Really? They'll play it again later? Then I've got to run and get the VCR set up to record. Thanks darling! Bye."

"Why was the sound off, Brad? Did you see us on TV?"

"Yeah, I did. Frank called. I was talking to him."

"You could have told me we were on," she scolded.

"What do you say to us taking a break from this?" he asked ignoring her mood. "Let's go to the Cape tomorrow and eat some fried clams, walk the beach like we used to. You enjoyed our trip to Nantucket, didn't you?"

"You're kidding right? Our pictures are on CNN and you want to runaway? Hide? Oh damn!" she said, suddenly distracted. "I'll need to press my grey pantsuit. The one like Hillary wears? And you better check your closet for a fresh suit. We need to be looking our best!"

That being said, she left the room with Brad wondering not for the first time, if his run for congress might not have been a mistake.

The home phone rang, jarring him from his thoughts of making different choices, of having a chance to do it all over again.

"Get that will you Brad? I'm in the laundry room." Maggie yelled.

Reaching for the house phone sitting conveniently next to his armchair Brad answered.

"Hello?" he said.

"Brad? It's Jessica." Her voice, which was naturally soft, was more of a whisper, making him push the receiver harder to his ear.

"Jessica?" he whispered back. "You're calling me at my home? What if my wife had—"

"I don't want to see you there tomorrow. Don't come," was all that he heard when the line went dead.

At the same time Brackton was delivering her demand to Sullivan, Kim Matson and Stan Ross were meeting at his office in Medfield. Sitting at her card table desk, Matson was staring wide-eyed at Ross.

"You think she was having an affair using the name Barbara Stanford?" she asked again.

"No, I know she was having an affair," Ross answered. "And the search engine says Barbara Stanford was the name of Jessica Brackton's mother. A bit too coincidental, don't you think?"

"But with him? Brad Sullivan. You think that's true?"

"Yep," Ross answered. "I spent the day checking. It's him alright."

"And that thing, that…" she couldn't recall the word navigator when looking at it, "that thing told you?" she asked in disbelief.

"No, the navigator led me to it," Ross said. "When I recognized the address, or at least the area it was in, I hopped over to Google maps and called up a street view of the address. And bam! There it was, the Exeter Hotel. And I thought no way," Ross shook his head for emphasis, "no way would a lady of Brackton's breeding have business at a place like that."

"And the doorman confirmed it was her?"

"The manager did!" Ross said excitedly. "Well, more of a handyman, front desk clerk, manager."

"And you believe him?" Matson asked.

"He thought I was law enforcement. He would have told me anything I wanted to know."

"That's what worries me, Stan. What if he was just telling you what you wanted to hear?"

"He would have been taking a big risk if he had and he knows it," Ross smiled as he said this.

"Why do you say that?"

"Cause he ain't in this country legally. I'll bet my laptop on it."

They continued to look at each other digesting what they learned.

"How can we use this Stan? There's nothing to come of this but ruined reputations, careers, marriages. It has nothing, really, to do with our case."

"Yeah, I thought the same thing. But you needed to know and I'm not much help to you at the trial. Sorry I spent the whole day chasing this down."

"Don't be." Matson said. "In fact, knowing what we do, let's make sure she was headed to her hairdressers that morning. Can you do that?"

"Only if she had it programmed. Otherwise, it will just get me to where the accident took place. Any who, I'll check it out."

"Take this along," Matson said while tossing a cell phone to Ross.

"Huh? What's this?" Ross asked. He opened the cell phone cover and a light came on illuminating the screen.

"It's not a biggie, Stan. Just don't tell your clients you have one. The phone itself is cheap and you're only billed for the minutes you use."

"Thanks. I think."

For the next two hours, Matson went over her questions for Kate Monroe, a local meteorologist and Randall Kelman, a Boston University climatologist. Adding a thought, deleting a line, and re-arranging the questions. She still has her summary to edit, but hated the thought the trial was moving so quickly. In her opinion, there was enormous room for doubt as to whether Michael Fitzpatrick should even be on trial let alone face punishment for what was clearly an act of God. She only had to convince the jury of that.

As she was reviewing and trying to memorize the most important points on her notes regarding black ice, Ross spoke.

"That don't look like no hair salon." Lifting his head form the screen of his PC he asked, "Where was that hair dresser located? Brookline wasn't it?"

"Yes," Matson answered. "Why?"

"She had a Brookline address entered into the system, but two things strike me as strange. One, she entered it for the first time that morning. Kind of an odd thing to do if she went there as a rule. And two, when I look at the address using Street View on Google? The building looks more like an office building."

"Lots of salons can be found in office buildings, Stan."

"Yeah...but. I don't know," Ross said shaken his head. "If it's all right with you, I'll take a run by it tomorrow morning. Unless you think you'll need some legal tax expertise during your questioning tomorrow?"

"Ah, I'll try to avoid that topic for the entire day. That's a promise. Actually, after the testimony of the few witnesses I have for tomorrow, we'll probably go into summation. It's going to be up the jury after that." Matson had a far off look in her eye as her mind returned to Brackton's affair.

Why would Brackton lie to her? Did she mix up her hair appointment dates? If there was some way she could have Jessica Brackton take the stand, without causing irreparable damage to her case, she would happily do it. But a mother grieving for her lost unborn baby was not the best person to grill on the witness stand. But what if she were on her way to meet with her lover that morning? Would it make enough of a difference to the jury?

"Go ahead and check it out, Stan. I'm not sure how I can use it at this point, but if she lied to us?" Matson let the question hang. She resigned herself to stop thinking about the affair. It simply had no bearing on the case.

"Any who," Ross said as he shut down his PC, "be sure to lock up."

As Ross headed down the stairs, Matson returned her attention to her notes, but not without the annoying thought that Jessica Brackton was a cheat and a liar."

TWENTY-FIVE

Judge Moretti's lower lip looked a bit swollen from his visit to the dentist. It was apparent the Novocain he received was still working as the judge absently slid his jaw from side to side.

"You may call your next witness, Mr. O'Brien." The judge said, pronouncing the word witness as witneth.

"Thank you your honor. State calls Maria Evans."

Maria Evans was a middle aged lady who had the air of a University Scholar which is what she was when she wasn't working on a documentary. White hair cut short and wearing black rimmed glasses with a silver chain attached to allow her to have them hang by her chest when not in use, she took the oath and turned to offer a small smile to the judge and the jurors. Many people in the courtroom recognized her as someone they had seen on the History Channel from time to time, but could not place her name.

"Ms. Evans," O'Brien's naturally loud voice made Evan's suddenly lean back in her chair.

"I'm sorry," O'Brien grinned, "It's sometimes necessary to speak loudly so the jury won't miss anything. But I'll try to lower the volume." He smiled widely at Evans as she nodded and reached into her shirt between two buttons and emerged with a small crucifix between her thumb and index finger. She rubbed it gently as O'Brien asked her to state her background and expertise.

"I'm a professor of religious studies at Boston College and I am involved in assisting with religious documentaries for the History Channel." Evans spoke so quietly that O'Brien was tempted to ask that she speak more loudly, but wasn't willing to take the chance his request might make her more nervous.

"Assisting in what way?" O'Brien asked.

"I have knowledge with the three major monotheistic religions practiced in the world today; Christianity, Judaism, and Islam."

"But it's more than a passing knowledge, isn't it?" O'Brien asked. "You are, in fact, acknowledged to be an expert in this field, isn't that right?"

"Yes, there are some who refer to me as an expert."

"And in your expert opinion, of the three major religions you mentioned, do any of them condone the taking of the life of a yet unborn child?"

"Objection, your honor!" Matson was on her feet. "Religious beliefs are not on trial here nor does defense have any issues with them."

"Your honor," O'Brien spoke before the judge could rule. "It is our attempt to clear up any doubt the jury may have as to whether a human life was ended as a result of Mr. Fitzpatrick's actions and not simply an embryo."

"Objection your honor!" Matson's face was turning red from the anger she was experiencing. "The guilt or innocence of my client has not been determined and to allow for Mr. O'Brien to make statements to the contrary is grounds for dismissal!"

"Careful, counselor," Judge Morreti growled at Matson.

"My apologies to both the court and my opponent," O'Brien said, "I will rephrase the question."

"Your honor?" Matson asked hoping to put an end to where she knew this was going.

"He may rephrase the question, counselor," Morreti answered.

"In your expert opinion, Ms. Evans, would any of the three major religions practiced today consider Mrs. Brackton's baby to be anything but a human being whose rights of life should be protected by society at large?"

"The sanctity of human life is a pivotal issue for these faiths. These religions would all consider a fetus to be equal in measure to a fully grown adult, yes," Evans answered. "But societies themselves have a different measure. For instance—"

"Yes, yes," O'Brien said quickly, "but where God is concerned, a fetus and an adult are equal, isn't that right?"

"Objection your honor. Speculation as to what *God* thinks?"

"Sustained."

O'Brien raised his eyes, took a breath, and asked again. "These major religions, all three, believe a fetus and an adult are equal, is that correct?"

"Yes."

"And by teaching this belief to their followers they are instructing them that it is what God expects?"

"Yes." Evans answered. A twitch had developed at the corner of her mouth as she rubbed the crucifix between her fingers.

"No more questions your honor."

"Counselor?" Judge Moretti asked Matson. She had done her research on Maria Evans and was prepared to confront her.

"Ms. Evans," Matson spoke as she approached her. "Before embarking on an educational career, you had another vocation. Would you please tell the court what that was?"

"I was a nun in the Catholic Church." Evans was looking at Matson's shoulder, avoiding her eyes.

"You were a nun, who left the order because you were disillusioned with your experience, isn't that right?"

"Yes," Evans answered.

"Would you care to tell us what it was that disillusioned you?"

"Objection your honor! Ms. Evans is considered an expert in the field of religions and her personal history is immaterial."

"The answer to my question will not reveal anything that can't be found in Ms. Evans' book, your honor, 'Walk with Me'. It's a personal history available to anyone willing to purchase it, written in her own words. To wit," Matson turned back to face Evans, "you left the order and your vows because you found the Church's views to be too narrow for you, isn't that right?"

"Yes, that is true," Evans answered quietly.

"In fact, according to your book, you went from nun to atheist before turning back to God. I have to wonder what your expert opinion would have been as an atheist regarding the right of a fetus."

Turning to the judge Matson said, "No more questions your honor."

"Mr. O'Brien," the judge asked expecting another witness to be called.

"We have no more witnesses, your honor," O'Brien stated.

"That being the case, we will recess until tomorrow morning when the defense will call their first witness."

"All rise!"

Jessica and John Brackton left the courthouse with Jack O'Brien and walked into a flurry of questions from the reporters gathered on the steps. It was the same yesterday, and without O'Brien's assistance they might never make it to their car.

"If you want a statement you'll have to come to my offices, otherwise, make way for these people," he said while indicating the Brackton's.

"Ms. Brackton? Ms. Brackton?" One of the female reporters spoke loudly. "Are you planning for another baby?"

Jessica, who was concentrating on the steps before her, raised her gaze to look at the woman. She wanted to take a swing at her. But with the number of reporters surrounding her she was uncertain as to who asked the question. Then, she caught her breath as her gaze fell upon someone she met while in the hospital; the psychologist, Doctor Bragg. He was standing at the bottom of the steps and to the right, speaking to another man while watching as she made her way through the crowd. When he realized he'd been spotted, he ducked behind the supporting column he stood next to.

Jessica was confused as to why he would be there. Was it to offer his services to her? She remembered that she liked him, but that he never came back to visit her. When she asked one of her attending doctors about him they said they were not aware of a Doctor Bragg but then, it was a big hospital.

Her curiosity peaked; she pushed her way through the reporters leaving her husband and lawyer's side, and made for the spot he was standing. But when she got there, he was hurriedly rounding the corner of the block and passed from her sight.

Her husband caught up to her at the same moment.

"Jessica? What's going on?"

"I just saw Doctor Bragg. You remember the psychologist that was meeting with me at the hospital when you arrived?"

Her husband cocked his head trying to place the name and the scene.

"The psychologist. He was there when you came in then you went to get coffee."

"Oh! Right. I remember now. He was here?"

"Yes, I think so. He was standing here, but when I came to speak with him he was gone."

"A psychologist?" A nearby reporter laughed. It was the same man Jeff Sailor had been talking to when Jessica spotted him.

"Jeff Sailor has been called a lot of things lady, but a psychologist isn't one of them. That was a reporter for The Hub standing there."

Jessica and her husband exchanged wide eyed glances at one another and continued with their speedy walk to their car.

After bolting the door locks and belting themselves in, he pulled his cell phone out of his breast pocket and dialed Hank Ryman. An attorney kept on retainer was always a useful thing when the unexpected popped up.

TWENTY-SIX

With Jeff Sailor unable to attend the trial in person for fear of being recognized by the Brackton's, which after the incident on the court steps he feared he already had been, he had to find a surrogate to cover the trial. The problem was that he needed someone who would not seek notoriety for their own benefit. He found the perfect candidate in Sean Foley. While somewhat illiterate, he has a mind that captured whatever was told to him and he was a natural story teller. He realized that after the first day of the trial when he attempted to read the notes Sean took during the proceedings. They were nearly indecipherable.

Sailor had decided the first meeting with Sean would be at the Black Orchid where Sailor was holding a private celebration for himself after just completing an in-depth story on the "Faith for Life" bill and how it would never makes its way to the floor of Congress for a vote. The politicians he spoke with, primarily Democrats, were adamant that the people had long since felt the Church was way off base on a woman's right to choose and to support the bill would be tantamount to resigning their seat.

The few Republicans who were willing to take his call spoke on the condition of anonymity. And, while they fundamentally supported the bill, they agreed with their Democratic opponents that to openly support it would end their political career.

But the House Speaker proved to be his best interviewee. She said she was "an ardent, practicing Catholic" and that abortion was something she had studied for a long time. And then Sailor read her a statement directly from the *Catechism of the Catholic Church*: "Since it must be treated from conception as a person, the embryo must be defended in its integrity, cared for, and healed, as far as possible, like any other human being."

To this she responded, "I understand. And this is like maybe 50 years or something like that. So again, over the history of the Church, abortion has been an issue of controversy."

Sailor realized when he was handling pure gold and went straight to his favorite source at the Church for a response; Bishop Connor. But before he could meet with Bishop Connor, he used the Speakers statement in his weekly column as filler, something that would allow him to make his deadline and get back to his research on the "Faith for Life". The statement, once made public, created a firestorm and was picked up nationally.

Church officials throughout the country responded to what they pointed out was a gross misinterpretation of teachings that had been in place since Christianity was founded.

When Sailor did meet with Bishop Connor, the Bishop, ever cool under pressure, simply handed Sailor a text he received via email from his friend, Charles Chaput, the Archbishop of Denver. It was a published response to the Speakers statement regarding the Church's ambiguity where abortion was concerned.

The following day, ten Republican congressmen crafted a statement demanding the Speaker "apologize for misrepresenting the Church's doctrine and misleading fellow Catholics."

It was a good story and had brought him the chance of winning a local media award. Not that he needed another one, but they did lend themselves to job security and competing offers for his talents.

The controversy brought Sailor into the national spotlight and ultimately, to the Black Orchid for his private celebration. He sat at the bar, the Orchid being only half filled with patrons as it was still early afternoon, where he listened to Sean Foley talk about Representative Brad Sullivan with the bartender.

"And he let me go, just like that!" Sean snapped his fingers to emphasize his statement.

"And after all you did for him?" The bartender said. "Shameful, is what it is. How did ya bride take it?"

"I never told her the truth. Mentioned something about budgets to her. Since then I've been keeping up with numbers," Sean winked at the barkeep to show he was referring to being a bookie. But even the bartender knew Sean was nothing more than a runner.

"Well, boy-o," I'll give ya credit for not wallowing in misery as most of the people in here. Ya brother-in-law left ya without a job, and with a wife to support to boot, but ya found a way to keep food on the table. More power to ya brother."

"Excuse me," Sailor said to Sean. "I couldn't help overhearing. Did you say that Brad Sullivan's your brother-in-law and that he fired you?"

Both Sean and the bartender turned their full attention to Sailor, and from their expressions, Sailor suddenly realized he was in danger. He not only intruded on what passed as a private conversation in the Black Orchid, but asked a personal question as well.

"I'm sorry," he spoke quickly. "What I mean to say is I may have job for you, if you're interested."

"Doing what?" Sean was blunt.

"I'm a reporter for The Hub and I can't be in two places at the same time. I need someone to take notes of an event, or to interview someone, when I'm not available to do it myself."

"Really? I can do that. I used to do that stuff for Brad. Go and talk to

Sheppard, he'd say to me, and find out what he thinks about this and that. What's the pay?"

Sailor had already given this some thought and offered Sean one hundred dollars to cover an event, fifty dollars for any interviews he sent him to do, and another fifty for any pictures he took that the paper used for publication.

"That's sounds good, I suppose." Sean glanced at the bartender to see if he had anything to offer and received a nod in response. The barkeep knew he was listening to a private conversation at this point and walked to the end of the bar to rinse glasses.

"I don't suppose there're many events that need covering though," Sean realized.

"On the contrary," Sailor answered. "You know that Fitzpatrick trial about to start? Well, I'll need you to attend every session reporting back to me each night. There is only one stipulation, you must not tell anyone what events I have you covering. No one! Interested?"

The deal was sealed with a shot of Jamison's and Sailor had the man he needed to cover the trial in his stead. But when they rendezvoused at their agreed upon meeting place, a restaurant on the expressway to Boston and near his offices at The Hub, Sailor was crestfallen to see that Sean's notes were useless to him.

"I can't read this, Sean. Most of these pages have half written sentences with words I can't decipher. Deals off, damn it!" Sailor moved to leave the booth they were sitting in.

"Hold on," Sean grabbed Sailor's arm holding him there. "I ain't a writer but I have a solid memory. I can tell you everything that was said." And as a way of proof he recited, word for word, the clerks opening statement announcing that court was in session.

Sailor relaxed in his seat, a glimmer of hope returning. He placed his miniature tape recorder on the table between them and said, "Okay, Sean. Take it from there."

When Sean had finished, Sailor marveled at how using Sean was like having a hidden tape recorder in court. So impressed was he that he handed Sean a hundred dollar bill and reminded him that paydays were on Friday, but that this was a bonus.

They met at the same place, directly after the close of trial each day.

It was during their fourth meeting, after Sailor had returned his tape recorder to his sports jacket pocket, when Sean insisted he buy his new employer a drink, when he brought up his dislike for Sullivan and how he had been used and then abused by being let go. Sailor realized that Sean must have stopped for a drink or two before their meeting as his eyes occasionally lost focus and how his face showed contempt whenever he mentioned Sullivan.

"I feel for you, Sean, but it's time for you to get used to the fact that Sullivan will be a congressman soon. He's leading Fitzpatrick in every poll. You might consider making amends with him; you know, swallow your pride and fall on your sword before him. He can do you a lot of good once he gets to Washington."

"Ain't nothing good about him, I'm telling ya! He drops friends he no longer has a use for; he only cares for himself and..."

Listening politely while occasionally stealing a glance at his watch Sailor was about to excuse himself when Sean dropped the bomb.

"...and if my sister were to learn about his other *fun* raising activities there'd be hell to pay. But I won't tell her. She's a good lady and I won't be the one to bring her pain."

"Did you say fund raising?" Sailor asked hoping he heard him correctly the first time.

"F-U-N," Sean replied. "He'd come back to the office smelling of perfume like I didn't have a nose."

Sailor signaled the waitress to bring another round of drinks, which brought a smile of appreciation to Sean, while Sailor reached into his coat pocket and reactivated his tape recorder.

"I had a brother-in-law doing the same thing to my sister," Sailor said to keep the topic fresh. "But she caught him at it and he's still paying dearly," he lifted his glass as a salute to Sean and sipped at his Jamison's. "But you know, Sean, thinking something is so is not the same as it being so, if you get my meaning."

"I won't argue with that, but that ain't the case with old Brad." Sean took a sip that finished half of his drink.

"How can you be sure?"

"'Cause I followed him is why," Sean said winking at Sailor.

"No kidding? Where'd he go? You want another before I have to skedaddle?"

"Sure! But I'm buying," Sean said while he concentrated on keeping his drooping head erect.

"So where'd he go?" Sailor asked again while holding one finger up to the waitress and then pointing at Sean.

"The Exeter Hotel. A real dump if you ask me."

"Did you see who he met with?" Sailor leaned forward to ask.

"Nope. But he met someone there and unless he's in to meeting men wearing perfume, it was another lady."

The waitress arrived with one shot and was reluctant to place it in front of Sean until Sailor tossed a fifty dollar bill on her tray and said, "Keep the change".

He excused himself telling Sean he had a deadline to meet at the paper, which was true. But he also had a new topic that may prove newsworthy, but required immediate further investigation.

Upon leaving his offices at The Hub, his story safely 'put to bed,' he drove to the Exeter Hotel with a four-by-six, full color image of Representative Bradford Sullivan in his overcoat pocket.

TWENTY-SEVEN

The next morning, court started later again, due to a juror's wife delivering their third child during the hours of day-break. O'Brien was unhappy with this set of events and would have challenged the man's selection as a juror to begin with, but he was the last one to be seated and the judge's impatience with the selection process was beginning to show. O'Brien relented and let the man be seated rather than to be in ill favor with the judge prior to the start of the trial.

Judge Moretti congratulated and then admonished the tardy man and warned all the participants of this trial the importance of being on-time. As it was, the proceedings didn't get underway until eleven o'clock.

Matson started the morning by calling Kate Monroe to the stand. She was attractive and whose face was known by juror members who watched the local morning weather report. Unfortunately, and according to the Neilson ratings, Monroe worked for the least watched morning news program in the region. Along with what she would bring as a good witness to the defense, she brought beauty in abundance. Her complexion was flawless and her natural blond hair hung just below the shoulders and turned in at the ends. Monroe smiled at the jurors, revealing teeth that were overly white, suggesting they had been bleached or capped. She was enjoying the undivided attention and was comfortable with it. Matson guessed she could just have easily landed a role on a soap opera if she found reporting the weather boring. But she was not a "dumb" blond as the jurors were about to find out.

After having Monroe state her credentials as a weatherperson, which consisted of an undergraduate degree in mathematics with a concentration in calculus, Matson began her questioning.

"Can you tell the court what you were doing the morning of February 15th?"

"Yes I can. I arrived at the station, WCBB, at four o'clock that morning and—"

"Four o'clock?" Matson interrupted. "Why so early?"

"In the world of TV personalities, that's a pretty normal start time for a six a.m. broadcast. I have to review the national weather reports that come out of Atlanta with particular attention to any weather alerts, as well as document the local observations."

"By local observations you mean?" Matson asked.

"There are a number of them actually. Mt Washington is generally used for the region, but local winds and temperatures are captured at the Blue Hills observatory in Milton, and of course there's Logan Airport, and—"

"Which observatory do you use for the Boston area?" Matson interrupted.

"Logan Airport."

"And what did you learn about from these reports related to conditions that morning?"

"That the temperature dropped to twenty-nine degrees for a low that night, and the expected high was thirty-nine that day."

"Pretty cold that day, wouldn't you agree?"

"Objection, your honor," O'Brien stated.

"Sustained."

"Sorry, your honor," Matson said. "Ms. Monroe, I need you to speak specifically about the weather conditions on and around Beacon Hill that morning. What did you report to your viewers regarding road conditions?"

"Well, I reviewed the tapes from my broadcast that morning and I specifically warned my viewers to be aware of black ice."

"Why would you do that?"

"I nearly had an accident myself on Storrow Drive that morning while coming into work. A car in front of me changed lanes without signaling and I hit my brakes a little too hard."

"What do you mean, a little too hard?"

"The road had a thin layer of ice on it, black ice, and I didn't know it. But I learned of it real quick when I hit my brakes."

O'Brien was about to object to her reference of black ice but decided to wait.

"Can you tell us what happened?"

"Sure," Monroe said, obviously warming to her role as the eyes of spectators and jury concentrated on her.

"The rear of my car started to slide to the left, that's when I knew I was on ice, but I was able to correct in time by tapping my brake pedal gently and steering into the slide. It was a very slight movement and easy to correct, but there was ice there all right."

"What typically happens when someone doesn't tap the brakes and turn into the slide as you did?"

"Objection, your honor," O'Brien spoke. "Conjecture."

"Sustained."

"Let me ask you then, what would have happened if you didn't tap your breaks gently and—"

"Objection, your honor! Counselor is now working on pure conjecture."

But Monroe answered over his objection with, "I would have spun out of control!"

"The jury will ignore that last comment from the witness," Judge Moretti said.

"No more questions your honor." Matson returned to her seat knowing the jurors would be unable to ignore that comment.

"Ms. Monroe," O'Brien approached the stand. "What was the temperature reading for downtown Boston at about nine o'clock that morning?"

"Thirty-five degrees," she answered.

"I'm no meteorologist, but if memory serves, that's above freezing isn't it?"

"Yes, but—"

"So road conditions, based on the rising temperature, would have improved from four a.m. to nine am, isn't that correct?"

"Somewhat, but—"

"Somewhat?" O'Brien asked in surprise. "Are you a certified meteorologist, Ms. Monroe?" he asked.

"Not certified, no."

"No more questions, your honor."

"Ms Monroe," Matson said as she passed O'Brien returning to his seat. "Did you receive a reprimand from your station manager for advising your viewers to be aware of black ice while driving that morning?"

"No, I did not." She met Matson's eyes and knew what she wanted to hear. "In fact, a viewer called later that day wanting to thank me for the warning. She was certain she would have had an accident due to black ice if not for my warning."

O'Brien rolled his eyes but didn't bother to object. The call was probably from some old lady who called to thank the weather 'girl' everyday, but with no way to prove it, he kept his objection silent.

Matson gave a brief smile Monroe to show her gratitude. "No more questions, your honor."

It was during the lunch break, which due to the late start began right after Monroe's testimony, when Ross used his new cell phone for the first time.

"Kim?" Ross asked.

"Hi Stan," Matson answered between bites of her corned-beef sandwich. "Where are—"

"Kim, listen!" Ross was excited and his voice an octave higher than normal. "Whatever happens in court today, do *not* rest your case! We've got to meet. There's too much to cover on this call. I've got what the movies call a surprise witness. And Kim? You ain't gonna believe it!"

Unable to get more information out of Ross, she agreed to meet him at his office directly after court adjourned for the day.

"Defense calls Randall Kelman," Matson announced upon the start of the afternoon session.

Kelman was a professor at Boston University who taught climatology at the Master's level. He was the key to Matson's defense that black ice was the most likely cause of the accident and as a result, totally unavoidable.

After he explained his credentials to the court, Matson's plan was to turn him lose.

"Can you tell us about black ice, professor?"

Clearing his throat Kelman answered.

"What we call black ice is frozen water, either sleet or rain or from melted snow, that freezes as a sheet and is not visible as ice," the professor said. "The road looks the same as it always does, which is why it's so hard to detect."

"Is there any signs to indicate black ice is present?"

"My advice is to look for signs of ice other than on the roadway. That means looking for ice on windshield wipers or side view mirrors, on road signs, trees or fences along the highway. If ice is forming on any of those things, it's possible that it may be on the road as well."

O'Brien's head was down while making a note and he smiled at what he was hearing.

"Then again, ice may not have formed on anything but the road. For example, it may have been a warm day during which the snow melted and then froze as ice after the temperature dropped at night."

"So," Matson asked, "it's possible for ice to be present on a road even as the temperature climbs above freezing?"

"Certainly, for a short period anyway."

"I suppose a person driving a four-wheel SUV would better luck operating on ice than sports car. Isn't that correct?" Matson asked.

"Not at all. Black ice is also one of the winter hazards that a four-wheel drive vehicle cannot overcome. I know that some of us get complacent because we have four-wheel drive, however, you need to be just as careful as the motorist who has a rear-wheel drive vehicle when it comes to ice on the roadway."

"Thank you, professor," Matson said, and turning to O'Brien, "Your witness."

"Mr. Kelman," O'Brien addressed him specifically not referring to his title. "You said that ice can remain on road tops only for a short time once the temperature gets above freezing? That's your professional opinion?"

"That's correct."

"The temperature that morning at nine a.m. was reported, by the defense's own witness, to be thirty-five degrees. Well above the temperature needed to thaw any ice, wouldn't you agree?"

"Certainly."

"Certainly," O'Brien repeated more loudly for the juror's benefit. "No more questions, your honor."

"Professor Kelman," Matson was on her feet approaching the witness before her opponent could take his seat. "Are there any circumstances that would allow ice to stay on a roadway after the temperature had risen above freezing? Say for an hour or even longer?"

"That's certainly true for the roads that run through Beacon Hill," the professor answered while nodding.

"Why is that?"

"Unless the sun is directly overhead, the brownstones on either side of those streets keep them in the shade."

"And by remaining in the shade, is it your professional opinion that it takes more than a change in air temperature to suddenly start the de-thawing process?"

"Certainly," the professor answered.

"Certainly," Matson repeated to the jury as she took her seat.

Matson requested a recess at that point due to an unforeseen problem with her lawyer slash investigator. He was to appear with her after lunch with information bearing on the case, she explained to the judge, but she had not seen nor heard from him.

"I will indulge you this one time, counselor," the judge spoke firmly, "provided Mr. O'Brien will agree."

Matson held her breath as she turned to see what O'Brien would say. If he nixed her request, then whatever Stan Ross had in the way of new information would be useless.

Fortunately for Matson, Jack O'Brien was delighted with the prospect of an early end to his day in court. He was meeting with a few select members of the press at his private golf club after court tomorrow in preparation of his winning this case, and he wanted all the publicity he could get while they still wanted to talk to him. An early break today would give him time to review his closing arguments for the jury and prepare another one for the reporters.

"I have no problem with it, your honor." O'Brien nodded towards Matson to show her his benevolence.

"The court will stand in recess until nine a.m. tomorrow," the judge said as he banged his gavel one time.

"All rise!"

TWENTY-EIGHT

Matson and Ross worked long into that night reviewing the new information Stan had uncovered during the day. The biggest problem Matson faced was how to present it to the court and the jury. Calling Jessica Brackton to the stand would have a heart-wrenching effect on everyone when it was her client who needed the sympathy, not the plaintiff. In addition, a new, last minute witness would need to be introduced and neither the judge nor O'Brien would be inclined to allow that.

"Tell me something, Kim," Ross asked. "Why did you take this case? Surely not to improve your win percentage. This case had 'loser' written all over it from the get-go."

"Yeah, it did," Matson answered quietly.

Ross waited while Matson stared at the screen of her laptop for several seconds, obviously thinking about his question. Finally, she spoke.

"When I told you my parents adopted me I didn't mention that they had another child, a son of their own. He was seventeen when he died in a car accident."

"Oh geez," Ross said. "I'm sorry. Forget I asked."

"No, it's okay. I was twelve years old and in the car with him at the time. He was driving me to a friend's house when we broached this hill. It was his first experience with winter driving. It was snowing, not heavily, but the roads were covered and it was so cold. As we crested the hill the car took on a life of its own. I could feel it in the speed that kept building even as Bobby nearly stood on the brakes. We hit a car, full bore, stopped at the traffic light at bottom of the hill. I was wearing my seat belt like any good girl scout does, but Bobby...he was a teen."

Matson stopped to dap at her eyes with a tissue.

"Please, Kim. Forgive me," Ross said. "I had no right to ask and—"

"Let me finish, Stan. It's only right that you know why I accepted this case seeing where this trial is headed. I don't want you thinking I took this case for my ego." Marston offered a weak smile.

"There was an older couple in the car, a husband and wife. She wasn't using a seat belt, either. Remember, this happened before wearing seatbelts in a car became the law. The impact snapped her neck.

"The husband was devastated, as our family was. We both lost loved ones. But he was unable, or unwilling, to accept it for what it was; an accident. He sued my family. As a result of attorney fees and a settlement, my parents had to sell our home. It wasn't right. We not only lost Bobby, but lost our home as well. My parents have never recovered from either.

"I took this case because I believe it to be what it is, an accident. It's tragic that the Brackton's lost their first baby, I know that. But Michael will spend the rest of his life carrying the fact that he is responsible for that. And that should be punishment enough. And knowing what we do now, maybe it will be."

***

The courtroom was packed as usual and the spectators sat quietly with as Marston rose to call the day's first witness. Bishop Connor sat in the back row wearing khaki pants, a blue shirt open at the collar, and a blue blazer. The sunglasses completed his efforts as going unnoticed and it seemed to be working. He instinctively knew his assistant, Farther Canalli, was being instructed to obstruct his relationship with Fitzpatrick and his interest in this trial. The Bishop could see that the man was internally shaken and growing weaker in appearance each passing day. He had pushed the Cardinal and the Archbishop's patience beyond the point of reason and knew the proverbial hammer would soon fall. He would use whatever favors owed to keep Canalli from falling with him.

"Defense calls Jessica Brackton," Marston announced.

Several voices could be heard as reporters and spectators mouthed their surprise. Calling Brackton to the witness stand was something that everyone knew as possible but not probable.

It was a surprise to Jack O'Brien, too, as he snapped his head to look at Matson and quickly turned in his seat to speak to his client.

"Can she do that?" Jessica Brackton asked in surprise. "I don't want to testify. I told you that!"

"It's actually better for us, Ms. Brackton," O'Brien said. Speaking quietly and soothingly as he could he added, "It will give the jury a chance to know you better, to understand your loss."

"I don't want to." Brackton said defiantly.

Sighing, O'Brien stood and faced the judge.

"Your honor, counselor's request for Ms. Brackton to take the stand comes as a bit of surprise to us. We ask that Ms. Matson explain her reasoning prior to putting my client through, what will obviously be an unnecessary stress."

"Your honor," Matson replied. "I have only a few questions for Ms. Brackton that will not directly refer to the accident."

"Exactly what I feared, your honor," O'Brien said. "Counselor wants to place a grieving mother on the stand to ask irrelevant questions? Where is the decency in that?"

"Your honor," Marston replied, "I have nothing but respect for the Brackton's and, like my client, have the deepest sympathy for their loss. I would, and Mr. O'Brien knows this better than most, I would avoid this step if it were at all possible. But as I stated, my questions, while pertinent to my client's case, will not refer directly to the accident itself."

The judge was listening to the arguments and nodded his head at Matson's last statement. O'Brien knew he was about to lose his argument and tried for time.

"Your honor, I would like to request a short recess to confer with my client. As I said, this comes as a surprise to us."

"Motion denied!" Judge Moretti snapped. "If you did not prepare your client for this eventuality it is not the responsibility of this court to see that you have the time to do it now."

O'Brien sat back down and whispered to Brackton. "I'm sorry. You have no choice. You must take the stand, but rest assured I'll make her pay dearly for doing this."

Jessica Brackton glared at O'Brien and stood. Turning her poisoned gaze to Kim Matson, she lifted her head and stepped into the witness box where she was administered the oath.

Matson took a sip of water from the glass on her table and took a deep breath. Walking towards Brackton, she offered a weak smile in an effort to show she was sorry for her being there, on the witness stand.

"Ms Brackton," she began, "Would you be kind enough to share with us your mother's maiden name?"

"Objection, your honor!" O'Brien shot to his feet. "The Billington name is one of the Commonwealth's most respected ones! To bring it before this court is nothing more than an attempt to slander history. That name can be found on the Mayflower Compact, for goodness sake!"

Judge Moretti thought a moment before answering, "Overruled."

"But your honor," O'Brien stated.

"I'm inclined to doubt counselor," the judge explained, "that it was Ms. Billington-Brackton's mother who signed the Compact. She may answer the question."

"Thank you, your honor," Matson said and turning to Brackton, "Ms. Brackton?"

As a result of the question and the arguments that followed, Jessica Brackton's face became drained of the defiant look she used upon taken the stand. She was looking at a spot on the floor several feet in front of where she stood when she answered.

"My mother's maiden name was Barbara Billington," Brackton answered.

"But she often used her middle name in an attempt to keep a low profile in public, didn't she? Could you tell the court her full name please?"

"Barbara Sanford Billington," Brackton nearly whispered.

"I'm sorry, Mrs. Brackton," the judge said. "You must speak loud enough for the court reporter to hear.

"My mother's maiden name was Barbara Sanford Billington," she spoke more loudly.

"And she kept that name when she married your father, didn't she?"

"Yes."

"On top of everything else, I know this next question will be difficult for you but I must ask it."

Brackton shifted her gaze to look directly at Matson while O'Brien leaned forward in his chair ready to object.

"Your mother died last year didn't she?"

"Objection, your honor! That question is totally irrelevant to this case and at best, is adding insult to unfathomable injury.

"Counselor?" Judge Moretti asked Matson.

"I promise this question, while undoubtedly painful to answer, your honor, is germane to the case before us."

"Objection overruled," the judge announced.

"My mother died last year after a long illness," Brackton answered.

"And you were the executor for her estate, weren't you?"

"Yes, I was," Brackton said and began to sob. She lifted her gaze to the spectators and found Brad Sullivan staring straight in front of him, not at her.

Marston could almost read her thoughts and a wave of sympathy washed through her. She wanted to reach out and take Brackton in her arms and offer her comfort. But that could not happen. Instead she asked quietly, "Is there anything you'd like to say, Ms. Brackton?"

"Objection! Your honor this line of questioning is not only meaningless but is causing undue stress on my client."

"No more questions, your honor," Matson stated and walked back to her table boldly staring at Bradford Sullivan who would not meet her eye.

"Do you have any questions, Mr. O'Brien?" The judge asked.

"I certainly do, your honor." But before he could walk the eight steps to the witness stand Brackton spoke.

"I do not want to answer any more questions." Her expression was sad but held a look of undeniable defiance. O'Brien stood frozen in place unsure of what he could do. He stood staring at Brackton as the sound of spectators mumbling brought the judge's gavel to play. The sound of its report on the top of the judge's bench sounded more like a gunshot than a hammer on wood. And it helped bring O'Brien back to the present.

"No more questions, your honor," he said as several people chuckled earning a stern look from the judge.

As Brackton returned to her seat, her husband whispered several questions into her ear, which were stonily ignored as she sat facing forward.

Judge Moretti was as confused as everyone else as to why Matson thought answers to her questions were directly related to her case. And, he was beginning to feel he had been set-up by a desperate defense lawyer with little more that they could offer their client in the way of defense. He was about to order both counselors to approach the bench when Marston spoke.

"Defense calls Ms. Kalisha Barnes," Matson announced.

"Objection, your honor!" O'Brien jumped to his feet. "Kalisha Barnes does not appear on our witness list."

"A result of intentional non-disclosure during the interview process, your honor," Matson explained.

"Are you implying Mrs. Brackton lied about—" O'Brien said heatedly but was cut off by the judge.

"Counselors will approach the bench!" The judge snapped.

The spectators and reporters began to chatter amongst each other, but as long they didn't let it get above a whisper, the judge allowed it knowing it would help to cover his discussion with the attorneys standing before him.

"I'm inclined to admonish you counselor," the judge spoke to Matson, "for your badgering of Ms. Brackton with what appears to be, your assurances aside, several questions unrelated to this case. This won't be the last you hear of it if my suspicions prove true."

O'Brien was elated to hear this from the judge.

"And what suspicions are you referring to, your honor?" Matson asked.

Ignoring her, the judge asked, "What's this about a new witness, counselor? And let me preface that question by saying I'm disinclined to allow new witnesses to appear in my court."

"I understand, your honor," Matson answered, "but this witness came to our attention in spite of a willful attempt on Jessica Brackton's part to lie about her destination when the accident occurred."

"What does her destination have to do with this?" O'Brien asked angrily. "This trial is about the accident caused by your client when—"

"Hush!" the judge barked at O'Brien.

The attorneys stood quietly facing the judge while O'Brien's elation faded. A surprise witness is never a good sign for the opposing side.

"I'm inclined to agree with Mr. O'Brien," the judge said.

"Thank you, your honor," O'Brien said feeling a surge of relief.

"However, am I to understand, Counselor," the judge asked Matson, "that your questions to Mrs. Brackton are related to your new witness? And that they will have a direct bearing on the outcome of this case? And let me warn you here and now," Judge Moretti pointed his finger at her face, "if the only result of this witness is to show to the jury that Mrs. Brackton told a falsehood, something that can be easily tied to the effect of her losing her baby, I will make a motion to have you disbarred." The judge lowered his finger and took a breath before finishing. "Knowing what you do now counselor, do you still wish for me to allow this witness?"

O'Brien's eyes widened noticeably with Kim Matson answer.

"Yes I do, your honor."

Kalisha Barnes walked into the court and down the aisle to the witness stand. Tall, black, and thin with a bandana tied over her hair she walked like royalty. She wore a richly decorated, but simple dress that hung from her shoulders to her ankles with the only adornment being her earrings; gold in color and long and slender like her body.

She held up her right hand, its palm noticeably white next to the complexion of her face, and took the oath performed by the court officer. She looked around the courtroom, confused and with a measure of fright as to why she was there.

"Ms. Barnes," Marston started, "Can you tell us where you are employed."

"I am a receptionist at Women's Health Services, Ma'am," Barnes answered with her rich Jamaican accent. "And I have my Green Card, as I told to that gentleman sitting there," she said pointing at Stan Ross.

"I've no doubt you're living and working here legally, Ms. Barnes. Your appearance here today has nothing to do with that. But please tell us how long have you been employed at Women's Health Services?"

"Nearly two years, ma'am."

"And were you working as the receptionist for Women's Health Services on the morning of February fifteenth, 2008?" Marston asked.

"I was, ma'am."

"Can you tell us if anyone called to cancel their appointments that morning?"

"No cancellations, ma'am," Barnes answered. "But there was one no show."

"Is that normal, to have patients with a scheduled appointment to simply not show up?"

"Sometimes. A person changes her mind and does not call us."

"Objection, your honor," O'Brien stated in a tired voice. "Is there a reason to subject us to this? Or even an end to this story?"

"I'm beginning to wonder the same thing, counselor," the judge said.

"Please indulge me, your honor. I promise to be done quickly."

"Objection overruled," Judge Moretti said as he looked pointedly at Matson.

"Can you tell us the name of the person in your appointment book that did not show up for her scheduled appointment that morning?"

"Her name was Barbara Sanford," Barnes answered confidently as she began to realize her court appointment wasn't about her.

The courtroom erupted in gasps and exclamations as they recognized the name of Jessica Brackton's deceased mother.

"I'd like to submit this as exhibit A, your honor." Matson passed the judge the appointment book from the medical center.

The judge took the book in one hand as the other slammed his gavel demanding silence.

"One last question, Ms. Barnes," Marston said to her. "What was the reason for Barbara Sanford's visit to the center?"

"The reason, ma'am?" Barnes replied, obviously confused by the question.

"Yes. What was the purpose of Barbara Sanford's appointment?"

"She was scheduled for an abortion, ma'am. That's the service we provide."

"No more questions, your honor," Matson hastily told the judge as the courtroom broke into pandemonium. People ignored, or simply forgot about the judge's warnings as they spoke aloud to one another and reporters pushed towards the exit.

Matson smiled to herself, believing that had the judge had two gavels, he would be able to effectively mimic the sound of machine gun fire.

TWENTY-NINE

Maggie Sullivan was too excited to drive directly home after the day's events in court and insisted that she and Brad eat out. He argued against it, stating he was suffering from a splitting headache. Maggie reached into her purse and handed him two aspirin of 500mg each and assured him he would be fine in no time. He didn't think that would be possible. Sitting at a booth on the upper floor of the Union House at Quincy Market, they sipped their wines.

The testimony of Jessica Brackton, and her reactions on the stand, along with Fitzpatrick's attorney staring through him, had set a very bad thought in motion. Was it possible that Jessica Brackton was carrying his baby? Was that why she wanted to meet with him, to tell him? She was on her way to have the baby aborted when the accident happened. He had to give her credit for that, he mused. Quietly arranging for the abortion on her own. But even if he had known that it was his baby, what other advice could she expect from him? And that Matson lady; did she know?

"Look Brad," Maggie whispered. "There's the Kennedy booth. We should have asked to be seated there."

Brad didn't bother to turn to look as he already knew about the booth in question. But he was happy for the distraction it provided his thoughts. When Jack Kennedy was a congressman, he often dined at the Union Oyster House, requesting to be seated at that booth. It was the oyster bar downstairs on the first floor that Sullivan held in greater regard. It's said that Daniel Webster sat there many a time shucking oysters and drinking beer. Now there was a legend worth aspiring to.

Sullivan began to relax as his mind slipped into the unique history of the area they were dining in. Across the street from the Oyster House was the Green Tavern Inn; still in operation from the days when Sam Adams and his gang of rowdies planned the Boston Tea Party. On the other side of the street sat Faneuil Hall, where he made his announcement to run for congress. It was the first "mall," so to speak, in the country where different merchants sold their crops and wares from the same spot. It was also the place where Sam Adams sang out, "This meeting can do nothing more to save the country" signaling that it was time for the Liberty Boys, thinly disguised as Indians, to head for Griffin's Wharf and start dumping tea into the harbor. His thoughts of those long ago patriots were interrupted by his wife's voice.

"I swear that Brackton lady was looking directly at you when she broke down on the stand!" Maggie said. "Didn't you think that? I swear I get goose bumps just thinking about it."

"I didn't think so," Brad answered, rubbing his temples. "She was just distraught."

"And that defense lawyer, too, now that I think about it. What was that all about?"

"You're imaging things. It was an exciting day. Everyone was surprised."

"Maybe. The Fitzpatrick's were sitting right in front of us. She may have been looking at them," she hesitated remembering the scene. "But why so angrily? And no," she added, "I didn't mean for us to sit there. They were the only seats left and Sean was kind enough to hold them open for us. If you had listened to me, we would have been there an hour earlier."

That's right, Sullivan thought. It was Sean who chose those seats. He hadn't thought of him in months. It was nearly a year since he let him go from his job as his aide at the State House. Sean had smiled at Brad as they took their seats, but that was natural enough, wasn't it? Or did Sean have some hidden agenda? What was he doing now?

"Speaking of Sean," he asked Maggie, "what's he been up to?"

"He's dyslexic, not useless." Maggie always became defensive when her brother was mentioned.

"Innocent question, Maggie."

"He's working as a freelance assistant for some reporter on The Hub." Sullivan's senses went on high alert.

"Freelancing for a newspaper reporter? That's not common. Which one?"

"Which one what?"

"Which reporter? For goodness sake, Maggie this may be important!"

"Don't get snippy with me! It's not my fault you let him go."

"I know. I'm sorry. I didn't mean to sound angry. I'll call Sean tomorrow. I'll work out something where we can work together again."

"I seem to recall you saying that when you fired him."

The waitress arrived at that moment with a seafood platter for him, and a bowl of clam chowder for Maggie. They sat in silence as they sampled their food.

Sullivan's debts were mounting to the point he had exhausted the second mortgage on their home to pay for advertising spots, print media, Ambrasio's excessive salary and a dozen other things that his campaign fund raising efforts couldn't cover. More than once, Ambrasio reminded him his money troubles would soon be over once he arrived in Washington.

"Soldier," Maggie said between sips of chowder.

"Excuse me?"

"The reporters name is Soldier or something."

"Do you mean Sailor? Jeff Sailor?"

"Yes! That's it. Sean says he's a real nice guy. He sends him to the trial in his place and he gives him assignments where he meets and interviews people. And if he takes a picture that the paper can use, he gets extra money. Sean really likes it."

"Do you know if Sailor asked Sean about me? About us?" Sullivan corrected himself. "At the moment were a couple of high-profile news makers, you know."

"You think so?" Maggie asked excitedly. "I know you are, but do you think I'm a high-profiler too? I mean, really?"

"Yes, you are. And because of that, we have to watch what we say and who we're talking to. If Sean says something about us, and it may seem innocent," Sullivan held up his hands to keep Maggie from getting defensive, "but things can be taken out of context, you know what I mean?"

"Like what?" Maggie asked.

"I just don't want to pick up the morning paper and find an article on a fight we may have had, or a problem you're experiencing with your organization, for instance. Some things aren't meant for public consumption."

Maggie nodded as she thought that. "You know, Brad, maybe we can use this reporter to our advantage. Through Sean, I mean."

"No! It's too dangerous a game, Maggie. We'd be over our heads. Don't even think about it."

"Oh foo! You needn't worry then. I won't use him to advance *your* cause."

Sullivan shook his head accepting defeat and made a mental note to call Sean first thing in the morning. He'd have to pay him out of pocket, but it made a lot more sense to have Sean nearby than it did having him "freelancing". What reporter worth his salt would send a ninny like Sean to cover a trial generating this kind of publicity? Nothing seemed to be adding up.

Maybe I'm just overtired, he considered. Most likely Jessica got impregnated by her husband, who he knew first hand that she was not crazy about, and decided to end her pregnancy. Now that he thought about it, that made the most sense. As for Sailor sending Sean to cover the trial in his place? Well, didn't Hunter Thompson write about events he never witnessed? A Super Bowl or something? What was that movie? Where the Buffalo Roam? Fear and Loathing? Maybe Sailor figures he can do the same thing.

Sullivan's cell phone rang earning him a disgusted look from Maggie.

"Honestly, Brad, can't we have a simple dinner together without you being available to the world?"

"Hello?" Brad spoke into the phone.

"Yo-ho Congressman!" Ambrasio's voice boomed. Sullivan quickly adjusted the volume.

"What's up? I'm having dinner with Maggie." Sullivan offered the information with little hope that it might discourage his campaign manager from continuing.

"Yeah? Where you at?"

"Union Oyster House. Look, can I call you back?"

"Only take a minute!"

"Then the reason you called?" Sullivan rolled his eyes to the ceiling.

"More good news, my friend. I just got a call from Sailor over at The Hub. He wanted a little more background on you and any quotes you wanted to offer."

"Quotes? Quotes about what?"

"The trial today. He says the Brackton lady nearly burnt a whole through you with her stare. Ain't that something? Broad's a kook."

"He's wrong, Frank! That never happened. Call him back and tell him to leave me out of his story."

"Are you nuts? Take a pass on free publicity? You're gonna be the democratic nominee, Brad! Get used to it buddy! You're leading in every poll and I plan to keep it that way. It's only gonna be you and Fitzpatrick from here out.

"Oh and say! This Sailor guy also wanted any comments you wished to offer about your meetings at the Exeter Hotel. What's that about? You aren't doing an end-run on me, are you? If so, let me remind you, buddy, that any meetings are my territory."

Sullivan felt his head swim as his vision blurred. "No! No!" he thought. And then quietly aloud, "This can't be happening."

"Never mind," Ambrasio said, feeling he may be pushing at the wrong time. "We'll talk about it tomorrow. Hey! Order the clam chowder, it's awesome." With that the connection was broken.

"What was that about?" Maggie asked. "Who's wrong about what?"

Sullivan stared open mouthed at her unable to think of anything coherent. His mind bounced from Sailor's query, to his candidacy, to Jessica Brackton, to his marriage and then back to his soon to be exposed affair with Jessica Brackton. Suddenly, a different synapse in his brain fired off a round that penetrated his circle of thoughts, bringing with it the realization he would soon be facing scandal, divorce, bankruptcy, and a failed run for congress. He felt a surge of bile in his mouth and instinctively swallowed, leaving a burning path of vomit down the length of his throat.

Maggie cell phone rang saving him from having to speak.

"Hi Carrie! Don't be silly. We were just finishing dinner. Did CNN show me leaving the courthouse?"

THIRTY

Jeff Sailor pulled into his coveted parking spot at The Hub and snubbed out his cigar in the car's ashtray before tossing it out of the window. Smoking cigars was a nasty habit, he knew, but it was more than a decade ago when he was introduced to it, and good habits, he reasoned, were as hard to kill as bad ones. And with the offers that were coming to him from the cable news networks, he saw no reason to reduce the quality items in his life. The best brandy a snifter could hold, the upscale restaurants, and the finest cigars were all on his horizon. Glancing at his watch, he noticed he was relatively early this morning by being only an hour or so past his scheduled start time. He felt confident that scheduled hours were about to be a thing of the past. His coverage of the Brackton-Fitzgerald story may well be the crowning point of his career and he had every intention of cashing in on it. And with the verdict due today, he was planning on very word above the fold of the newspaper devoted to his every word.

Finding Sean to cover the trial for him was surely an act of divine guidance. Without Sean's photographic memory, he wouldn't have nearly enough detail to write about it using his unique style. His boss and editor of The Hub, John Congdon, would have a hissy fit if he knew about his use of Sean as his eyes and ears at the trial, but unless he chose to tell him, and that was never going to happen, he had nothing to worry about. In fact, Sean proved himself to be so valuable that Sailor planned to use his unique talent in the future.

For years he had been covering the parades in Boston's North End to honor the Saints, Southie's St. Patrick's Day celebrations, and numerous other annual events where the real, every day people gathered. Some of his best pieces came from the unemployed, the crack addicts, AIDS victims, and husbandless mothers. But he could only be at one place at a time and there were so many stories that he was missing. Using Sean as his personal assistant, with his ability to repeat back everything said or overheard, he would have twice as much material to work with.

Posing as a doctor at the hospital was the biggest blunder of his career and could have well ended it had he not found Sean. But, assuming different personalities came so easy to him. He had planned to only get a quote from Jessica Brackton, but when an opportunity as ripe as being mistaken for the hospital's psychologist presented itself? Well, he reminded himself, good stories didn't write themselves.

He stepped out of the elevator and was passing the receptionists desk when a hand grabbed his arm, stopping him in mid-step. Turning, he saw Angela with a look of near panic on her face.

"Angela?" he asked. "What is it?"

"Mr. Congdon's been waiting over an hour for you," she whispered. "You're to go straight to his office."

Sailor smiled believing that the paper's editor had gotten wind of his recent offers of employment with cable news. Nothing like a little competition to fatten the wallet, he thought.

"Well you can relax," he told Angela. "I have a feeling I know what he wants with me and it's all good."

"Really?" she said. "Whew! I was worried when the lawyers..." But Sailor had already turned the corner towards his own office.

Throwing his sports coat over his desk chair he sat down and noticed a sticky note on his PC's monitor. "Come to my office ASAP, Congdon" it said. A smile spread across Sailor's face as he considered just how worried Congdon was about losing him to a competitor.

Standing he donned his jacket, put on a tie that he kept in his desk drawer, and walked to the office where only the powerful were allowed to tread. And at this moment, Sailor felt as powerful as he ever had. He had been thinking about this meeting for weeks, and originally planned to ask for a twenty percent raise plus a four day work week. But now that Congdon showed his cards, those terms would be the least he'd accept.

As Sailor opened the glass doors to the editor's private reception area, he could see someone was already with the editor sitting in a chair facing the huge mahogany desk. He was about to take a seat outside the office when the administrative assistant placed her hand over the phone receiver she was speaking into and told him to go straight in.

The first thing that Sailor realized was that the editor had more than one guest in his office. There was the man he saw while approaching the office sitting in the guest chair in front of the editor's desk and another one, a lady in a smart business suit, on the sofa situated against the wall.

"Hello, Jeff," Congdon greeted him then looked at his visitors and announced, "Mr. Ryman, this is Jeff Sailor. Jeff, this is Mr. Ryman who represents the Brackton's.

The man in the guest chair didn't bother to stand, but offered a nod of his head in Sailor's direction.

"Pleased to meet you Mr. Ryman," Sailor said while trying to think of what use he could be to him or, better yet, what use he could use from his visit. Obviously, Ryman's presence was related to his story running this morning exposing the affair Brackton was having with Sullivan.

"If you're here in the hopes of getting the names of my sources, I'm afraid you're wasting your time," Sailor spoke to Ryman.

Then Sailor turned to the lady sitting on the sofa and recognized her as one of the attorneys retained by The Hub. He had met with her from time to time over his years when free speech needed to be defended. Her presence confirmed for him that his instincts were right; Ryman was here for a rebuttal from him and The Hub.

"Hello, Alice," he said offering a warm smile. "If it will help speed things up, I want to state now that I stand by my story."

"Hi, Jeff," she responded coldly. Turning her attention to the editor she said, "I have a conference call with the attorney's for Mass General in less than an hour Mr. Congdon."

"The Mass General?" Sailor asked as his mind started to race through numerous scenarios to account for her visit with none of them being good for him.

"Have you a psychologist degree, Jeff?" Congdon asked. "Something we don't know about perhaps?"

Sailor shook his head, confused and very concerned.

"That's unfortunate I'm afraid. There's a report circulating that you posed as a psychologist to get access to Mrs. Brackton. Would you know anything about that?"

"Nonsense!" he laughed. "Who came up with that one?" This was not good at all, Sailor realized.

"I did!" Ryman shot back. "I have a copy of you on tape taken from one of the hospital's security cameras, wearing a stethoscope going into and then leaving Mrs. Brackton's hospital room. The Brackton's have already identified you as the one on the tape as well as the "doctor" who asked questions of a very personal nature."

Sailor stood there, his mind racing, unable to think of anything to say.

"It will interests you to know, Mr. Sailor, that John Brackton has had you followed these past few weeks and—"

"Had *me* followed? What is this, Nazi Germany? It may interest Mr. Brackton to know that I have a very large audience who read my columns faithfully. They wouldn't take too kindly to these accusations or that your client has had me followed. I can pretty much guarantee that he'll regret any negative allegations he—"

"Who's Sean Foley, Jeff?" Congdon interrupted. "Mr. Ryman says you've been using him as your eyes and ears at the trial."

"What?"

"Have you been actually at the trial each day, Jeff?" Congdon asked.

"Look, Mr. Congdon, all of this can be explained, but I think it's something we should discuss between the two of us," Sailor suggested. "I've been an employee here for how many years now? I still remember—"

"I don't think that would be a good idea, Jeff. What I suggest you do is go home and engage an attorney to represent you. You'll be on paid leave until—"

"An attorney?" Sailor repeated. "I don't need an attorney, Mr. Congdon. And even if I did, Alice here represents us when someone comes after us reporters. Right, Alice?"

"You're partially right, Jeff. I represent employees who are attacked unjustly while covering newsworthy events or when our free speech rights come under fire. But this isn't about your rights or the rights of the paper being abused; it's about the rights of a citizen. If what Mr. Ryman says is true, Jeff, you've brought irreparable harm to the paper."

"I can't believe this!" Sailor shouted. Turning his attention to Ryman he said, "I can't believe you'd take the word of this, this, shyster over mine."

"This shyster," Ryman said while smiling at Sailor, "has arranged for Sean Foley to drop by here later this morning to have a chat with Mr. Congdon. It seems Mr. Foley is under the impression that a job offer will be forthcoming."

"Fine! I used Foley to gather some background info for my pieces. It's done all the time."

"At a trial you reported each day but never attended?" Ryman asked. "I read those articles and I couldn't find anything that mentioned that you weren't there."

"I write in third person," Sailor began to argue. "Whether I'm there or not doesn't impact what I write about."

"I think your readers would disagree," Ryman answered.

Sailor opened his mouth to speak but his editor cut him off with, "I agree." His face had turned a darker shade as Sailor, and everyone else in the complex, knew was a prelude to an explosion. Sailor knew it was time to fold his cards.

"You'll be on paid leave until we can learn more about these allegations. But for what it's worth, Jeff, I suggest you clean out your office on your way out. If I learn from this Foley character you were using him to cover the trial, you're employment here is through."

"Fine," Sailor said and gave his boss a smirk. "I've been planning on a career change anyway. Cable news will jump at the chance to get me."

"You might want to turn on your TV when you get home, Jeff," Alice said. "Cable news is already running with this story. I believe they referenced you as an unscrupulous rogue reporter. But if it's any consolation, they made certain to mention the word 'alleged' several times."

Sailor's eyes went involuntarily wide as he comprehended what that would mean; no offers from cable or any other media outlet would be forthcoming.

"You can thank this shyster for that, too, Mr. Sailor." Standing, he brushed past Sailor on his way out of the office. Turning at the door he smiled, "As they say in the movies, I'll see you all in court. Always wanted to say that!"

THIRTY-ONE

The next morning the court displayed the usual hubbub of spectators lucky enough to gain a seat in the court. Most all of them spent the night standing outside on the sidewalk, and reporters jockeyed for seats near the exit allowing them to deliver their reports on-air first. The primary difference in today's proceedings was the number of news vans outside the court. Their satellite antennas sticking up from their roofs, they appeared to be nothing more than technically equipped recreational vehicles, but for the logos painted prominently on their sides. All of the mainstream networks were accounted for, along with the cable stations.

This trial was made for a nation who had become accustomed to sound bites, zip files, and compacted news stories. This trial had started last Monday and closing arguments were to begin today, a Friday. And a good thing too, the journalists agreed, as the following Monday began Holy Week, the most sacred days on the Christian calendar. It was pretty much assumed that jury deliberations would be quick, with a decision no later than Monday afternoon.

Sitting at his table looking like he had been up all night, sat Jack O'Brien. He was still memorizing his closing statements even as he edited them. He remained certain in his decision not to cross-exam Kalisha Barnes after her explosive testimony. Get the damage off the stand as soon as possible, he remembered his favorite law professor stating. And that it was better to have testimony look bad for your side, than to cross-examine and remove all doubt of it.

In his past, and quite recently if he was to be honest with himself, he directed, or more accurately stated, he nudged some clients to lie. But never had he been fully aware of being lied to by his own client prior to going to trial. It was humiliating in the best of light. And there wasn't much light to share. He couldn't very well take on the appearance that it was his suggestion to keep Brackton's appointment from being exposed. That could only lead to obstruction of justice.

Glancing at his clients, he noticed coldness between them that hadn't been visible before. They both sat upright, facing straight ahead, with only the husband exposing betrayed signs of unease. He'd glance at his wife, open his mouth to speak, and just as quickly turn to the face front again. This marriage is over, O'Brien thought, as he inwardly shuddered at the image of his meeting with them at his offices last night.

John Brackton went white at the trial. O'Brien hadn't missed that but, hopefully, the jurors did. They arrived at his offices just as O'Brien cancelled his planned media interview at his golf club. They were shown to his office and chose separate chairs rather than share the sofa.

O'Brien had read her the riot act. What was she thinking! If she had mentioned her plans to visit the abortion clinic to him upfront, they would still have a case. A very strong case. Her destination was immaterial, justifiable, a woman's right. Hiding it from the jurors led to a sense of mistrust. And here's the weird thing, he mused. She had hid it from her husband as well.

He was just warming up to his tirade, both of them hardly paying attention, when she said she wanted to drop the charges. It stopped O'Brien cold.

"That's not going to happen, Jessica," her husband said quietly. "You can drop your family heritage in the trash, but I won't offer mine up."

"All's not lost, Mrs. Brackton," O'Brien added hastily. "Your, er, destination that morning is immaterial."

"Is it?" she asked. "After all of your pontificating about the church's stance on abortion? Do you have any idea now as to what I was going through when you had that Evans lady testify?" Tears began to glisten at the corners of her eyes.

"I want that bastard in jail!" her husband yelled.

"Why?" she shouted back at him. "So you can talk about how you single handedly brought the congressman down? Because you'll get the ear of even wealthier clients than you have now? That's what this is about, isn't it?" She paused and spoke evenly as understanding came to her. "You're using this trial as a springboard."

"He took my son from me!" John Brackton yelled.

"Okay. We need to calm down and think about our next steps," O'Brien was trying to get them focused on tomorrow when closing arguments would be heard.

"It was your first pregnancy, Mrs. Brackton," he said. "You were distraught, unsure you were ready. You made the appointment, but never really intended to go through with it. It was just something you used to steady your nerves, a way out. But being the lady you are you, would never had chosen that option."

"Why won't anyone listen to me?" Jessica Brackton shouted at the ceiling. "I didn't want this trial! I don't want it to go on!"

"I'm afraid your husband is right," O'Brien answered sternly. "If we drop the charges now, you'll both be facing humiliation you'll never recover from. You might even find yourself in a courtroom reliving this all over again should Congressman Fitzpatrick seek damages for wrongful—"

"Enough!" John Brackton said. "We're seeing this through till the end, O'Brien, and if you hope to see the fruits of our little deal, you'll still have to earn it."

Brackton stood up to leave and expected Jessica to join him. But she lay hunched over her knees sobbing. Gently taking her by the elbow, she stood as he guided her out the door.

O'Brien thought of the little deal John Brackton had alluded to. In fact, he had been thinking of hardly anything else since learning of Jessica's plan to abort the baby the day of the accident. He was to be paid one million dollars by John Brackton for his successful conviction of Michael Fitzpatrick. A highly illegal, and therefore covert deal, that only he and Brackton knew about. It didn't take much arm twisting on Brackton's part to get him to agree to it. Brackton knew the value of brownstones on Beacon Hill and that a run for the governor's office wouldn't come cheaply. But this deal came with a catch. If he failed to get a conviction, he would not only be out a million dollars, but any future contributions from Brackton as well. And it was Brackton's money that got him elected as district attorney. John Brackton was not a man you wanted to have supporting an opponent. No matter, he consoled himself, withholding information as important as a planned abortion was breach of contract, so to speak, and he was going to get that million come hell or high water.

O'Brien's cell phone vibrated against his desk top indicating someone was calling. Thank goodness for 'silent modes', he thought as he read the number on the screen. What the heck, he thought, and answered.

"Mr. O'Brien, Jeff Sailor from The Hub calling. I'm sorry you couldn't make it to your club this evening. Is everything all right?"

O'Brien rolled his eyes and was tempted to hang up, but he would have to face this guy sooner or later, and he didn't want to aggravate him unnecessarily.

"Everything's fine, Mr. Sailor. What can I do for you?"

"I wondered if you'd care to make a statement about today at court. Something that will appear in the morning paper," he hinted. "You know, about your client's plan to—"

"There was no plan, Mr. Sailor," O'Brien interrupted. "She never had any intent to have her infant aborted. It was more of a failsafe, you know? First time mother and all that. Now I promise to give you a full briefing tomorrow, but right now, I really am busy. Goodbye."

Having heard himself use the explanation he had been thinking about for his closing arguments he felt more confident. He took from his desk the notes he had been preparing to use as a summary and began to read them, crossing out sentences and whole paragraphs that could no longer be used.

In Medfield, Matson and Ross had just ushered out the Fitzpatrick family who were naturally elated at the new turn of events. Matson tried to keep their expectations for success reasonable, but the congressman wouldn't stop smiling. He slapped Stan Ross on the back so many times she was sure Stan would be sore in the morning.

"Well, Kim," the Congressman said, "I suspect the thing to do now is to forget about the loss of the baby and concentrate on this being what it is, an unavoidable accident."

"Sound right to me, Kim," Ross offered. "The loss of her child is a non-issue after what we learned today."

Kim shook her head and answered, "That would be a huge mistake. She lost the baby as a result of the accident regardless her plans to have an abortion. When the jury begins its deliberations, sooner or later, someone is going remember that. We need to concentrate on the baby."

"I don't understand," the Congressman stated. "How can that help?"

"First of all, the District Attorney helped us in that regard. All of that talk about the sanctity of life is about to bite him in the butt. Our roles have been reversed. He can't very well make reference to his religious expert without bringing attention to the jurors that his client was about to end a life on her own. And we need to use that fact to our advantage."

"I hope you know what you're doing Kim," the Congressman said just prior to leading his family out the door.

"You know, Stan," Matson said after the Fitzpatrick's had gone. "You really are responsible should we win this case. Even if we lose, you've more than earned the congressman's praise. And mine, too. You've been awesome!"

"It's me that wants to thank you, Kim. I've never felt more alive or proud of my profession! I want to celebrate!"

"Stan?" Matson spoke quietly. "We haven't won. At least not yet. There was nothing illegal about Brackton planning to abort her baby."

"But aren't we better off than we were? People were falling all over themselves in that court today."

"They were just responding to news."

"You're saying we're no better off, Kim?"

"Not at all. But we have one big advantage going for us."

"And that would be?" Ross asked as his euphoria vanished.

"The DA was as surprised today as everyone else. Forget about everything we've planned up to this point. This verdict is going to rest on summations to the jury."

THIRTY-TWO

Keep it short and sweet, O'Brien recalled his law professor saying. More sales have been lost due to an agent's overselling a product. Remind them what your witnesses said to prove your facts of the case and sit down.

"Ladies and gentleman. It's only been a few days since we first met and I spoke to you about the facts of this case. Since then, I have presented witnesses to support those facts. As a result, my opponent has resorted to directing your attention to facts that do not relate to the case before us.

"We all know, thanks to Ms. Matson's utter disrespect for a person's privacy, that Mrs. Brackton had made an appointment with a clinic that provides alternatives to women who are not ready to become mothers. We also know that her appointment was scheduled for February fifteenth, the very day Michael Fitzpatrick decided to drive after having spent a night celebrating with his friends and even after downing a shot of booze moments before the accident.

"These are facts that we know and I assure you, Ms. Matson will not dispute them. But allow me to point out some things, important information, you may not know.

"Ms. Brackton was experiencing a pregnancy for the first time. She was scared, unsure, not unlike most women facing pregnancy for the first time, if she were really ready to become a mother. She made the appointment at Women's Health Services, but never intended to keep it. That's right. She never would have kept that appointment and do you know why? She's a devout Christian. She believes in the sanctity of life. What's more, she's one of societies leading ladies. Not just here in the Bay State but in the country. I can assure you that Jessica Brackton was simply using that appointment to ease her concerns about motherhood.

"But let's suppose, for a moment, that I'm simply making all of this up. Let's consider for a moment, that she had every intention of aborting her baby.

"So *what*? It's not for us to decide the right or wrong of that. And where the law is concerned, our Supreme Court justices determined the legality of a woman's right to terminate a pregnancy back in 1973. More than 20 years ago! And while the Church condemns the practice, we must, each of us, ask ourselves 'am I to cast the first stone?'

"On February fourteenth, Michael Fitzpatrick met with his friend Timothy Jenkins, and together, they drank so heavily that it required his friend to offer his living room couch as a bed so Michael could sleep it off. The next morning, with hardly enough time for the alcohol from the previous night's binge to work its way through his system, what does he do? Drink some orange juice? Go for a jog and let the bitter cold clear his head? No! He gets up from the sofa and downs a shot of bourbon. And then what does he do? He jumps in his car! Does that sound like the actions of the respectable man his defense attorney has tried to fool you with? Where can anyone, I have to ask, find anything at all responsible about his actions that morning?

"Lee Harvey Oswald was certainly to be executed for taking the life of our beloved president John Kennedy, and yet his assassin, Jack Ruby was tried and went to prison for killing him. Imprisoned for doing what the courts surely would have, terminating Oswald's life.

O'Brien walked to his desk and took a sip of water while he debated the pros and cons of mentioning the Church, or simply wrapping up. He was feeling confident and decided he could use his next statement as a stepping stone to a higher office. Something that will show the people he was up-to-speed with current thoughts and popular belief.

Stepping towards the jurors he spoke again.

"Church beliefs have no bearing on this trial today, nor should they. Why? Because it has fallen woefully out of step with what we as a people have come to understand. The Supreme Court knows this, and no matter how hard the Church tries to keep blinders on us, we know it, too. Terminating a fetus is a woman's choice. Driving under the influence is a choice as well. Which of these do you wish to support?

"You are charged here today with a heavy burden. It's important to your future piece of mind that you make the right choice. In your hands lay the responsibility of choosing what you know is right, or providing another easy out for the privileged son of a congressman.

"Whether Jessica Brackton was to abort her baby, or carry it to term, is not what you need to consider. It is immaterial to this case. Rather, in your hands, ladies and gentlemen, lays the burden of protecting the long fought for rights of women everywhere. Not the right for a spoiled, drunken son of wealthy politician to decide, but the right for women to make their own choice.

"Thank you."

***

Kim Matson was scribbling notes throughout O'Brien's speech and could only wish she was allowed to preview it prior to this morning. What an ass he is, she thought.

"Counselor?" Judge Moretti spoke in her direction.

Without acknowledging the judge, she rose from her chair and approached the jury.

"Good morning. I had, as you can imagine, a well prepared summary of this case prepared to present to you this morning." Matson paused as she walked to the end of the jurors' row and turned so she could see them all.

"But the prosecutor's statement has made me realize a prepared speech won't be necessary. He has conceded to us what I have been arguing about from the start; this trial was never about the guilt or innocence of Michael Fitzpatrick, but the weight of responsibility we assign when an unavoidable accident occurs.

"He conceded it when his summary ignored the facts that were presented here, the facts *he* presented, and concentrated instead on a woman's right to choose. Did you notice that? I suspect you did. But this case isn't about a women's right to vote, to own land, to earn equal wages. It's about an accident.

"He mentioned our Supreme Court recognizing the right of a woman to chose abortion back 1973. More than twenty years ago. My, my, that is a long time. And if you'll recall your middle school history lessons, it was Chief Justice Roger Taney who ruled that slaves were property and not citizens. That the United States Congress had no authority to prohibit slavery. Gee that was way back in 1857, more than one-hundred years ago! Well it took a few years and a civil war to overturn that blunder!" Matson smiled while nodding her head.

"You see? The Supreme Court justices sometimes get things wrong, too. Just like each of us. History tells us that while justice is blind, it sometimes takes a peak from behind the blindfold to see what the populace is thinking. Not to base a decision on the meaning of an old age law, one that may well have kept this country from foundering, but whether it should apply today, to *modern* times.

"And yet my esteemed and nationally known opponent, Mr. Jack O'Brien, would have you believe that the law supersedes anything the Church would ask of you. Let's think about that a moment.

"It's not against the law for a man to cheat on his wife, is it? Or for a wife to have an extramarital affair? We know it's wrong, but hey, the law's okay with it.

"You want to impregnate several different women but not marry any of them? You're going to face some hefty child support payments, but as far the law's concerned, good luck.

"You know why the law doesn't have specific punishments for people who do these things? Because it relies on the teachings of the Church to keep people from doing them!

"Mr. O'Brian states the Church is woefully out-of-step because, I assume, right or wrong, it is a woman's choice to abort a fetus. I would be curious to know if he feels the Church is woefully behind the times in believing in the sanctity of marriage. Honor thy father and mother? Thou shall not steal?

"There's something that bothers me about all of this and I'll share it with you. Why is it against the law to sell a baby, when it's okay to murder one? I can't make sense of that."

Matson stopped a moment to look over at Mrs. Brackton. Her head bowed, she seemed the perfect victim. Glancing at Michael, she was pleased to see his head lowered as well, giving the impression of being contrite, lonely, and ready to cry. In fact, she realized, there were tears at the corner of his eyes. She hoped the jury had followed her gaze, but not wanting to lose her cadence, she spoke again.

"The prosecutor brought a recognized known expert on Church beliefs to testify, but does he make reference to anything she said during his summation? Perhaps you'll be kind enough to allow me to remind you.

"Life is sacred. That's what the church believes and teaches. In fact, as we heard from Ms. Evans, the sanctity of life is the foundation of all Christian and Judaism religions.

"Yes, we go to Church and pray together, offer money when the collection plate is passed, some of us may even tithe while others volunteer their time. Oh! Let's not forget that we offer prayers for the wicked and the wayward to see the light. But how easy is it for us to see and follow that same light? The Church teaches us that it is a sin to steal, a sin to dishonor our mother's and father's, a sin to commit adultery, a sin to commit murder and I say *Amen to That!* The Church and I see eye-to-eye when it comes to those sins. Yup, they know what they're talking about." Matson paused to give the jurors a chance to think about what she said.

"But wait a minute. An unborn baby doesn't apply to that murder thing does it? Well then, hold on a minute! That's my decision! Sure, I'll still go to Church and agree with everything said about God's laws and the Church's interpretation of them as long as it's convenient for me. As long as my parish priest or minister or rabbi doesn't know how I feel, what I'm thinking, or what I've done. But after the service and when I'm back in my home *I'll* decide what God meant by, *Thou Shall Not Kill*.

"Hard to believe for some of you, I'm sure. Yet, some people think they know better than God." Matson slowly shook her head to emphasize the difficulty she had in acknowledging that truth.

"Now, you'll recall Mr. O'Brien mentioning Jack Ruby being found guilty and sentenced to prison for murdering President Kennedy's assassin, Lee Harvey Oswald. But he failed to mention that Oswald never had a chance for a trial to determine his guilt. And that's what this country is all about. It's been ingrained in us from childhood; we're innocent until proven guilty. I am not a conspiracy theory advocate, but as far as the law is concerned, Oswald was never tried for the murder of President Kennedy and therefore remained innocent until he was found guilty."

She turned to face Jack O'Brien.

"And you'll excuse me, ladies and gentleman of the jury, if I take this moment to point out to Mr. O'Brien that Oswald was not walking to the gas chamber when he was shot, but in a manner of speaking, Jessica Brackton's baby *was!*"

A murmur arose in the courtroom that was snuffed out when Judge Moretti reached for his gavel.

"This trial isn't about a woman's right to choose to abort an unborn *baby*. It's about a different right from wrong. Yes, Michael Fitzpatrick was involved in the accident that prematurely ended the life of Jessica Brackton's baby, a baby whose own mother was on her way to have murdered!

"I have too much respect for each of you to relate in detail how tongs are used to crush the baby's skull, ending his life prematurely. *Deliberately*."

Matson paused to let that image sink in as one of the female jurors pressed her fingers to her lips in dismay.

"When a child drowns, we are told that it's God's will. It was an unforeseen accident that took the child's life. There's no one to blame, no one to put on trial. There's simply no other answer for it but God's will. We can accept that.

"But I think I stand on pretty firm ground with Church teachings to support me when I say it has never been God's will to have the Brackton baby, or any baby, murdered!"

Matson stopped to catch her breath and to gage the impact of what she was saying to the jurors. But it was always the same, she could not tell.

"I am not so arrogant to think for one moment that I know God's intentions any better than the next person. But isn't it possible, just maybe, that God intervened to prevent the Brackton baby from being subjected to the horror of an abortion and he used Michael Fitzpatrick as his instrument?

"Why? Because he was in the right place, at the right time, and had the type of character we know through our Bible teachings that God prefers to work with, faithful, humble, and giving of himself to others.

"God didn't put Michael on trial for his part in this accident, society did. The same society that wants a measure of revenge for the murder of any baby, as it should, but turns a blind eye if that murder is a mother's will. Not God's will, mind you, but the mother's.

"If we are to punish Michael Fitzpatrick for being part of an unavoidable accident, an accident that may very well have been God's will, then what does that say about us?

"You're burden today is not as heavy as Mr. O'Brien would have you believe. It's relatively simple. But the decision you make will have a far greater impact on your own future piece of mind, along with the conscience of a country, than any impact it could possibly have on the women's movement.

"Thank you."

THIRTY-THREE

The jury spent the remainder of that day debating the facts as they heard them. When it approached five o'clock, the judge had them led back into the courtroom to check on their progress. When it was apparent they would not reach a verdict even if they stayed late that day, he dismissed them for the evening, reminding them that they were forbidden to talk about this case with anyone including their significant others.

That evening at his home, Michael Fitzpatrick attempted to write a letter to John and Deborah Brackton explaining how devastated he was that he was involved in the loss of their baby. Of any human life. But when he finished and re-read it, he realized that it would only serve to remind Mrs. Brackton that she was about to end her baby's life that same morning. How could he tell her how badly he felt about his role when she was apparently at ease with her decision regarding baby Brackton's life?

He heard his father's voice coming from the living room downstairs as he spoke loudly to Stan Ross, who dropped by earlier. He was unable to hear Stan's reply, but knowing he was there, Michael's mind drifted through the events of the trial until he recalled the conversation with his attorney, Kim Matson, when it was disclosed that Deborah Brackton was on her way to an abortion clinic.

"I don't understand," he said to Matson as they sat in Stan Ross' office earlier that night. "Why am I still being tried? She was about to have her baby aborted, Ms. Matson. Why am I being tried for what would have been the same result?" Michael sat facing her with an expression that conveyed a difficult problem was being internally contemplated. "It's not fair," he said at last.

"I'm sorry," Matson said, "But it's not about fairness, Michael. An accident occurred that ended the life, or the promise of life, of another. Someone must be held accountable. Unfortunately, that someone is you."

Michael let his head fall as he contemplated his future.

"Will I be found guilty do you think?" he asked.

"I can't say for certain, but let's keep a good thought. The jury is considering the same bizarre chain of events that you and I are."

"What will happen to me if I'm found guilty?"

"The judge will take into consideration the facts as we uncovered them as well as whether you are a threat to the community," she smiled to provide him some hope.

"But worst case?" he asked.

"It could be something as simple as probation for a few months. But Michael," she waited till she had his attention, "you should know that it could be jail time, too. Whatever the verdict, I want you to hold your head high and say nothing. Do you understand? Not a word."

"Okay," Michael sighed.

Stan Ross sat in the Fitzpatrick's living room providing what comfort and hope he could. The Congressman was as perplexed as Michael at this point and wanted to know why Kim Matson didn't call for a mistrial. "She was on her way to have the baby aborted for heaven's sake!" the congressman barked.

"It's not that easy, Frank," Ross answered. "Ms. Brackton's intentions that morning are not on trial. The law looks at what happened as a crime." Then he held up his hands to finish his thoughts before the congressman could speak. "A life was lost possibly due to negligent driving while impaired. You and I know that is not what happened but..." Ross let his voice trail off and shook his head.

"This trial is a travesty!" the congressman added as more of a way to have the last word.

Stan Ross tried to think of something to say that would put what was happening into better perspective, but by the time he opened his mouth to respond, he realized that he could only come to the same conclusion.

On Beacon Hill, Deborah and John Brackton sat across from each other at the dining room table in their plush condominium. John Brackton ordered Chinese food and when it arrived, he opened the boxes and placed them in the middle of the kitchen table. In his opinion, eating Chinese food ordered from a take-out restaurant did not belong on a thirty-five thousand dollar dining room table. Leaving the dining room, his wife took her place at the kitchen table, but made no move to fill her plate. She sat there looking intently at her empty plate.

"Why were you going to do it Deborah?" John asked. Neither had spoken since leaving the courthouse and his voice startled Deborah back to the present.

"I wasn't sure I was ready to have a baby," she answered in her typically soft voice.

"How about me?" he asked. "Didn't you think I might be ready?"

Deborah lifted her head and looked him in the eyes when she said, "If the Fitzpatrick boy goes to jail tomorrow, I am going to leave you."

"What!" he responded, "You lose our baby and now you want to leave me?"

"It was an accident," she said and then murmured, "All of this was an accident."

"Huh? What's that?"

She met his eyes again and suddenly realized that she would be leaving him regardless of the verdict. Marrying him was one mistake she could rectify. Her other mistakes, she theorized, would take more time.

The following day, not more than an hour after the lunch break, the jury foreman informed the judge they had reached a verdict. All of the parties were present, except for John Brackton, and each felt the heat that a packed courtroom held. Even the reporters stopped whispering as the jury were ushered into the courtroom and took their seats.

Deborah Brackton had been sitting quietly throughout the day and remained in her seat during the lunch recess. When the DA asked earlier in the day if her husband would be joining them she said, "I have no idea." That was the last question Jack O'Brien attempted with her.

"Has the jury reached a verdict, Mr. Foreman?" the judge asked.

"We have, your honor."

The court officer took the verdict sheet from the foreman and handed to the judge. Judge Moretti glanced at its contents and asked the foreman, "How do you find the defendant."

"Guilty, your honor."

Pandemonium is the only word that could actually describe the next few moments as Emily Fitzpatrick, Michael's mother, cried out and reporters jammed the exit to be the first to report the news. The judge banged his gavel and yelled for silence. As the reporters continued to push their way toward the exit he told the court officers to bar the door. Once quiet took hold, the judge thanked the jury for doing their civic duty and dismissed them. Once they left the courtroom, he turned his attention back to the defendant.

"Please stand, Mr. Fitzpatrick," the judge instructed. "Normally, I would call for a recess at this point to consider an appropriate sentence. But giving the notoriety this case has generated, I have taken ample time to review the guidelines in preparation of a guilty verdict. It's time to end this and let everyone get on with their lives. Have you anything to say before I announce sentencing?"

"No, your honor," Michael answered remembering Kim Matson's instructions.

"In that case," the judge began, but stopped when Deborah Brackton stood.

"Mrs. Brackton?" the judge asked.

"I have something to say," she stated as all eyes turned to the most beautiful woman in the building.

Jack O'Brien placed his hand on her wrist and motioned for her to sit, but she flicked her hand as she would shoo a fly. The DA released his hold on her and sat facing forward.

"I'm sorry for this to have happened. Not for the loss of my baby, but for this to come to court." She shook her head slowly trying to comprehend how she came to be here.

"It's true that I was going to the abortion clinic that morning to end my pregnancy. I was not ambivalent about it," she glanced briefly at O'Brien, "I was certain." She looked over at Michael who remained standing, but was perhaps the only person not looking at her as he studied a spot near his shoes. It made her heart break to see him.

The judge fiddled with his gavel wondering if he should stop her but he quickly reminded himself this was not his ordinary citizen. With money, came power.

"I know I may not be considered to be the best person by some for my actions and others will call me a hero. I came to realize that this trial isn't about Michael, Judge. It's not even about me or my baby." She turned to the empty juror box and said softly, "What were they thinking?"

"Mrs. Brackton," the judge interrupted. "This has not been easy on anyone and…"

"It's about a women's right to choose, isn't it?" she asked. "And because of that, this poor boy was found guilty for an unavoidable accident."

"Mrs. Brackton, please sit down," the judge intoned.

"I want the Fitzpatrick family to know," she spoke while looking at the parents, "I want this court and the millions of people who will hear my words tonight to know that I will do everything in my power to see that Michael is eventually found innocent. Whatever the costs may be."

Brackton at last sat while the judge and the spectators continued to look at her.

The judge cleared his throat and turned a steely gaze to the DA. "And what does the district attorney think about those sentiments?"

Jack O'Brien stood and was about to make a statement concerning justice being blind and a guilty verdict demanding punishment. But knowing that he had already won his "bonus fee" from John Brackton with the guilty verdict, he simply couldn't care less what the judge or Deborah Brackton wanted. But Deborah Brackton was not someone he wished to antagonize. Her net worth alone was rumored to be twice that of her husband's.

"The state feels that justice has been served, your honor."

"Does it now," the judge said.

The spectators, along with the lucky reporters who were barred from leaving the court earlier, began to speak to one another as Judge Moretti fiddled with his gavel with eyes that were no longer in the same dimension as they. Finally, he took a loud breath that brought the court to silence immediately.

"Mr. Fitzpatrick," he said looking at Michael. "You were brought to the police station directly after the accident. Is that not so?"

"Ah, yes. Yes sir, I was."

"Then it is the opinion of this court that you will be incarcerated for the time already served. Case dismissed!"

With a rapt of his gavel the judge stood and walked briskly to his chambers as reporters ran for the exit, accidently knocking one of the court officers to his butt.

Deborah Brackton walked over to where the Fitzpatrick family was standing while they were alternating shared hugs with each other and Michael's attorneys. She walked to where Michael stood and, forcing herself to look into his eyes, said, "I'm sorry." At that, she started to cry.

"I am too, Mrs. Brackton," Michael said. "I tried to tell you in a letter but I..." he stopped speaking as Deborah turned and began the long walk from the courtroom, past the reporters, to where she parked her car. She didn't feel she would ever be able to stop crying from this point on, knowing it would be a long time before she reached home again. Her affair, her baby, and her marriage were all gone. And they were all, in her opinion, nothing more than a mistake, an accident.

THIRTY-FOUR

Bishop Connor sat in his easy chair with several of the latest ordained priests seated about the floor around him. This group had arrived nearly ten days ago and would be leaving for their assignments shortly. It was to be the last group to participate in his program. The Arch Diocese would be returning to the standard procedure for assignments which consisted of reviewing a parish need and assigning a name to it. End of story. This would be the last time he gathered the newly ordained. The Cardinal and Archbishop had made that abundantly clear. Being caught on camera leaving the courthouse had apparently been the last straw. He was being reassigned. To where and for what purpose was still being discussed, but he had no doubt any active role he would have in the Church would be greatly curtailed.

Forty years of learning and trying to instruct, communicating with parishes, fellow priests and, of course, God. The timing was good for retirement, to take a less active role, he reflected. Maybe now that the Fitzpatrick verdict was in, it was all everyone was talking about, the Congressman could get back to fighting for his Faith for Life bill. But no, he thought with regret. That opportunity had come and gone. Fitzpatrick will have little support now for this bill. It all comes back to relying on the individual and a conscientious decision. How many future medical researchers, Nobel laureates, and priests even will have their life's terminated for the sake of convenience? How many would have grown to become good citizens, soldiers, Christians, and moms and dads? There was a time, the Bishop reflected, that war and disease accounted for early death statistics. Now the individual does. Advances in medicine allow us to see the sex of the baby along with any malformations. Has an expectant mother ever shown the pictures from an ultrasound to a friend and exclaimed, "This is my embryo!" Unlikely. Chilling really, he thought with distaste.

That Matson is pretty sharp; he absently nodded as his mind skipped to the defense attorney. I think I'll have father Canelli see if she'd be interested in representing our diocese from time to time. If only they allowed him to stay on here, he thought, remembering Canalli's punishment; a parish priest in one of the poorest sections of the state. It wouldn't hurt to have a sharp mind like Matson's on the Church's side. I may find I need her myself, he suddenly thought and it made him smile. No, he realized, whatever hope I have for redemption is about to be cast into the wind this Easter Sunday when I announce the excommunication of those who openly support abortion. The very gates of hell will open!

And more than a few politicians will be affected, he considered, while absently nodding his head. Knowing they will be unable to receive the sacraments or have a Catholic burial may be the medicine they need. It will be the last Mass I officiate, of that I'm sure. But it's been done before in Corpus Christi, he reasoned. Thank the lord for men like Bishop Garcida for giving us strength. It's within my power and I will do it regardless what becomes of me. I seriously doubt that the Cardinal or Archbishop will find the will or a way to rescind my action. Yes, the church will be hurt, I suppose, but there's no getting around that. How many will leave to fill the pews of the protestant sects is anybody's guess, but we can't be expected to change the teachings of Christ to meet the current mores, whims, and secular interests so as to be popular! We've been kidding ourselves too long. In time and with God's help and divine guidance, we will come back stronger with a congregation willing to listen. To learn. To believe again in what we've believed and known to be true for more than two-thousand years. "They'll come back," he muttered aloud.

Father Canelli focused his whole attention on the bishop as Connor's mind wandered over the past several months from the accident, to the trial, to the young priests staying with him, when it stopped on the warning he gave to each of the classes. Yes, he acknowledged again, it's the decisions based upon the easy path that you'll find leads to evil. Not based on what is right by God or what is good for my country, but what is best for me. "How did we lose them so completely?" he mumbled aloud.

"Excuse me, Bishop Connor?" Father Canalli asked quietly. He could see, as they all could, the Bishop was disturbed by the deep thoughts that held him.

Looking about, Bishop Connor wondered how long they sat there waiting for him. Rubbing his eyes with his heels of his hands, he raised his head and offered a weak smile.

"I'm sure you are all aware of what happened at the Fitzpatrick trial this morning" he began. "And if not, I'll tell you. Mrs. Brackton was apparently on her way to an appointment she made to have her pregnancy aborted when the car accident made that visit unnecessary." Bishop Connor continued to wear a look of consternation as he slowly shook his head.

The young men sat unmoving with their attention focused solely on the Bishop as Father Canalli, leaning on the doorframe to the room, watched with apprehension. He had never seen the Bishop look so tired or pale. Perhaps he was getting sick, Father Canalli feared. He may be the one man Gandhi had been searching for, Canalli reflected. He suddenly grasped what Bishop Connor may have been saying all along. He was 'listening' and realized that the studying, the vows, the robes, the prayers were all important, but how you *lived* your life was what it was all about. And believing that meant everyone was born a man of God, a teacher, and a priest. He was suddenly, and for the first time in many years, anxious to be assigned a parish. He had a lot of teaching to do.

"You know a story occurs to me that seems to fit the circumstances of events today," the Bishop said. "Not just about the Fitzpatrick case, but circumstances surrounding us everywhere.

"It seems that Satan held a meeting with all of his lieutenants to review the progress they had made during the prior year in their effort to hasten man's destruction. Once they had finished their reports, Satan chastised them for not doing enough and ordered each of them to report back in a week's time with a plan that would speed the ruin of mankind.

"When they met again, a week later, he had each of them state their plans.

"We can release a super resilient locust strain upon the land that will eat their crops and have them starve," one suggested.

"I have a better idea Master where we can introduce a new virus, similar to the black plague that will have them in our grasps in less than a year."

"And still another offered to replace the world leaders with their own members and start a world ending war.

"Additional plans were tendered until, hearing enough, Satan held up his hands signaling an end to the exercise.

"Those are all good plans," Satan said, "but during the past week I have taken a tour of Earth and have a better idea."

His apprentices all leaned forward to better hear what their master had in mind, knowing it would be far more destructive, and undoubtedly more evil, than anything they had suggested.

With his forefinger and thumb massaging his lower lip he appeared to be looking off into the future.

"Let's just leave them be," Satan spoke. "They're doing a fine job all on their own."

About the Author

Rich was a Boston native for more than 40 years and is now a resident of Colorado with his wife and daughter. When not writing, Rich enjoys fishing in the mountains, golf, and the occasional Rockies game.

www.ingramcontent.com/pod-product-compliance
Lightning Source LLC
Chambersburg PA
CBHW031111260626
47172CB00001B/312